# REASSURING TALES

## E X P A N D E D   E D I T I O N

by

# T.E.D. KLEIN

ISBN-10: 1-953215-16-5
ISBN-13: 978-1-953215-16-1
Published by Pickman's Press, Edgewood, NM, USA
Visit us at http://www.pickmanspress.com.

# COPYRIGHT INFORMATION

# CONTENTS

# THE EVENTS AT POROTH FARM

As soon as the phone stops ringing, I'll begin this affidavit. Lord, it's hot in here. Perhaps I should open a window...

Thirteen rings. It has a sense of humor.

I suppose that ought to be comforting.

Somehow I'm not comforted. If it feels free to indulge in these teasing, tormenting little games, so much the worse for me.

The summer is over now, but this room is like an oven. My shirt is already drenched, and this pen feels slippery in my hand. In a moment or two the little drop of sweat that's collecting above my right eyebrow is going to splash onto this page.

Just the same, I'll keep the window closed. Outside, through the dusty panes of glass, I can see a boy in red spectacles sauntering toward the courthouse steps. Perhaps there's a telephone booth in back...

A sense of humor—that's one quality I never noticed in it. I saw only a deadly seriousness and, it's clear, an intelligence that grew at terrifying speed, malevolent and inhuman. If it now feels itself safe enough to toy with me before doing whatever it intends, so much the worse for me. So much the worse, perhaps, for us all.

I hope I'm wrong. Though my name is Jeremy, derived from Jeremiah, I'd hate to be a prophet in the wilderness. I'd much rather be a harmless crank.

But I believe we're in for trouble.

I'm a long way from the wilderness now, of course. Though perhaps not far enough to save me. I'm writing this affidavit in room 2-K of the Union Hotel, overlooking Main Street in Flemington, New Jersey, twenty miles south of Gilead. Directly across the street, hippies lounging on its steps, stands the county courthouse where Bruno Hauptmann was tried back in 1935. (Did they ever find the body of that child?) Hauptmann undoubtedly walked down those very steps, now lined with teenagers savoring their last week of summer vacation. Where that boy in the red spectacles sits sucking on his cigarette—did the killer once halt there, police and reporters around him, and contemplate his imminent execution?

For several days now I have been afraid to leave this room.

I have perhaps been staring too often at that ordinary-looking boy on the steps. He sits there every day. The red spectacles conceal his eyes; it's impossible to tell where he's looking.

I know he's looking at me.

But it would be foolish of me to waste time worrying about executions when I have these notes to transcribe. It won't take long, and then, perhaps, I'll sneak outside to mail them—and leave New Jersey forever. I remain, despite all that's happened, an optimist. What was it my namesake said? "Thou art my hope in the day of evil."

There *is,* surprisingly, some real wilderness left in New Jersey, assuming one wants to be a prophet. The hills to the west, spreading from the southern swamplands to the Delaware and beyond to Pennsylvania, provide shelter for deer, pheasant, even an occasional bear—and hide hamlets never visited by outsiders: pockets of ignorance, some of them, citadels of ancient superstition utterly cut off from news of New York and the rest of the state, religious communities where customs haven't changed appreciably since the days of their settlement a century or more ago.

It seems incredible that villages so isolated can exist today on the very doorstep of the world's largest metropolis—villages with nothing to offer the outsider, and hence never visited, except by the occasional hunter who stumbles on them unwittingly. Yet as you speed down one of the state highways, consider how few of the cars slow down for the local roads. It is easy to pass the little towns without even a glance at the signs; and if there are no signs...? And consider, too, how seldom the local traffic turns off onto the narrow roads that emerge without warning from the woods. And when those untraveled side roads lead into others still deeper in wilderness; and when those in turn give way to dirt roads, deserted for weeks on end... It is not hard to see how tiny rural communities can exist less than an hour from major cities, virtually unaware of one another's existence.

Television, of course, will link the two—unless, as is often the case, the elders of the community choose to see this distraction as the Devil's tool and proscribe it. Telephones put these outcast settlements in touch with their neighbors—unless they choose to ignore their neighbors. And so in the course of years they are...forgotten.

New Yorkers were amazed when in the winter of 1968 the *Times* "discovered" a religious community near New Providence that had existed in its present form since the late 1800s—less than forty miles from Times Square. Agricultural work was performed entirely by hand, women still wore long dresses with high collars, and town worship was held every evening.

I, too, was amazed. I'd seldom traveled west of the Hudson and still thought of New Jersey as some dismal extension of the Newark slums, ruled by gangsters, foggy with swamp gases and industrial waste, a grey land that had surrendered to the city.

Only later did I learn of the rural New Jersey, and of towns whose solitary general stores double as post offices, with one or two gas pumps standing in front. And later still I learned of Baptistown and Quakertown, their old religions surviving unchanged, and of towns like Lebanon, Landsdown, and West Portal, close to Route 22 and civilization but heavy with secrets undreamt of by city folk; Mt. Airy, with its network of hidden caverns, and Mt. Olive, bordering the infamous Budd Lake; Middle Valley, sheltered by dark cliffs, subject of the recent archaeological debate chronicled in *Natural History*, where a wanderer may still find peculiar relics of pagan worship and, some say, hear the chants that echo from the cliffs on certain nights; and towns with names like Zaraphath and Gilead, forgotten communities of bearded men and black-robed women, walled hamlets too small or obscure for most maps of the state. This was the wilderness into which I traveled, weary of Manhattan's interminable din; and it was outside Gilead where, until the tragedies, I chose to make my home for three months.

Among the silliest of literary conventions is the "town that won't talk"—the Bavarian village where peasants turn away from tourists' queries about "the castle" and silently cross themselves, the New England harbor town where fishermen feign ignorance and cast "furtive glances" at the traveler. In actuality, I have found, country people love to talk to the stranger, provided he shows a sincere interest in their anecdotes. Storekeepers will interrupt their activity at the cash register to tell you their theories on a recent murder; farmers will readily spin tales of buried bones and of a haunted house down the road. Rural townspeople are not so reticent as the writers would have us believe.

Gilead, isolated though it is behind its oak forests and ruined walls, is no exception. The inhabitants regard all outsiders with an initial suspicion, but let one demonstrate a respect for their traditional reserve and they will prove friendly enough. They don't favor modern fashions or flashy automobiles, but they can hardly be described as hostile, although that was my original impression.

When asked about the terrible events at Poroth Farm, they will prove more than willing to talk. They will tell you of bad crops and polluted well water, of emotional depression leading to a fatal argument. In short, they will describe a conventional rural murder, and will even volunteer their opinions on the killer's present whereabouts.

But you will learn almost nothing from them—or almost nothing that is true. They don't know what really happened. I do. I was there.

I had come to spend the summer with Sarr Poroth and his wife. I needed a place where I could do a lot of reading without distraction, and

Poroth's farm, secluded as it was even from the village of Gilead two miles down the dirt road, appeared the perfect spot for my studies.

I had seen the Poroths' advertisement in the *Hunterdon County Democrat* on a trip west through Princeton last spring. They advertised for a summer or long-term tenant to live in one of the outbuildings behind the farmhouse. As I soon learned, the building was a long low cinderblock affair, unpleasantly suggestive of army barracks but clean, functional, and cool in the sun; by the start of summer ivy sprouted from the walls and disguised the ugly grey brick. Originally intended to house chickens, it had in fact remained empty for several years until the farm's original owner, a Mr. Baber, sold out last fall to the Poroths, who immediately saw that with the installation of dividing walls, linoleum floors, and other improvements, the outbuilding might serve as a source of income. I was to be their first tenant.

The Poroths, Sarr and Deborah, were in their early thirties, only slightly older than I, although anyone who met them might have believed the age difference to be greater; their relative solemnity, and the drabness of their clothing, added years to their appearance, and so did their hair styles: Deborah, though possessing a beautiful length of black hair, wound it all in a tight bun behind her neck, pulling the hair back from her face with a severity which looked almost painful, and Sarr maintained a thin fringe of black beard that circled from ears to chin in the manner of the Pennsylvania Dutch, who leave their hair shaggy but refuse to grow moustaches lest they resemble the military class they've traditionally despised. Both man and wife were hardworking, grave of expression, and pale despite the time spent laboring in the sun—a pallor accentuated by the inky blackness of their hair. I imagine this unhealthy aspect was due, in part, to the considerable amount of inbreeding that went on in the area, the Poroths themselves being, I believe, third cousins. On first meeting, one might have taken them for brother and sister, two gravely devout children aged in the wilderness.

And yet there was a difference between them—and, too, a difference that set them both in contrast to others of their sect. The Poroths were, as far as I could determine, members of a tiny Mennonitic order outwardly related to the Amish, though doctrinal differences were apparently rather profound. It was this order that made up the large part of the community known as Gilead.

I sometimes think the only reason they allowed an infidel like me to live on their property (for my religion was among the first things they inquired about) was because of my name; Sarr was very partial to Jeremiah, and the motto of their order was "Stand ye in the ways, and see, and ask for the old paths, where is the good way, and walk therein." (VI:16)

Having been raised in no particular religion except a universal skepticism, I began the summer with a hesitancy to bring up the topic in conversation, and so I learned comparatively little about the Poroths' beliefs. Only toward the end of my stay did I begin to thumb through the Bible in odd moments and take to quoting jeremiads. That was, I suppose, Sarr's influence.

I was able to learn, nonetheless, that for all their conservative aura the Poroths were considered, in effect, young liberals by most of Gilead. Sarr had a bachelor's degree in religious studies from Rutgers, and Deborah had attended a nearby community college for two years, unusual for women of the sect. Too, they had only recently taken to farming, having spent the first year of their marriage near New Brunswick, where Sarr had hoped to find a teaching position and, when the job situation proved hopeless, had worked as a sort of handyman and carpenter. While most inhabitants of Gilead had never left the farm, the Poroths were coming to it late—their families had been merchants for several generations—and so were relatively inexperienced.

The inexperience showed. The farm comprised some ninety acres, but most of that was forest, or fields of weeds too thick and high to walk through. Across the backyard, close to my rooms, ran a small, nameless stream nearly choked with green scum. A large cornfield to the north lay fallow, but Sarr was planning to seed it this year, using borrowed equipment. His wife spent much of her time indoors, for though she maintained a small vegetable garden, she preferred keeping house and looking after the Poroths' great love, their seven cats.

As if to symbolize their broad-mindedness, the Poroths owned a television set, very rare in Gilead; in light of what was to come, however, it is unfortunate they lacked a telephone. (Apparently the set had been received as a wedding present from Deborah's parents, but the monthly expense of a telephone was simply too great.) Otherwise, though, the little farmhouse was "modern" in that it had a working bathroom and gas heat. That they had advertised in the local newspaper was considered scandalous by some of the order's more orthodox members, and indeed a mere subscription to that innocuous weekly had at one time been regarded as a breach of religious conduct.

Though outwardly similar, both of them tall and pale, the Poroths were actually so different as to embody the maxim that opposites attract. It was that carefully nurtured reserve that deceived one at first meeting, for in truth Deborah was far more talkative, friendly, and energetic than her husband. Sarr was moody, distant, silent most of the time, with a voice so low that one had trouble following him in conversation. Sitting as stonily as one of their cats, barely moving, seldom speaking, remote and inscrutable, he tended to frighten visitors to the farm until they learned that he was not really sitting in judgment on them; his reserve was born not of surliness but of shyness.

Where Sarr was catlike, his wife hid beneath the formality of her order the bubbly personality of a kitten. Given the smallest encouragement— say, a family visit—she would plunge into animated conversation, gesticulating, laughing easily, hugging whatever cat was nearby or shouting to guests across the room. When drinking—for both of them enjoyed liquor and, curiously, it was not forbidden by their faith—their innate differences were magnified: Deborah would forget the restraints placed upon women in the order and would eventually dominate the conversation, while her husband would seem to grow increasingly withdrawn and morose.

Women in the region tended to be submissive to the men, and certainly the important decisions in the Poroths' lives were made by Sarr. Yet I really cannot say who was the stronger of the two. Only once did I ever see them quarrel...

Perhaps the best way to tell it is by setting down portions of the journal I kept this summer. Not every entry, of course. Mere excerpts. Just enough to make this affidavit comprehensible to anyone unfamiliar with the incidents at Poroth Farm.

The journal was the only writing I did all summer; my primary reason for keeping it was to record the books I'd read each day, as well as to examine my reactions to relative solitude over an extended period. All the rest of my energies (as you will no doubt gather from the notes below) were spent reading, in preparation for a course I plan to teach at Trenton State this fall. Or *planned*, I should say, because I don't expect to be anywhere around here come fall.

Where will I be? Perhaps that depends on what's beneath those rose-tinted spectacles.

The course was to cover the gothic tradition from Shakespeare to Faulkner, from *Hamlet* to *Absalom, Absalom!* (And why not view the former as gothic, with its ghost on the battlements and concern for lost inheritance?) To make the move to Gilead, I'd rented a car for a few days and had stuffed it full of books—only a few of which I ever got to read. But then, I couldn't have known...

How pleasant things were, at the beginning.

## June 4

Unpacking day. Spent all morning putting up screens, and a good thing I did. Night now, and a million moths tapping at the windows. One of them as big as a small bird—white—largest I've ever seen. What kind of caterpillar must it have been? I hope the damned things don't push through the screens.

Had to kill literally hundreds of spiders before moving my stuff in. The Poroths supposedly renovated this building only a couple of months ago, and already it's infested. *Arachnidae*—hate the bastards. Why? We'll take that one up with Sigmund someday. Daydreams of Revenge of the Spiders, writhing body covered with a frenzy of hairy brown legs. "Egad, man, that face! That bloody, torn face! And the missing eyes! It looks like—no! Jeremy!" Killing spiders is supposed to bring bad luck. (Insidious Sierra Club propaganda masquerading as folk myth?) But can't sleep if there's anything crawling around... so it's swat or stamp on whatever I can.

Supper with the Poroths. Began to eat, then heard Sarr saying grace. Apologies—but things like that don't embarrass me as much as they used to. Is that because I'm nearing thirty?

Chatted about crops, insects, humidity. (Very damp area—band of purplish mildew already around bottom of walls out here.) Sarr told of plans to someday build a larger house when Deborah has a baby, three or four years from now. Intends to build it out of stone. Then he shut up, and I had to keep the conversation going. (Hate eating in silence—animal sounds of mastication, bubbling stomachs.) Deborah joked about cats being her surrogate children. All seven of them hanging around my legs, rubbing against ankles. My nose began running and my eyes itched. Goddamned allergy. Must remember to start treatments this fall, when I get to Trenton. Deborah sympathetic, Sarr merely watchful; she told me my eyes were bloodshot, offered antihistamine. Told them I was glad they at least believe in modern medicine—I'd been afraid she'd offer herbs or mud or something. Sarr said some of the locals still use "snake oil." Asked him how snakes were killed, quoting line from *Vathek:* "The oil of the serpents I have pinched to death will be a pretty present." We discussed wisdom of pinching snakes. Apparently there's a copperhead out back, near the brook.

The meal was good—lamb and noodles. Not bad for twenty dollars a week, since I detest cooking. Spice cake for dessert, home-made, of course. Deborah is a good cook. Handsome woman, too.

Still light when I left their kitchen. Fireflies already on the lawn—I've never seen so many. Knelt and watched them a while, listening to the crickets. Think I'll like it here.

Took nearly an hour to arrange my books the way I wanted them. Alphabetical order by authors? No, chronological... But anthologies mess that system up, so back to authors. Why am I so neurotic about my books?

Anyway, they look nice there on the shelves.

Sat up tonight finishing *The Mysteries of Udolpho*. Figure it's best to get the long ones out of the way first. Radcliffe has unfortunate penchant for explaining away all her ghosts and apparitions—really a mistake and a bore. All in all, not exactly the most fascinating reading, though a good study in

Romanticism. Montoni the typical Byronic hero/villain. But can't demand students read *Udolpho*—too long. In fact, had to keep reminding myself to slow down, have patience with the book. Tried to put myself in frame of mind of 1794 reader with plenty of time on his hands.

It works, too—I do have plenty of time out here, and already I can feel myself beginning to unwind. What New York does to people...

It's almost two a.m. now, and I'm about ready to turn in. Too bad there's no bathroom in this building—I hate pissing outside at night. God knows what's crawling up your ankles... But it's hardly worth stumbling through the darkness to the farmhouse and maybe waking up Sarr and Deborah. The nights out here are really pitch-black.

...Felt vulnerable, standing there against the night. But what made me even uneasier was the view I got of this building. The lamp on the desk casts the only light for miles, and as I stood outside looking into this room, I could see dozens of flying shapes making right for the screens. When you're inside here, it's as if you're in a display case—the whole night can see you, but all you can see is darkness. I wish this room didn't have windows on three of the walls—though that does let in the breeze. And I wish the woods weren't so close to the windows by the bed. I suppose privacy is what I wanted—but feel a little unprotected out here.

Those moths are still batting themselves against the screens, but as far as I can see the only things that have gotten in are a few gnats flying around this lamp. The crickets sound good—you sure don't hear them in the city. Frogs are croaking in the brook.

My nose is only now beginning to clear up. Those goddamned cats. I'll walk to town tomorrow; must remember to buy some Contac. Even though the cats are all outside during the day, that farmhouse is full of their scent. But I don't expect to be spending that much time inside the house anyway; this allergy will keep me away from the TV and out here with the books.

Just saw an unpleasantly large spider scurry across the floor near the foot of my bed. Vanished behind the footlocker. Must remember to buy some insect spray.

## June 11

Hot today, but at night comes a chill. The dampness of this place seems to magnify temperature. Sat outside most of the day finishing the Maturin book, *Melmoth the Wanderer*, and feeling vaguely guilty each time I heard Sarr or Deborah working out there in the field. Well, I've paid for my reading time, so I guess I'm entitled to enjoy it. Though some of these old gothics are a bit hard to enjoy. The trouble with *Melmoth* is that it wants you to hate. You're especially supposed to hate the Catholics. No doubt its picture of the Inquisition is accurate, but all a book like this can do is put you in an unconstructive rage. Its cast of vicious characters have been dead for centuries, and there's no way to punish them. Still, it's a nice, cynical book for those who like atrocity scenes—starving prisoners forced to eat their girlfriends, etc. And narratives within narratives within narratives within narratives. I may assign some sections to my class.

Just before dinner, in need of a break, read a story by Arthur Machen. Born a century ago in rural Wales, though not sure exactly where the story's set: old house in the hills, dark woods with secret paths and hidden streams. God, what an experience! I was a little confused by the framing device and all its high-flown talk of "cosmic evil," but the sections from the young girl's notebook were...staggering. That air of paganism, the malevolent little faces peeping from the shadows, and those rites she can't dare talk about... It's called "The White People," and it must be the most persuasive horror tale ever written.

Afterward, strolling toward the farmhouse—the Poroths had already gone in to get dinner ready—I was moved to climb the old tree in the side yard and stood upright on a great heavy branch near the middle, making strange gestures and faces that no one could see. Can't say exactly what it was I did, or why. It was getting dark—fireflies below me and a mist rising off the field. I must have looked like a madman's shadow as I made signs to the woods and the moon.

Lamb tonight, and damned good. I may find myself getting fat. Offered, again, to wash the dishes, but apparently Deborah feels that's her role, and I don't care to dissuade her. So talked a while with Sarr about his cats—the usual subject of conversation, especially because, now that summer's coming, they're bringing in dead things every night. Field mice, moles, shrews, birds, even a little garter snake. They don't eat them, just lay them out on the porch for the Poroths to see—sort of an offering, I guess. Sarr tosses the bodies in the garbage can, which, as a result, smells indescribably foul. Deborah wants to put bells around their necks; she hates mice but feels sorry for the birds. When she finished the dishes, she and Sarr sat down to watch one of their godawful TV programs, so I came out here to read.

Spent the usual ten minutes going over this room, spray can in hand, looking for spiders to kill. Found a couple of little ones, then spent some time spraying bugs that were hanging on the screens hoping to get in. Watched a lot of long-legged things curl up and die. Tended not to kill the moths, unless they were making too much of a racket banging against the screen; I can tolerate them okay, but it's the fireflies I really like. I always feel a little sorry when I kill one by mistake and see it hold that cold glow too long. (That's how you know they're dead: the dead ones don't wink. They just keep their light on till it fades away.)

The insecticide I'm using is made right here in New Jersey, by the Ortho Chemical Company. The label on the can says, "WARNING: For Outdoor Use Only." That's why I bought it—figured it's the most powerful brand available.

Sat in bed reading Algernon Blackwood's witch/cat story "Ancient Sorceries" (nowhere near as good as Machen, or as his own tale "The Willows"), and it made me think of those seven cats. The Poroths have around a dozen names for each of them, which seems a little ridiculous, since the creatures barely respond even to one. Sasha, for example, the orange male, is also known as Butch, which comes from *bouche*, mouth. And that's short for Eddie la Bouche, so he's also called Ed or Eddie— which in turn come from some friend's mispronunciation of the cat's original name, Itty, short for Itty Bitty Kitty, as he was quite small when they got him. And Zoë, the cutest of the kittens, is also called Bozo and Bisbo. Let's see, how many others can I remember? (I'm just learning to tell some of them apart.) Felix, or Flixie, was originally called Paleface; and Phaedra, his mother, is sometimes known as Phuddy, short for Phuddy Duddy.

Come to think of it, the only cat that hasn't got multiple names is Bwada, Sarr's cat. (All the others were acquired after he married Deborah, but Bwada was his pet years before.) She's the oldest of the cats, and the meanest. Fat and sleek, with fine grey fur darker than silver grey, lighter than charcoal. She's the only cat that's ever bitten anyone—Deborah, as well as friends of the Poroths—and after seeing the way she snarls at the other cats when they get in her way, I decided to keep my distance. Fortunately she's scared of me and retreats whenever I approach. I think being spayed is what's messed her up and given her an evil disposition.

Sounds are drifting from the farmhouse. I can vaguely make out a psalm of some kind. It's late, past eleven, and I guess the Poroths have turned off the TV and are singing their evening devotions…

And now all is silence. They've gone to bed. I'm not very tired yet, so I guess I'll stay up a while and read some—

Something odd just happened. I've never heard anything like it. While writing for the past half hour I've been aware, if half-consciously, of the crickets. Their regular chirping can be pretty soothing, like the sound of a well-tuned machine. But just a few seconds ago they seemed to miss a beat. They'd been singing along steadily, ever since the moon came up, and all of a sudden they just *stopped* for a beat—and then they began again, only they were out of rhythm for a moment or two, as if a hand had jarred the record or there'd been some kind of momentary break in the natural flow…

They sound normal enough now, though. Think I'll go back to *Otranto* and let that put me to sleep. It may be the foundation of the English gothics, but I can't imagine anyone actually reading it for pleasure. I wonder how many pages I'll be able to get through before I drop off.

## June 12

Slept late this morning, and then, disinclined to read Walpole on such a sunny day, took a walk. Followed the little brook that runs past my building. There's still a lot of that greenish scum clogging one part of it, and if we don't have some rain soon I expect it will get worse. But the water clears up considerably when it runs past the cornfield and through the woods.

Passed Sarr out in the field—he yelled to watch out for the copper-head, which put a pall on my enthusiasm for exploration... But as it happened I never ran into any snakes, and have a fair idea I'd survive even if bitten. Walked around half a mile into the woods, branches snapping in my face. Made an effort to avoid walking into the little yellow caterpillars that hang from every tree. At one point I had to get my feet wet, because the trail that runs alongside the brook disappeared and the undergrowth was thick. Ducked under a low arch made by decaying branches and vines, my sneakers sloshing in the water. Found that as the brook runs west it forms a small circular pool with banks of wet sand surrounded by tall oaks, their roots thrust into the water. Lots of animal tracks in the sand—deer, I believe, and what may be a fox or perhaps some farmer's dog. Obviously a watering place. Waded into the center of the pool—it only came up a little past my ankles—but didn't stand there long because it started looking like rain.

The weather remained nasty all day, but no rain has come yet. Cloudy now, though; can't see any stars.

Finished *Otranto*, began *The Monk*. So far so good—rather dirty, really. Not for readers today, of course, but I can imagine the sensation it must have caused back at the end of the eighteenth century.

Had a good time at dinner tonight, since Sarr had walked into town and brought back some wine. (Medical note: I seem to be less allergic to cats when mildly intoxicated.) We sat around the kitchen afterward playing poker for matchsticks—very sinful indulgence, I gather; Sarr and Deborah told me, quite seriously, that they'd have to say some extra prayers tonight by way of apology to the Lord.

Theological considerations aside, though, we all had a good time, and Deborah managed to clean us both out. Women's intuition, she says. I'm sure she must have it—she's the type. Enjoy being around her, and not always so happy to trek back outside to this room, through the high grass, the night dew, the things in the soil... I've got to remember, though, that they're a couple, I'm the single one, and I mustn't intrude too long. So left them tonight at eleven—or actually a little after that, since their clock is slightly out of kilter. They have this huge grandfather-type clock, a wedding present from Sarr's parents, that has supposedly been keeping perfect time for a century or more. You can hear its ticking all over the house when everything else is still. Deborah said that last night, just as they were going to bed, the clock seemed to slow down a little, then gave a couple of faster beats and started in as before. Sarr examined it—he's pretty good with mechanical things—but said he saw nothing wrong. Guess everything's got to wear out a bit, after years and years.

Back to *The Monk*. May Brother Ambrosio bring me pleasant dreams.

## June 13

Read a little in the morning, loafed during the afternoon. At four thirty watched *The Thief of Bagdad*—ruined on TV and portions omitted, but still a great film. Deborah puttered around the kitchen, and Sarr spent most of the day outside. Before dinner I came back out here with a scissors and cut away a lot of ivy that has tried to grow through the windows of this building. The little shoots fasten onto the screens and really cling.

Beef with rice tonight, and apple pie for dessert. Great. I stayed inside the house after dinner to watch the late news with the Poroths. The announcer mentioned that today was Friday the thirteenth, and I nearly gasped. I'd known on some dim automatic level that it was the thirteenth, if only from keeping this journal; but I hadn't had the faintest idea it was Friday. That's how much I've lost track of time out here; day drifts into day, and every one but Sunday seems completely interchangeable. Not a bad feeling, really, though at certain moments this isolation makes me feel somewhat adrift. I'd been so used to living by the clock and the calendar.

We tried to figure out if anything unlucky happened to any of us today. About the only incident we could come up with was Sarr's getting bitten by some animal a cat had left on the porch. The cats had been sitting by the front door waiting to be let in for their dinner, and when Sarr came in from the field, he was greeted with the usual assortment of dead mice and moles. As he always did, he began gingerly picking the bodies up by the tails and tossing them into the garbage can, meanwhile scolding the cats for being such natural-born killers. There was one body, he told us, that looked different from the others: rather like a large shrew, only the mouth was somehow askew, almost as if it were vertical instead of horizontal, with a row of little yellow teeth exposed. He figured that, whatever it was, the cats had pretty well mauled it, which probably accounted for its unusual appearance; it was quite tattered and bloody by this time.

In any case, he'd bent down to pick it up, and the thing had twisted itself and bitten him on the thumb. Apparently it had just been feigning death, like an opossum, because as soon as he yelled and dropped it, the thing sped off into the grass, with Bwada and the rest in hot pursuit. Deborah had been afraid of rabies—always a real danger around here, rare though it is—but fortunately the bite hadn't even pierced Sarr's skin. Just a nip, really. Hardly a Friday-the-thirteenth tragedy.

Lying in bed now, listening to sounds in the woods. The trees come really close to my windows in the back, and there's always some kind of sound coming from the underbrush in addition to the tapping at the screens. A million creatures out there, after all—most of them insects and spiders, a colony of frogs in the swampy part of the woods, and perhaps even skunks and raccoons. Depending on your mood, you can either ignore the sounds and just go to sleep or—as I'm doing now—remain awake listening to them. When I lie here thinking about what's out there, I feel more protected with the light off. So I think I'll put away this writing...

## June 15

Something really weird happened today. I still keep trying to figure it out.

Sarr and Deborah were gone almost all day; Sunday worship is, I assume, the center of their religious activity. They walked into Gilead early in the morning and didn't return until after four. They'd left, in fact, before I woke up. Last night they'd asked me if I'd like to come along, but I got the impression they were inviting me mainly to be polite, so I declined. I wouldn't want to make them uncomfortable during their services, but perhaps someday I'll accompany them anyway, since I'm curious to see a fundamentalist church in action.

I was left to share the farm with the Poroths' seven cats and the four hens they'd bought last week. From my window I could see Bwada and Phaedra chasing after something near the barn; lately they've taken to stalking grasshoppers. As I do every morning, I went into the farmhouse kitchen and made myself some breakfast, leafing through one of the Poroths' religious magazines, and then returned to my rooms out back for some serious reading. I picked up *Dracula* again, which I'd started yesterday, but the soppy Victorian sentimentality began to annoy me. The book had begun so well, on such a frightening note—Jonathan Harker trapped in that Carpathian castle, inevitably the prey of its terrible owner—that when Stoker switched the locale to England and his main characters to women, he simply couldn't sustain that initial tension.

With the Poroths gone I felt a little lonely and bored, something I hadn't felt out here before. Though I'd brought cartons of books to entertain me, I felt restless and wished I owned a car. I'd have gone for a drive; surely there must be plenty of places worth exploring. As things stood, though, I had nothing to do except watch television or take a walk.

So I followed the stream again into the woods, and eventually came to the circular pool. There were some new animal tracks in the wet sand, and, ringed by oaks, the place was very beautiful, but still I felt bored. Again I waded to the center of the pool and looked up at the sky through the trees. Feeling myself alone, I began to make some of the odd signs with face and hands that I had made that evening in the tree—but I felt that these movements had been unaccountably robbed of their power. Standing there up to my ankles in water, I felt foolish.

Worse than that, upon leaving the place, I found a red-brown leech clinging to my right ankle. It wasn't large and I was able to scrape it off with a stone, but it left me with a little round bite that oozed blood, and a feeling of—how shall I put it?—physical helplessness. I felt that the woods had somehow become hostile to me and, more important, would forever remain hostile. Something had passed.

I followed the stream back to the farm, and there I found Bwada, lying on her side near some rocks along the bank. Her legs were stretched out as if she were running, and her eyes were wide and astonished-looking. Flies were crawling over them.

She couldn't have been dead for long, since I'd seen her only a few hours before, but she was already stiff. There was foam around her jaws. I couldn't tell what had happened to her until I turned her over with a stick and saw, on the side that had lain against the ground, a gaping red hole that opened like some new orifice. The skin around it was folded back in little triangular flaps, exposing the pink flesh beneath. I backed off in disgust, but I could see even from several feet away that the hole had been made *from the inside.*

I can't say that I was very upset at Bwada's death, because I'd always hated her. What did upset me, though, was the manner of it—I can't figure out what could have done that to her. I vaguely remember reading about a kind of slug that, when eaten by a bird, will bore its way out through the bird's stomach... But I'd never heard of something like this happening with a cat. And even more peculiar, how could—

Well, anyway, I saw the body and thought, Good riddance. But I didn't know what to do with it. Looking back, of course, I wish I'd buried it right there. But I didn't want to go near it again. I considered walking into town and trying to find the Poroths, because I knew their cats were like children to them, even Bwada, and that they'd want to know right away. But I really didn't feel like running around Gilead asking strange people where the Poroths were—or worse yet, stumbling into some forbidding-looking church in the middle of a ceremony.

Finally I made up my mind to simply leave the body there and pretend I'd never seen it. Let Sarr discover it himself. I didn't want to have to tell him when he got home that his longtime pet had been killed; I prefer to avoid unpleasantness. Besides, I felt strangely guilty, the way one often does at someone else's misfortune.

So I spent the rest of the afternoon reading in my room, slogging through the Stoker. I wasn't in the best mood to concentrate. Sarr and Deborah got back after four—they shouted hello and went into the house. When Deborah called me for dinner, they still hadn't come outside.

When I entered the kitchen, all the cats were inside having their evening meal—all except Bwada—and Sarr asked me if I'd seen her during the day. I lied and said I hadn't. Deborah suggested that occasionally Bwada ignored the supper call because, unlike the other cats, she sometimes ate what she killed. "Maybe she's just full," said Deborah, and laughed. That rattled me a bit, but I had to stick to my lie.

Sarr seemed more concerned, and when he told Deborah he intended to search for the animal after dinner (it would still be light), I readily offered my help. I figured I could lead him to the spot where the body lay…

And then, in the middle of our dinner, came that scratching at the door. Sarr got up and opened it. Bwada walked in.

Now, I know she was dead. She was *stiff* dead. That wound in her side had been unmistakable, and now it was only a reddish swelling, hairless. Luckily the Poroths didn't notice my shock; they were busy fussing over her, seeing what was wrong. "Look, she's hurt herself," said Deborah. "She's bumped into something." The animal didn't walk well, and there was a clumsiness in the way she held herself. When Sarr put her down after examining the swelling, she slipped when she tried to walk away.

The Poroths decided that she must have run into a jagged rock or some other object and had badly bruised herself; they believe her lack of coordination is due to the shock, or perhaps to a pinching of the nerves. It sounds logical enough. Sarr told me, before I came out here for the night, that if she's worse tomorrow, he'll take her to the local vet, even though he'll have trouble paying for treatment. I immediately offered to lend him money, or even pay for the visit myself, because I desperately want to hear a doctor's opinion.

My own conclusion is really not that different from theirs. I tend to think now that maybe, just maybe, I was wrong in assuming the cat was dead. I'm no scientist—maybe what I mistook for rigor mortis was some kind of fit. Maybe she really did run into something sharp and then went into some kind of shock whose effect hasn't yet worn off. It's possible, I guess.

But I could swear that hole came from inside her.

I couldn't continue dinner and told the Poroths my stomach hurt, which was partly true. We all watched Bwada stumble around the kitchen floor, ignoring the food Deborah put before her as if it weren't there. Her movements were stiff, tentative, like a newborn animal still unsure how to move its muscles. I suspect that's the result of her fit.

When I left the house tonight, a little while ago, she was huddled in the corner staring at me. Deborah was crooning over her, but the cat was staring at me.

Killed a monster of a spider behind my suitcase tonight. That Ortho bug spray really does a job. When Sarr was in here a few days ago he said the room smelled of spray, but I guess my allergy's too bad for me to smell it.

I enjoy watching the zoo outside my screens. Put my face close and stare at the bugs eye to eye. Zap the ones whose faces I don't like.

Tried to read more of the Stoker—but one thing keeps bothering me. The way that cat stared at me. Deborah was brushing its back, Sarr fiddling with his pipe, and that cat just stared at me and never blinked. I stared back, said, "Hey, Sarr? Look at Bwada. That damned cat's not blinking." And just as he looked up, it blinked. Heavily.

Hope we can go to the vet tomorrow, because I want to ask him whether cats can impale themselves on a rock or a stick, and if such an accident might cause a fit of some kind that would make them rigid.

Cold night. Sheets are damp and the blanket itches. Wind from the woods—ought to feel good in the summer, but it doesn't feel like summer. That damned cat didn't blink till I mentioned it. Almost as if it understood me.

## June 17

...Swelling on her side's all healed now. Hair growing back over it. She walks fine, has a great appetite, shows affection to the Poroths. Sarr says her recovery demonstrates how the Lord watches over animals—affirms his faith. Says if he'd taken her to a vet he'd just have been throwing away money.

Read some LeFanu—"Green Tea," about the phantom monkey with eyes that glow, and "The Familiar," about the little staring man who drives the hero mad. Not the smartest choices right now, the way I feel, because for all the time that fat grey cat purrs over the Poroths, it just stares at me.

And snarls. I suppose the accident may have addled its brain a bit. I mean, if spaying can change a cat's personality, certainly a goring on a rock might.

Spent a lot of time in the sun today. The flies made it pretty hard to concentrate on the stories, but figured I'd get a suntan. I probably have a good tan now (hard to tell, because the mirror in here is small and the light dim), but suddenly it occurs to me that I'm not going to be seeing anyone for a long time anyway, except the Poroths, so what the hell do I care how I look?

Can hear them singing their nightly prayers now. A rather comforting sound, I must admit, even if I can't share the sentiments.

Petting Felix today—my favorite of the cats, real charm—came away with a tick on my arm which I didn't discover till taking a shower before dinner. As a result, I can still feel imaginary ticks crawling up and down my back. Damned cat.

## June 21

...Coming along well with the Victorian stuff. Zipped through "The Uninhabited House" and "Monsieur Maurice," both very literate, sophisticated. Deep into the terrible suffering of "The Amber Witch," poor priest and daughter near starvation, when Deborah called me in for dinner. Roast beef, with salad made from garden lettuce. Quite good. And Deborah was wearing one of the few sleeveless dresses I've seen on her. So she has a body after all...

A rainy night. Hung around the house for a while reading in their living room while Sarr whittled and Deborah crocheted—like the way Victorians used to spend their evenings, all sitting around together, everyone doing their thing. Rain sounded better from in there than it does out here, where it's not so cozy.

At eleven we turned on the news, cats purring around us, Sarr with Zoë on his lap, Deborah petting Phaedra, me sniffling... Halfway through the broadcast I pointed to Bwada, curled up at my feet, and said, "Look at her. You'd think she was watching the news with us." Deborah laughed and leaned over to scratch Bwada behind the ears. As she did so, Bwada turned to look at me.

The rain is letting up slightly. I can still hear the dripping from the trees, leaf to leaf to the dead leaves lining the forest floor. It will probably continue on and off all night. Occasionally I think I hear a kind of thrashing in one of the oaks near the barn, but then the sound turns into the falling of the rain.

Mildew higher on the walls of this place. Glad my books are on shelves off the ground. So damp in here my envelopes are ruined—glue moistened, sealing them all shut. Stamps I've kept in my wallet are stuck to the dollar bills. At night my sheets are clammy and cold, but each morning I wake up sweating.

Finished "The Amber Witch," really fine. Would that all lives had such happy endings.

## June 22

Rain continued through most of the morning. After the Poroths returned from church (looking, with their black clothes and large old-fashioned black umbrellas, like figures out of Edward Gorey), I passed some time indoors by helping them prepare strips of molding for their upstairs study. We worked in the tool shed, one of the old wooden outbuildings. I measured, Sarr sawed, Deborah sanded. All in all, hardly felt useful, but I was in the mood for some companionship.

While they were busy, I stood staring out the window. The day had finally cleared. There's a narrow cement walk running from the shed to the main house, and two of the kittens—Felix, I think, and Minnie, the little orange one—were crouched in the middle of it, drying themselves in the late afternoon sun. Suddenly Bwada appeared around the side of the house and began slinking along the walk in our direction, tail swishing from side to side. When she neared the kittens, she gave a snarl—I could see her mouth working—and they leaped to their feet, bristling, and ran off into the grass.

Called this to the Poroths' attention. They said, in effect, Yes, we know, she's always been nasty to the kittens, probably because she never had any of her own. And besides, she's getting older.

When I turned back to the window, Bwada was gone. Asked the Poroths if they didn't think she'd gotten meaner lately. Realized that, in speaking, I'd unconsciously dropped my voice, as if someone might be listening through the chinks in the floorboards.

Deborah conceded that, yes, the cat is behaving worse these days toward the others. And not just toward the kittens, as before. Butch, the adult orange male, seems particularly afraid of her.

...Later, good Sunday dinner—chicken breast, rice, slice of rhubarb pie—and came back here.

Yet now am a little irritated at the Poroths. They claim they never come into these rooms, respect privacy of a tenant, etc. etc., but one of them must have been in here, because I've just noticed my can of insect spray is missing. I don't mind their borrowing it, but I like to have it by my bed on nights like this. Went over the room looking for spiders, just in case; had a fat copy of *American Scholar* in my hand to crush them (only thing it's good for), but found nothing.

Tried to read some *Walden* as a break from all the horror stuff, but found my eyes too irritated, watery. Keep scratching them as I write this. Nose pretty clogged, too—damned allergy's worse tonight.

Probably it's the dampness. Expect I'll have trouble getting to sleep.

## June 24

Writing this in the morning. Slept very late, as noise from outside kept me up last night. (Come to think of it, the Poroths' praying was unusually loud as well, but that wasn't what bothered me.) I'd been in the middle of doing this journal—some notes on De la Mare—when it came. I immediately stopped writing and shut off the light.

At first it sounded like something in the woods near my room—an animal? a child? I couldn't tell, but smaller than a man—shuffling through the dead leaves, kicking them around as if it didn't care who heard it. There was a snapping of branches and, every so often, a silence and then a bump, as if it were hopping over fallen logs. I stood in the dark listening to it, then crept to the window and looked out. Thought I noticed some bushes moving, back there in the undergrowth, but it may have been the wind.

The sound grew farther away. Whatever it was must have been walking directly out into the deepest part of the woods, where the ground gets swampy and treacherous, because, very faintly, I could hear the sucking sounds of feet slogging through the mud.

I stood by the window for almost an hour, occasionally hearing what I thought were movements off there in the swamp, but finally all was quiet except for the crickets and the frogs. I had no intention of going out there with my flashlight in search of the intruder, that's only for guys in the movies, and I wondered if I should call Sarr. But by this time the noise had stopped, and whatever it was had obviously moved on. Besides, I figured he'd have been angry if I'd awakened him and Deborah just because some stray dog had wandered near the farm. I recalled how annoyed he'd been earlier when—maybe not all that tactfully—I'd asked him what he'd done with my bug spray. (Will walk to town later and pick up a new one; clearly I must've misplaced the old.)

I went over to the windows on the other side and watched the moon-light on the barn for a while; my nose probably looked cross-hatched from pressing against the screen. In contrast to the woods, the grass looked peaceful under the full moon. Then I lay in bed, but had a hard time falling asleep. Just as I was getting relaxed, the sounds started again. High-pitched wails and caterwauls, from deep within the woods. Even after thinking about it a lot today, I still don't know whether the noise was human or animal. There were no actual words, of that I'm certain, but nevertheless there was the impression of *singing*. In a crazy, tuneless kind of way the sound seemed to carry the same solemn rhythm as the Poroths' prayers earlier that night.

The noise only lasted a minute or two, but I lay awake till the sky began to get lighter. Probably should have read a little more De la Mare, but was reluctant to turn on the lamp.

… After I returned from town, the farm looked very lonely. Wish they had a library in Gilead with more than religious tracts. Or a stand that sold the *Times*. Truth is, though, after a week or two you no longer miss it.

At dinner (pork chops, home-grown string beans, and pudding—quite good), mentioned the noise of last night. Sarr acted very concerned and went to his room to look up something in one of his books. Deborah and I discussed the matter at some length, and she suggested that the shuffling sounds weren't necessarily related to the wailing. The former were almost definitely those of a dog—dozens in the area, and they love to prowl around at night, exploring, hunting coons—and as for the wailing… well, it's hard to say. She thinks it may have been an owl or whippoorwill, while I suspect it may have been that same stray dog. I've heard the howl of wolves and I've heard hounds baying at the moon, and both have the same element of, I suppose, *worship* in them that these did.

Sarr came back downstairs and said he couldn't find what he'd been looking for. Said that when he moved into this farm he'd had "a fit of piety" and had burned a lot of old books he'd found in the attic; now he wishes he hadn't.

Looked up something on my own after leaving the Poroths. *Field Guide to Mammals* lists both red and grey foxes and, believe it or not, coyotes as surviving here in New Jersey. No wolves left, though—but the guide might be wrong.

Then, on a silly impulse, opened another reference book, Barbara Byfield's *Glass Harmonica*. Sure enough, my hunch was right: looked up June twenty-third, and it said, "St. John's Eve. Sabbats likely."

I'll stick to the natural explanation. Still, I'm glad Mrs. Byfield lists nothing for tonight; I'd like to get some sleep. There is, of course, a beautiful full moon—werewolf weather, as Maria Ouspenskaya might have said. But then, there are no wolves left in New Jersey…

(Which reminds me, really must read some Marryat and Endore. But only after *Northanger Abbey*; the course always comes first.)

## June 25

Slept all morning and, in the afternoon, followed the road in the opposite direction from Gilead, seeking anything of interest. But the road just gets muddier and muddier till it disappears altogether by the ruins of an old homestead—rocks and cement covered with moss—and it looked so much like poison ivy around there that I didn't want to risk tramping through.

Overheated from walk—am I getting out of shape? Or is it just the hot weather? Took a cold shower. When I opened the bathroom door, I accidentally let Bwada out; I'd wondered why the chair was propped against it. She raced into the kitchen, pushed open the screen door by herself, and I had no chance to catch her. (Wouldn't have attempted to anyway; her claws are wicked.) I apologized later when Deborah came in from the fields. She said Bwada had become vicious toward the other cats and that Sarr had confined her to the bathroom as punishment. The first time he'd shut her in there, Deborah said, the cat had gotten out; apparently she's smart enough to turn the doorknob by swatting at it a few times. Hence the chair.

Sarr came in carrying Bwada, both obviously out of temper. He'd seen a streak of orange running through the field toward him, followed by a grey blur. Butch had stopped at his feet and Bwada had pounced on him, but before she could do any damage, Sarr had grabbed her around the neck and carried her back here. He'd been bitten once and scratched a lot on his hands, but not badly; maybe the cat still likes him best. He threw her back in the bathroom and shoved the chair against the door, then sat down and asked Deborah to join him in some silent prayer. I thumbed uneasily through a religious magazine till they were done, and we sat down to dinner.

I apologized again, but he said he wasn't mad at me, that the Devil had gotten into his cat. It was obvious he meant that quite literally.

During dinner (omelet—the hens have been laying well) we heard a grating sound from the bathroom, and Sarr ran in to find the cat almost out the window; somehow she must have been strong enough to slide the sash up part way. She seemed so placid, though, when Sarr pulled her down from the sill—he'd been expecting another fight—that he let her out into the kitchen. At this she simply curled up near the stove and went to sleep; I guess she'd worked off her rage for the day. Still, the other cats gave her a wide berth.

Watched a couple of hours of television with the Poroths. They may have gone to college, but the shows they find interesting... God! I'm ashamed of myself for sitting there like a cretin in front of that box. I won't even mention what we watched, lest history record the true level of my taste.

And yet I find that the TV draws us closer, as if we were having an adventure together. Shared experience, really. Like knowing the same people or going to the same school.

But there's duplicity in those Poroths—and I don't mean just religious hypocrisy, either. Came out here after watching the news, and though I hate to accuse anyone of spying on me, there's no doubt that Sarr or

Deborah has been inside this room today. I began tonight's entry with great irritation, because I found my desk in disarray; this journal wasn't even put back in the right drawer. I keep all my pens on one side, all my pencils on another, ink and erasers in the middle, etc., and when I sat down tonight I saw that everything was out of place. Thank God I haven't included anything too personal in here... What I assume happened was that Deborah came in to wash the mildew off the walls—she's mentioned doing so several times, and she knew I'd be out walking part of the day—and got sidetracked into reading this, thinking it must be some kind of secret diary. (I'm sure she was disappointed to find that it's merely a literary journal, with nothing about her in it.)

What bugs me is the difficulty of broaching the subject. I can't just walk in and charge Deborah with being a sneak—Sarr is moody enough as it is—and even if I hint at "someone messing up my desk," they'll know what I mean and perhaps get angry. Whenever possible I prefer to avoid unpleasantness. I guess the best thing to do is simply hide this book under my mattress from now on and say nothing. If it happens again, though, I'll definitely move out of here.

...I've been reading some *Northanger Abbey*. Really quite witty, as all her stuff is, but it's obvious the mock-gothic bit isn't central to the story; I'd thought it was going to be a real parody. Love stories always tend to bore me, and normally I'd be asleep right now, but my damned nose is so clogged tonight that it's hard to breathe when I lie back. Usually being out here clears it up. I've used this goddamned inhaler a dozen times in the past hour, but within a few minutes I sneeze and have to use it again. Wish Deborah'd gotten around to cleaning off the mildew instead of wasting her time searching in here for True Confessions and deep dark secrets...

Think I hear something moving outside. Best to shut off my light.

**June 30**

Slept late. Read some Shirley Jackson stories over breakfast, but got so turned off at her view of humanity that I switched to old Aleister Crowley, who at least keeps a sunny disposition. For her, people in the country are callous and vicious, those in the city are callous and vicious, husbands are (of course) callous and vicious, and children are little sadists. The only ones with feelings are her put-upon middle-aged heroines, with whom she obviously identifies. Good thing she writes so well, otherwise the stories wouldn't sting so.

Inspired by Crowley, walked back to the pool in the woods. Had visions of climbing a tree, swinging on vines, anything to commemorate his exploits... Saw something dead floating in the center of the pool and ran back to the farm. Copperhead? Caterpillar? It had somehow opened up...

From far off could hear the echo of Sarr's axe, and joined him chopping stakes for tomatoes. He told me Bwada hadn't come home last night, and no sign of her this morning. Good riddance, as far as I'm concerned. Helped him chop some stakes while he was busy peeling off bark. That axe can get heavy fast! My arm hurt after three lousy stakes, and Sarr had already chopped fifteen or sixteen. Must start exercising. But I'll wait till my arm's less tired.

## July 2

Unpleasant day. Two a.m. now and still can't relax.

Sarr woke me up this morning—stood at my window calling "Jeremy... Jeremy..." over and over very quietly. He had something in his hand which, through the screen, I first took for a farm implement; then I saw it was a rifle. He said he wanted my help. For what? I asked.

"A burial."

Last night, after he and Deborah had gone to bed, they'd heard the kitchen door open and someone enter the house. They both assumed it was me, come to use the bathroom—but then they heard the cats screaming. Sarr ran down and switched on the light in time to see Bwada on top of Butch, claws in his side, fangs buried in his neck. From the way he described it, sounds almost sexual in reverse. Butch had stopped struggling, and Minnie, the orange kitten, was already dead. The door was partly open, and when Bwada saw Sarr, she ran out.

Sarr and Deborah hadn't followed her; they'd spent the night praying over the bodies of Minnie and Butch. I *thought* I'd heard their voices late last night, but that's all I heard, probably because I'd been playing my radio. (Something I rarely do—you can't hear noises from the woods when it's on.)

Poroths took deaths the way they'd take the death of a child. Regular little funeral service over by the unused pasture. (Hard to say if Sarr and Deborah were dressed in mourning, since that's the way they always dress.) Must admit I didn't feel particularly involved—my allergy's never permitted me to take much interest in the cats, though I'm fond of Felix—but I tried to act concerned: when Sarr asked, appropriately, "Is there no balm in Gilead? Is there no physician there?" (Jeremiah VIII:22), I nodded gravely. Read passages out of Deborah's Bible (Sarr seemed to know them all by heart), said "amen" when they did, knelt when they knelt, and tried to comfort Deborah when she cried. Asked her if cats could go to heaven, received a tearful "Of course." But Sarr added that Bwada would burn in hell.

What concerned me, apparently a lot more than it did either of them, was how the damned thing could get into the house. Sarr gave me this stupid, earnest answer: "She was always a smart cat." Like an outlaw's mother, still proud of her baby...

Yet he and I looked all over the land for her so he could kill her. Barns, tool shed, old stables, garbage dump, etc. He called her and pleaded with her, swore to me she hadn't always been like this.

We could hardly check every tree on the farm—unfortunately—and the woods are a perfect hiding place, even for animals far larger than a cat. So naturally we found no trace of her. We did try, though; we even walked up the road as far as the ruined homestead.

But for all that, we could have stayed much closer to home.

We returned for dinner, and I stopped at my room to change clothes. My door was open. Nothing inside was ruined, everything was in its place, everything as it should be—except the bed. The sheets were in tatters right down to the mattress, and the pillow had been ripped to shreds. Feathers were all over the floor. There were even claw marks on my blanket.

At dinner the Poroths demanded they be allowed to pay for the damage—nonsense, I said, they have enough to worry about—and Sarr suggested I sleep downstairs in their living room. "No need for that," I told him. "I've got lots more sheets." But he said no, he didn't mean that: he meant for my own protection. He believes the thing is particularly inimical, for some reason, toward me.

It seemed so absurd at the time... I mean, nothing but a big fat grey cat. But now, sitting out here, a few feathers still scattered on the floor around my bed, I wish I were back inside the house. I did give in to Sarr when he insisted I take his axe with me. But what I'd rather have is simply a room without windows.

I don't think I want to go to sleep tonight, which is one reason I'm continuing to write this. Intend to sit up all night on my new bedsheets, my back against the Poroths' pillow, leaning against the wall behind me, the axe beside me on the bed, this journal on my lap... The thing is, I'm rather tired out from all the walking I did today. Not used to that much exercise.

I'm pathetically aware of every sound. Every few minutes some snapping of a branch or rustling of leaves makes me jump.

"Thou art my hope in the day of evil."

At least that's what the man said.

## July 3

Woke up this morning with the journal and the axe cradled in my arms. What awakened me was the trouble I had breathing—nose all clogged, gasping for breath. Down the center of one of my screens, facing the woods, was a huge slash...

## July 15

Pleasant day, St. Swithin's Day—and yet my birthday. Thirty years old, lordy lordy lordy. Today I am a man. First dull thoughts on waking: "Damnation. Thirty today." But another voice inside me, smaller but more sensible, spat contemptuously at such an artificial way of charting one's life. "Ah, don't give it another thought," it said. "You've still got plenty of time to fool around." Advice I took to heart.

Weather today? Actually, somewhat nasty. And thus the weather for the next forty days, since "If rain on St. Swithin's Day, forsooth, no summer drouthe," or something like that. My birthday predicts the weather. It's even mentioned in *The Glass Harmonica*.

As one must, took a critical self-assessment. First area for improvement: flabby body. Second? Less bookish, perhaps? Nonsense—I'm satisfied with the progress I've made. "And seekest thou great things for thyself? Seek them not." (Jeremiah XLV:5) So I simply did what I remembered from the RCAF exercise series and got good and winded. Flexed my stringy muscles in the shower, certain I'll be a Human Dynamo by the end of summer. Simply a matter of willpower.

Was so ambitious I trimmed the ivy around my windows again. It's begun to block the light, and someday I may not be able to get out the door.

Read Ruthven Todd's *Lost Traveller*. Merely the narrative of a dream turned to nightmare, and illogical as hell. Wish, too, there'd been more than merely a few hints of sex. On the whole, rather unpleasant; that gruesome ending is so inevitable... Took me much of the afternoon. Then came upon an incredible essay by Lafcadio Hearn, something entitled "Gaki," detailing the curious Japanese belief that insects are really demons or the ghosts of evil men. Uncomfortably convincing!

Dinner late because Deborah, bless her, was baking me a cake. Had time to walk into town and phone parents. Happy birthday, happy birthday. Both voiced first worry—mustn't I be getting bored out here? Assured them I still had plenty of books and did not grow tired of reading.

"But it's so...*secluded* out there," Mom said. "Don't you get lonely?"

Ah, she hadn't reckoned on the inner resources of a man of thirty. Was tempted to quote *Walden*—"Why should I feel lonely? Is not our planet in the Milky Way?"—but refrained. How can I get lonely, I asked, when there's still so much to read? Besides, there are the Poroths to talk to.

Then the kicker: Dad wanted to know about the cat. Last time I'd spoken to them, it had sounded like a very real danger. "Are you still sleeping inside the farmhouse, I hope?"

No, I told him, really, I only had to do that for a few days, while the thing was prowling around at night. Yes, it had killed some chickens—a hen every night, in fact. But there'd been only four of them, and then it stopped. We haven't had a sign of it in more than a week. (I didn't tell him that it had left the hens uneaten, dead in the nest. No need to upset him further.)

"But what it did to your sheets," he went on. "If you'd been sleeping… Such savagery."

Yes, that was unfortunate, but there's been no trouble since. Honest. It was only an animal, after all, just a house cat gone a little wild. It posed the same kind of threat as (I was going to say, logically, a wildcat; but for Mom said) a nasty little dog. Like Mrs. Miller's bull terrier. Besides, it's probably miles and miles away by now. Or dead.

They offered to drive out with packages of food, magazines, a portable TV, but I made it clear I needed nothing. Getting too fat, actually.

Still light when I got back. Deborah had finished the cake, Sarr brought up some wine from the cellar, and we had a nice little celebration. The two of them being over thirty, they were happy to welcome me to the fold.

It's nice out here. The wine has relaxed me, and I keep yawning. It was good to talk to Mom and Dad again. Just as long as I don't dream of *The Lost Traveller*, I'll be content. And happier still if I don't dream at all.

## July 30

Well, Bwada is dead—this time for sure. We'll bury her tomorrow. Deborah was hurt, just how badly I can't say, but she managed to fight Bwada off. Tough woman, though she seems a little shaken. And with good reason.

It happened this way: Sarr and I were in the tool shed after dinner, building more shelves for the upstairs study. Though the fireflies were out, there was still a little daylight left. Deborah had gone up to bed after doing the dishes; she's been tired a lot lately, falls asleep early every night when they're watching TV. He thinks it may be something in the well water.

It had begun to get dark, but we were still working. Sarr dropped a box of nails, and while we were picking them up, he thought he heard a scream. Since I hadn't heard anything, he shrugged and was about to start sawing again when—fortunately—he changed his mind and ran off to the house. I followed him as far as the back porch, not sure whether to go upstairs, until I heard him pounding on their bedroom door and calling Deborah's name. As I ran up the stairs, I heard her say, "Wait, don't come in. I'll unlock the door…soon." Her voice was extremely hoarse, practically a croaking. We heard her rummaging in the closet—finding her bathrobe, I suppose—and then she opened the door.

She looked absolutely white. Her long hair was in tangles and her robe buttoned incorrectly. Around her neck she had wrapped a towel, but we could see patches of blood soaking through it. Sarr helped her over to the bed, shouting at me to bring up some bandages from the bathroom.

When I returned, Deborah was lying in bed, still pressing the towel to her throat. I asked Sarr what had happened; it almost looked as if the woman had tried suicide.

He didn't say anything, just pointed to the floor on the other side of the bed. I stepped around for a look. A crumpled grey shape was lying there, half covered by the bedclothes. It was Bwada, a wicked-looking wound in her side. On the floor next to her lay one of the Poroths' old black umbrellas—the thing Deborah had used to kill her.

She told us she'd been asleep when she felt something crawl heavily over her face. It had been like a bad dream. She'd tried to sit up, and suddenly Bwada was at her throat, digging in. Luckily she'd had the strength to tear the animal off and dash to the closet, where the first weapon at hand was the umbrella. Just as the cat sprang at her again, Deborah said, she'd raised the weapon and lunged. Amazing; how many women, I wonder, would have had such presence of mind? The rest sounds incredible to me, but it's probably the sort of crazy thing that happens in moments like this: somehow the cat had impaled itself on the umbrella.

Her voice, as she spoke, was barely more than a whisper. Sarr had to persuade her to remove the towel from her throat; she kept protesting that she wasn't hurt that badly, that the towel had stopped the bleeding. Sure enough, when Sarr finally lifted the cloth from her neck, the wounds proved relatively small, the slash marks already clotting. Thank God that thing didn't really get its teeth in.

My guess—only a guess—is that it had been weakened from days of roaming around the woods. (It was obviously incapable of feeding itself adequately, as I think was proved by its failure to eat the hens it had killed.) While Sarr dressed Deborah's wounds, I pulled back the bedclothes and took a closer look at the animal's body. The fur was matted and patchy; odd that an umbrella could make a puncture like that, ringed by flaps of skin, the flesh seeming to push outward. Deborah must have had the extraordinary good luck to have jabbed the animal precisely in its old wound, which had reopened. Naturally I didn't mention this to Sarr.

He made dinner for us tonight—soup, actually, because he thought that was best for Deborah. Her voice sounded so bad he told her not to strain it any more by talking, at which she nodded and smiled. We both had to help her downstairs, as she was clearly weak from shock.

In the morning, Sarr will go and get the doctor. He'll have to examine the cat, too, to check for rabies, so we put the body in the freezer to preserve it as well as possible. Afterward we'll bury it.

Deborah seemed okay when I left. Sarr was reading through some home medical guides, and she was just lying on the living room couch gazing at her husband with a look of purest gratitude—not moving, not saying anything, not even blinking.

I feel quite relieved. God knows how many nights I've lain here thinking every sound I heard was Bwada. I'll feel more relieved, of course, when that demon's safely underground; but I think I can say, at the risk of being melodramatic, that the reign of terror is over.

Hmm, I'm still a little hungry—am used to more than soup for dinner. These daily push-ups burn up energy. I'll probably dream of hamburgers and chocolate layer cakes.

## July 31

...The doctor collected scrapings from Bwada's teeth and scolded us for doing a poor job of preserving the body. Said storing it in the freezer was a sensible idea but that we should have done so sooner, since it was already decomposing. The dampness, I imagine, must act fast on dead flesh.

He pronounced Deborah in excellent condition—the marks on her throat are, remarkably, almost healed—but he said her reflexes seemed a little off. Sarr invited him to stay for the burial, but he declined—and quite emphatically, at that. He's not a member of their order, doesn't live in the area, and apparently doesn't get along too well with the people of Gilead, most of whom mistrust modern science. (Not that the old geezer sounded very representative of modern science. When I asked him for some good exercises, he recommended "chopping wood and running down deer.")

Standing under the heavy clouds, Sarr looked like a revivalist minister. His sermon was from Jeremiah XXII:19—"He shall be buried with the burial of an ass." The burial took place far from the graves of Bwada's two victims, and closer to the woods. We sang one song, Deborah just mouthing the words (still mustn't strain throat muscles). Sarr solemnly asked the Lord to look mercifully upon all His creatures, and I muttered an "amen." Then we walked back to the house, Deborah leaning on Sarr's arm; she's still somewhat stiff.

It was grey the rest of the day, and I sat in my room reading *The King in Yellow*—or rather, Chambers' collection of the same name. One look at the *real* book, according to Chambers, and I might not live to see the morrow, at least through the eyes of a sane man. (That single gimmick—masterful, I admit—seems to be his sole inspiration.)

I was disappointed that dinner was again made by Sarr; Deborah was upstairs resting, he said. He sounded concerned, felt there were things wrong with her the doctor had overlooked. We ate our meal in silence, and I came back here immediately after washing the dishes. Feel very drowsy and, for some reason, also rather depressed. It may be the gloomy weather— we are, after all, just animals, more affected by the sun and the seasons than we care to admit. More likely it was the absence of Deborah tonight. Hope she feels better soon.

Note: The freezer still smells of the cat's body. Opened it tonight and got a strong whiff of decay.

## August 1

Writing this, breaking habit, in early morning. Went to bed last night just after finishing the entry above, but was awakened around two by sounds coming from the woods. Wailing, deeper than before, followed by a low, guttural monologue. No words, at least that I could distinguish. If toads could talk... For some reason I fell asleep before the sounds ended, so I don't know what followed. Could very well have been an owl of some kind, and later a large bullfrog. But I quote, without comment, from *The Glass Harmonica*: "July 31: Lammas Eve. Sabbats likely."

Little energy to write tonight, and even less to write about. (Come to think of it, I slept most of the day: woke up at eleven, later took an afternoon nap. Alas, senile at thirty!) Too tired to shave, and haven't had the energy to clean this place, either; thinking about work is easier than doing it. The ivy's beginning to cover the windows again, and the mildew's been climbing steadily up the walls. It's like a dark green band that keeps widening. Soon it will reach my books...

Speaking of which: opened M. R. James at lunch today—*Ghost Stories of an Antiquary*—and a silverfish slithered out. Omen?

Played a little game with myself this evening—

I just had one hell of a shock. While writing the above, I heard a soft tapping, like nervous fingers drumming on a table, and discovered an enormous spider, biggest of the summer, crawling only inches from my ankle. It must have been living behind this desk.

When you can hear a spider walk across the floor, you *know* it's time to keep your socks on. Thank God for insecticide.

Oh, yeah, that game—the What If game. I probably play it too often. (Vain attempt to enlarge realm of the possible? Heighten my own sensitivity? Or merely work myself into an icy sweat?) I pose unpleasant questions for myself and consider the consequences—e.g., what if this glorified chicken coop is sinking into quicksand? (Wouldn't be at all surprised.) What if the Poroths are tired of me? What if I woke up inside my own coffin?

What if I never see New York again?

What if some horror stories aren't really fiction? If Machen sometimes told the truth? If there *are* White People, malevolent little faces peering out of the moonlight? Whispers in the grass? Poisonous things in the woods? Perfect hate and evil in the world?

Enough of this foolishness. Time for bed.

## August 9

...Read some Hawthorne in the morning and, over lunch, reread this week's *Hunterdon County Democrat* for the dozenth time. Sarr and Deborah were working somewhere in the fields, and I felt I ought to get some physical activity myself; but the thought of starting my exercises again after more than a week's laziness just seemed too unpleasant... I took a walk down the road, but only as far as a smashed-up cement culvert half buried in the woods. I was bored, but Gilead just seemed too far away.

Was going to cut the ivy surrounding my windows when I got back, but decided the place looks more artistic covered in vines. Rationalization?

Chatted with Poroths about politics, the World Situation, a little cosmology, blah blah blah. Dinner wasn't very good, probably because I'd been looking forward to it all day. The lamb was underdone and the beans were cold. Still, I'm always the gentleman, and was almost pleased when Deborah agreed to my offer to do the dishes. I've been doing them a lot lately.

I didn't have much interest in reading tonight and would have been up for some television, but Sarr's recently gotten into one of his religious kicks and began mumbling prayers to himself immediately after dinner. (Deborah, more human, wanted to watch the TV news. She seems to have an insatiable curiosity about world events, yet she claims the isolation here appeals to her.) Absorbed in his chanting, Sarr made me uncomfortable—I didn't like his face—and so after doing the dishes, I left.

I've been listening to the radio for the last hour or so... I recall days when I'd have gotten uptight at having wasted an hour, but out here I've lost all track of time. Feel adrift—a little disconcerting, but healthy, I'm sure.

...Shut off the radio a moment ago, and now realize my room is filled with crickets. Up close their sound is hardly pleasant—cross between a radiator and a tea kettle, very shrill. They'd been sounding off all night, but I'd thought it was interference on the radio.

Now I notice them; they're all over the room. A couple of dozen, I should think. Hate to kill them, really—they're one of the few insects I can stand, along with ladybugs and fireflies. But they make such a racket! Wonder how they got in.

## August 14

Played with Felix all morning—mainly watching him chase insects, climb trees, doze in the sun. Spectator sport. After lunch, went back to my room to look up something in Lovecraft and discovered my books were out of order. (Saki, for example, had been filed under "S," whereas— whether out of fastidiousness or pedantry—I've always preferred to file him as "Munro.") This is definitely one of the Poroths' doing. I'm pissed they didn't mention coming in here, but also a little surprised they'd have any interest in this stuff.

Arranged them correctly again, then sat down to reread Lovecraft's essay on "Supernatural Horror in Literature." It upset me to see how little I've actually read, how far I still have to go. So many obscure authors, so many books I've never come across... Left me feeling depressed and tired, so I took a nap for the rest of the afternoon.

Over dinner—vegetable omelet, rather tasteless—Deborah continued to question us on current events. It's getting to be like junior high school, with daily newspaper quizzes... Don't know how she got started on this, or why the sudden interest, but it obviously annoys the hell out of Sarr.

Sarr used to be a sucker for her little-girl pleadings—I remember how he used to carry her upstairs, becoming pathetically tender, the moment she'd say, "Oh, honey, I'm so tired"—but now he just becomes angry. Often he goes off morose and alone to pray, and the only time he laughs is when he watches television.

Tonight, thank God, he was in a mood to forgo the prayers, and so after dinner we all watched a lot of offensively ignorant programs. I was disturbed to find myself laughing along with the canned laughter, but I have to admit the TV helps us get along better together. Came back here after the news.

Not very tired, having slept so much of the afternoon, so began to read John Christopher's *The Possessors;* but good though it was, my mind began to wander to all the books I *haven't* yet read, and I got so depressed I turned on the radio. Find it takes my mind off things.

## August 19

Slept long into the morning, then walked down to the brook, scratching groggily. Deborah was kneeling by the water, lost, it seemed, in daydream, and I was embarrassed because I'd come upon her talking to herself. We exchanged a few insincere words and she went back toward the house.

Sat by some rocks, throwing blades of grass into the water. The sun on my head felt almost painful, as if my brain were growing too large for my skull. I turned and looked at the farmhouse. In the distance it looked like a picture at the other end of a large room, the grass for a carpet, the ceiling the sky. Deborah was stroking a cat, then seemed to grow angry when it struggled from her arms. I could hear the screen door slam as she went into the kitchen, but the sound reached me so long after the visual image that the whole scene struck me as, somehow, fake. I gazed up at the maples behind me, and they seemed trees out of a cheap postcard, the kind in which paint is thinly dabbed over a black-and-white photo; if you look closely, you can see that the green in the trees is not merely in the leaves, but rather floats as a vapor over leaves, branches, parts of the sky... The trees behind me seemed the productions of a poor painter, the color and shape not quite meshing. Parts of the sky were green, and pieces of the green seemed to float away from my vision. No matter how hard I tried, I couldn't follow them.

Far down the stream I could see something small and kicking, a black beetle, legs in the air, borne swiftly along in the current. Then it was gone.

Thumbed through the Bible while I ate my lunch—mostly cookies. By late afternoon I was playing word games while I lay on the grass near my room. The shrill twitter of the birds, I would say, the birds singing in the sun... And inexorably I'd continue with the sun dying in the moonlight, the moonlight falling on the floor, the floor sagging to the cellar, the cellar filling with water, the water seeping into the ground, the ground twisting into smoke, the smoke staining the sky, the sky burning in the sun, the sun dying in the moonlight, the moonlight falling on the floor—melancholy progressions that held my mind like a whirlpool.

Sarr woke me for dinner; I had dozed off, and my clothes were damp from the grass. As we walked up to the house together he whispered that, earlier in the day, he'd come upon his wife bending over me, peering into my sleeping face. "Her eyes were wide," he said. "Like Bwada's." I said I didn't understand why he was telling me this.

"Because," he recited in a whisper, gripping my arm, "the heart is deceitful above all things, and desperately wicked: who can know it?"

I recognized that. Jeremiah XVII:9.

Dinner was especially uncomfortable; the two of them sat picking at their food, occasionally raising their eyes to each other like children in a staring contest. I longed for the conversations of our early days, inconsequential though they must have been, and wondered where things had gone wrong.

The meal was dry and unappetizing, but the dessert looked delicious—chocolate mousse, made from an old family recipe. Deborah had served it earlier in the summer and knew that both Sarr and I loved it. This time, however, she gave none to herself, explaining that she had to watch her weight.

"Then we'll not eat any!" Sarr shouted, and with that he snatched my dish from in front of me, grabbed his own, and hurled them both against the wall, where they splattered like mud balls.

Deborah was very still; she said nothing, just sat there watching us. Thank heaven, she didn't look particularly afraid of this madman—but *I* was. He may have read my thoughts, because as I got up from my seat, he said much more gently, in the soft voice that once had been normal to him, "Sorry, Jeremy. I know you hate scenes. We'll pray for each other, all right?"

"Are you okay?" I asked Deborah, with more bravado than I felt. "I'm going out now, but I'll stay if you think you'll need me for anything." She stared at me, smiled slightly, and shook her head. Trying to convey as much meaning as I could, I nodded toward her husband. She shrugged.

"Things will work out," she said. I could hear Sarr laughing as I shut the door.

When I snapped on the light out here, I took off my shirt and stood in front of the little mirror. It had been nearly a week since I'd showered, and I'd become used to the smell of my body. My hair had wound itself into greasy brown curls, my beard was at least two weeks old, and my eyes... well, the eyes that stared back at me looked like those of an old man. The whites were turning yellow, like old teeth. I looked at my chest and arms, flabby at thirty, and I thought of the frightening alterations in my friend Sarr. I knew I'd have to get out of here.

Just glanced at my watch. It's now quite late: two thirty. I've been packing my things.

## August 20

I woke about an hour ago and continued packing. Lots of books to put away, but I'm just about done. It's not even nine a.m. yet, much earlier than I normally get up, but I guess the thought of leaving here fills me with energy.

The first thing I saw on rising was a garden spider whose body was as big as some of the mice the cats have killed. It was sitting on the ivy that grows over my window sill—fortunately on the other side of the screen. Apparently it had had good hunting all summer, preying on the insects that live in the leaves. Concluding that nothing so big and fearsome has a right to live, I held the spray can against the screen and doused the creature with poison. It struggled halfway up the screen, then stopped, arched its legs, and dropped backwards into the ivy.

I plan to walk into town this morning and telephone the office in Flemington where I rented my car. If they can have one ready today, I'll hitch there to pick it up; otherwise I'll spend tonight here and pick it up tomorrow. I'll be leaving a little early in the season, but the Poroths already have my month's rent, so they shouldn't be too offended.

And anyway, how could I be expected to stick around here with all that nonsense going on, never knowing when my room might be ransacked, having to put up with Sarr's insane suspicions and Deborah's moodiness?

Before I go into town, though, I really must shave and shower for the good people of Gilead. I've been sitting inside here waiting for some sign the Poroths are up, but as yet—it's almost nine—I've heard nothing. I wouldn't care to barge in on them while they're having breakfast or, worse, just getting up... So I'll just wait here by the window till I see them.

...Ten o'clock now, and they still haven't come out. Perhaps they're having a talk. I'll give them half an hour more, then I'm going in.

Here my journal ends. Until today, almost a week later, I have not cared to set down any of the events that followed. But here in the temporary safety of this hotel room, protected by a heavy brass travel-lock I had sent up from the hardware store down the street, watched over by the good people of Flemington—and perhaps by something not good—I can continue my narrative.

The first thing I noticed as I approached the house was that the shades were drawn, even in the kitchen. Had they, I wondered, decided to sleep late this morning? Throughout my thirty years I have come to associate drawn shades with a foul smell, the smell of a sickroom, of shamefaced poverty and food gone bad, of people lying too long beneath blankets; but I was not ready for the stench of decay that met me when I opened the kitchen door and stepped into the darkness. Something had died in that room—and not recently.

At the moment the smell first hit, four little shapes scrambled across the linoleum toward me and out into the daylight. The Poroths' cats.

By the other wall a lump of shadow moved; a pale face caught light penetrating the shades. Sarr's voice, its habitual softness exaggerated to a whisper: "Jeremy. I thought you were still asleep."

"Can I—"

"No. Don't turn on the light." He got to his feet, a black form towering against the window. Fiddling nervously with the kitchen door—the tin doorknob, the rubber bands stored around it, the fringe at the bottom of the drawn window shade—I opened it wider and let in more sunlight. It fell on the dark thing at his feet, over which he had been crouching: Deborah, the flesh at her throat torn and wrinkled like the skin of an old apple.

Her clothing lay in a heap beside her. She appeared long dead. The eyes were shriveled, sunken into sockets black as a skull's.

I think I may have staggered at that moment, because he came toward me. His steady, unblinking gaze looked so sincere—but why was he *smiling?* "I'll make you understand," he was saying, or something like that; even now I feel my face twisting into horror as I try to write of this. "It needed to be done."

"You—"

"She tried to kill me," he went on, silencing all questions. "The same thing that possessed Bwada...possessed her."

My hand played behind my back with the bottom of the window shade. "But her throat—"

"That happened long ago. Bwada did it. I had nothing to do with...that part." Suddenly his voice rose. "Don't you understand? She tried to stab me with the bread knife." He turned, stooped over, and, clumsy in the darkness, began feeling about him on the floor. "Where is that thing?" he was mumbling. "I'll show you..." As he crossed a beam of sunlight, something gleamed like a silver handle on the back of his shirt.

Thinking, perhaps, to help him search, I pulled gently on the window shade, then released it; it snapped upward like a gunshot, flooding the room with light. From deep within the center of his back protruded the dull wooden haft of the bread knife, buried almost completely but for an inch or two of gleaming steel.

He must have heard my intake of breath—that sight chills me even today, the grisly absurdity of the thing—he must have heard me, because immediately he stood, his back to me, and reached up behind himself toward the knife, his arm stretching in vain, his fingers curling around nothing. The blade had been planted in a spot he couldn't reach.

He turned towards me and shrugged in embarrassment, a child caught in a foolish error. "Oh, yeah," he said, grinning at his own weakness. "I forgot it was there."

With an odd jerking movement he suddenly thrust his face closer, fixing me in a gaze that never wavered, eyes wide as if with candor. "It's easy for us to forget things," he explained—and then, still smiling, eyes still staring into mine, he volunteered that last trivial piece of information, that final message whose words released me from inaction and left me free to dash from the room, to sprint in panic down the road to town, pursued by what had once been the farmer Sarr Poroth.

It serves no purpose here to dwell on my flight down that twisting road, breathing in such deep gasps that I was soon moaning with every breath; how, with my enemy racing behind me, not even winded, his steps never flagging, I veered into the woods; how I finally lost him, perhaps from the inexperience of whatever thing now controlled his body, and was able to make my way back to the road, only to come upon him again as I rounded a bend; his laughter as he followed me, and how it continued long after I had evaded him a second time; and how, after hiding until nightfall in the old cement culvert, I ran the rest of the way in pitch-darkness, stumbling in the ruts, torn by vines, nearly blinding myself when I ran into a low branch, until I arrived in Gilead filthy, exhausted, and nearly incoherent.

Suffice it to say that my escape was largely a matter of luck, a physical wreck fleeing something oblivious to pain or fatigue; but beyond mere luck, I had been impelled by an almost ecstatic sense of dread produced by his last words to me, that last communication, from an alien face smiling inches from my own, which I chose to take as his final warning:

"Sometimes we forget to blink."


You can read the rest in the newspapers. The *Hunterdon County Democrat* covered most of the story, though its man wrote it up as merely another lunatic wife-slaying, the result of loneliness, religious mania, and a mysteriously tainted well. (Traces of insecticide were found, among other things, in the water.) The *Somerset Reporter* took a different slant, implying that I had been the third member of an erotic triangle and that Sarr had murdered his wife in a fit of jealousy.

Needless to say, I was by this time past caring what was written about me. I was too haunted by visions of that lonely, abandoned farmhouse, the wails of its hungry cats, and by the sight of Deborah's corpse, discovered by the police, protruding from that hastily dug grave beyond the cornfield.

Accompanied by state troopers, I returned to my ivy-covered outbuilding. A bread knife had been plunged deep into its door, splintering the wood on the other side. The blood on it was Sarr's.

My journal had been hidden under my mattress and so was untouched, but (I look at them now, piled in cardboard boxes beside my suitcase) my precious books had been hurled about the room, their bindings slashed. My summer is over, and now I sit inside here all day listening to the radio, waiting for the next report. Sarr—or his corpse—has not been found.

One might think the evidence was clear enough to corroborate my story, but I suppose I should have expected the reception it received from the police. They didn't laugh at my theory of "possession"—not to my face, anyway—but they ignored it in obvious embarrassment. Some see a nice young bookworm gone slightly deranged after contact with a murderer; others believe my story to be the desperate fabrication of an adulterer trying to avoid the blame for Deborah's death.

I can understand their reluctance to accept my explanation of the events, for it's one that goes a little beyond the natural, a little beyond the scientific considerations of motive, *modus operandi*, and fingerprints. But I find it quite unnerving that at least one official—an assistant district attorney, I think, though I'm afraid I'm rather ignorant of these matters—believes I am guilty of murder.

There has, of course, been no arrest. Still, I've been given the time-honored admonition against leaving town.

The theory proposing my own complicity in the events is, I must admit, rather ingenious—and so carefully worked out that it will surely gain more adherents than my own. This public official is going to try to prove that I killed poor Deborah in a fit of passion and, immediately afterward, disposed of Sarr. He points out that their marriage had been an observably happy one until I arrived, a disturbing influence from the city. My motive, he says, was simple lust—unrequited, to be sure—aggravated by boredom. The heat, the insects, and, most of all, the oppressive loneliness—all constituted an environment alien to any I'd been accustomed to, and all worked to unhinge my reason.

I have no cause for fear, however, because this affidavit will certainly establish my innocence. Surely no one can ignore the evidence of my journal (though I can imagine someone of implacable hostility maintaining that I wrote it not at the farm but here in the Union Hotel, this very week).

What galls me is not the suspicions of a few detectives but the predicament their suspicions place me in. Quite simply, *I cannot run away.* I am compelled to remain locked up in this room, potential prey to whatever the thing that was Sarr Poroth has now become—the thing that was once a cat, and once a woman, and once...what? A large white moth? A serpent? A shrewlike thing with wicked teeth?

A police chief? A president? A boy with eyes of blood that sits beneath my window?

Lord, who will believe me?

It was that night that started it all, I'm convinced of it now. The night I made those strange signs in the tree. The night the crickets missed a beat.

I'm not a philosopher, and I can supply no ready explanation for what has been released into the world. I'm only a poor scholar, a bookworm, and I must content myself with mumbling a few phrases that keep running through my mind, phrases out of books read long ago when such abstractions meant, at most, a pleasant shudder. I am haunted by scraps from the myth of Pandora, and by a semantic discussion I once read comparing "unnatural" and "supernatural."

And something about "a tiny rent in the fabric of the universe." Just large enough to let something in. Something not of nature, and hard to kill. Something with its own obscure purpose.

Ironically, the police may be right. Perhaps it was my visit to Gilead that brought about the deaths. Perhaps I had a hand in letting loose the force that, to date, has snuffed out the lives of four hens, three cats, and at least two people—but will hardly be content to stop there.

I've just checked. He hasn't moved from the steps of the courthouse; and even when I look out my window, the rose spectacles never waver. Who knows where the eyes beneath them point? Who knows if they remember to blink?

Lord, this heat is sweltering. My shirt is sticking to my skin, and droplets of sweat are rolling down my face and dripping onto this page, making the ink run.

My hand is tired from writing. I think it's time to end this affidavit.

If, as I now believe possible, I inadvertently called down evil from the sky and began the events at Poroth Farm, my death will only be fitting. And after my death, many more. We are all, I'm afraid, its destined prey. Please, then, forgive this prophet of doom, old at thirty, his last jeremiad: "The harvest is past, the summer is ended, and we are not saved."

# ONE SIZE EATS ALL

The words had been emblazoned on the plastic wrapper of Andy's new sleeping bag, in letters that were fat and pink and somewhat crudely printed. Andy had read them aloud as he unwrapped the bag on Christmas morning.

" 'One size eats all.' What's that supposed to mean?"

Jack, his older brother, had laughed. "Maybe it's not really a sleeping bag. Maybe it's a *feed* bag!"

Andy's gaze had darted to the grotesquely large metal zipper that ran along the edge of the bag in rows of gleaming teeth. He'd felt a momentary touch of dread.

"It's obviously a mistake," Andy's father had said. "Or else a bad translation. They must have meant 'One size *fits* all.' "

He was sure that his father was right. Still, the words on the wrapper had left him perplexed and uneasy. He'd slept in plenty of sleeping bags before, but he knew he didn't want to sleep in this one.

And now, as he sat huddled in his tent halfway up Wendigo Mountain, about to slip his feet into the bag, he was even more uneasy. What if it *wasn't* a mistake?

He and Jack had been planning the trip for months; it was the reason they'd ordered the sleeping bags. Jack, who was bigger and more athletic and who'd already started to shave, had picked an expensive Arctic Explorer model from the catalogue. Nothing but the best for Jack. Andy, though, had hoped that if he chose an obscure brand manufactured overseas, and thereby saved his parents money, maybe they'd raise his allowance.

But they hadn't even noticed. The truth was, they'd always been somewhat inattentive where Andy was concerned. They barely seemed to notice how Jack bullied him.

Jack did bully him—in a brotherly way, of course. His bright red hair seemed to go with his fiery temper, and he wasn't slow to use his fists. In bicycle races, he would swerve, knocking Andy off his bike; in basketball, he'd been known to bounce the ball off Andy's head. He seemed to best the younger boy in just about everything, from boxing to campfire-building.

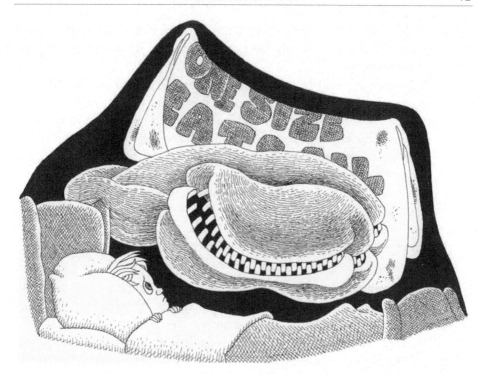

Which was why, just before they'd set out for Wendigo Mountain, Andy had invited his friend Willie along. Willie was small, pale, and even less athletic than Andy. His head seemed much too big for his body. On a strenuous overnight hike like this one, Andy thought, it was nice to have somebody slower and weaker than he was.

True to form, Willie lagged behind the two brothers as they trudged single-file up the trail, winding their way among the tall trees that covered the base of the mountain, keeping their eyes peeled for the occasional dark green trail-markers painted on the trunks. It was a sunny morning, and the air had begun to lose some of the previous night's chill.

By the time Willie caught up, winded and sweating beneath his down jacket, Andy and Jack had taken off their backpacks and stopped for a rest.

"It's *your* tough luck," Jack was telling him. "You've heard the old saying, 'You made your bed, now lie in it'?"

Andy nodded glumly.

"Well, it's the same thing," said Jack. "You *wanted* the damn bag, so tonight you're just gonna have to lie in it."

All morning, that's exactly what Andy had been worrying about. He eyed the pack at his feet, with the puffy brown shape strapped beneath it, and wished the night would never come. *You made your bed,* he told himself. *Now die in it.*

"Andy, for God's sake, stop obsessing about that bag!" said Willie. "You're letting your fears get the best of you. Honest, it's a perfectly ordinary piece of camping gear."

"Willie's right," said Jack. Hoisting his backpack onto his shoulders, he grinned and added cruelly, "And the people it eats are perfectly ordinary, too!"

As they continued up the trail, the trees grew smaller and began to thin; the air grew cooler. Andy could feel the weight of the thing on his back, heavier than a sleeping bag ought to be and pressing against him with, he sensed, a primitive desire—a creature impatient for its dinner.

Ahead of him, Jack turned. "Hey, Willie," he yelled. "Did Andy tell you where his bag is from?"

"No," said Willie, far behind them. "Where?"

Jack laughed delightedly. "Hungary!"


They made camp at a level clearing halfway up the mountain. Andy and Willie would be sharing a tent that night; Jack had one to himself. Late afternoon sunlight gleamed from patches of snow among the surrounding rocks.

The three unrolled their sleeping bags inside the tents. Andy paused before joining the others outside. In the dim light of the tent his bag lay brown and bloated, a living coffin waiting for an occupant. Andy reminded himself that it was, in fact, a fairly normal-looking bag—not very different, in truth, from Jack's new Arctic Explorer. Still, he wished he had a sleeping bag like Willie's, a comfortable old thing that had been in the family for years.

Willie lagged behind again as the brothers left camp and returned to the trail. They waited until he'd caught up. Both younger boys were tired and would have preferred to stay near the tents for the rest of the day, but Jack, impatient, wanted to press on toward the summit while it was still light.

The three took turns carrying a day pack with their compasses, flashlights, emergency food, and a map. The slope was steeper here, strewn with massive boulders, and the exertion made them warm again. Maybe, thought Andy, he wouldn't even need the bag tonight.

The terrain became increasingly difficult as they neared Wendigo's peak, where the trail was blanketed by snow. The air seemed to be growing thinner. They were exhausted by the time they reached the top—too exhausted to appreciate the sweeping view, the stunted pines, and the small mounds of stones piled in odd patterns across the rock face.

They raised a feeble shout of triumph, rested briefly, then started down. Andy sensed that they would have to hurry; standing on the summit, he'd been unnerved at how low the sun lay in the sky.

The air was colder now, and shadows were lengthening across the snow. Before they'd gotten very far, the sun had sunk below the other side of the mountain.

They'd been traveling in shadow for what seemed nearly an hour, Jack leading the way, when the older boy paused and asked to see the map. Andy and Willie looked at one another and realized, with horror, that they had left the day pack at the top of the mountain, somewhere among the cairns and twisted trees.

"I thought you had it," said Andy, aghast at the smaller boy's carelessness.

"I thought *you* did," said Willie.

No matter; it was Andy that Jack swore at and smacked on the side of the head. Willie looked pained, as if he, too, had been hit.

Jack glanced up the slope, then turned and angrily continued down the trail. "Let's go!" he snapped over his shoulder. "Too late to go back for it now."

They got lost twice coming down, squeezing between boulders, clambering over jagged rocks, and slipping on patches of ice. But just as night had settled on the mountain and Andy could no longer make out his brother's red hair or his friend's pale face, they all felt the familiar hard-packed earth of the trail beneath their boots.

They were dog-tired and aching by the time they stumbled into camp. They had no flashlights and were too fatigued to try to build a fire. Poor Willie, weariest of all, felt his way to the tent and crawled inside. Andy hung back. In the darkness he heard Jack yawn and slip into the other tent.

He was alone now, with no light but the stars and a sliver of moon, like a great curved mouth. The night was chilly; he knew he couldn't stay out here. With a sigh, he pushed through the tent flaps, trying not to think about what waited for him inside.

The interior of the tent was pitch black and as cold as outdoors. Willie was already asleep. The air, once crisp, seemed heavy with an alien smell; when he lifted the flap of his sleeping bag, the smell grew stronger. Did all new bags smell like this? He recognized the odors of canvas and rubber, but beneath them lurked a hint of something else: fur, maybe, or the breath of an animal.

No, he was imagining things. The only irrefutable fact was the cold. Feeling his way carefully in the darkness, Andy unlaced his boots, barely noticing that his socks were encrusted with snow. Gingerly he inserted one foot into the mouth of the bag, praying he'd feel nothing unusual.

The walls of the bag felt smooth and, moments later, warm. *Too* warm. Surely, though, it was just the warmth of his own body.

He pushed both legs in further, then slipped his feet all the way to the bottom. Lying in the darkness, listening to the sound of Willie's breathing, he could feel the bag press itself against his ankles and legs, clinging to them with a weight that seemed, for goose down, a shade too heavy. Yet the feeling was not unpleasant. He willed himself to relax.

It occurred to him, as he waited uneasily for sleep, what a clever disguise a bag like this would make for a creature that fed on human flesh. Like a spider feasting upon flies that had blundered into its web, such a creature might gorge contentedly on human beings stupid enough to disregard its warning: *One size eats all…* Imagine, prey that literally pushed itself into the predator's mouth!

Human stomach acid, he'd read, was capable of eating through a razor blade; and surely this creature's would be worse. He pictured the thing dissolving bones, draining the very life-blood from its victim, leaving a corpse sucked dry of fluids, like the withered husk a spider leaves behind.

Suddenly he froze. He felt something damp—no, *wet*—at the bottom of the bag. Wet like saliva. Or worse.

Kicking his feet, he wriggled free of the bag. Maybe what he'd felt was simply the melted snow from his socks, but in the darkness he was taking no chances. Feeling for his boots, he laced them back on and curled up on top of the bag, shivering beneath his coat.

*     *     *

Willie's voice woke him.

"Andy? Are you okay?"

Andy opened his eyes. It was light out. He had survived the night.

"Why were you sleeping like that?" said Willie. "You must be frozen."

"I was afraid to get back in the bag. It felt…weird."

Willie smiled. "It was just your imagination, Andy. That's not even your bag."

"Huh?" Andy peered down at the bag. A label near the top said *Arctic Explorer.* "But how—"

"I switched your bag with Jack's when the two of you were starting for the summit," said Willie. "I meant to tell you, but I fell asleep."

"Oh my God," cried Andy, "Jack'll be furious. He'll kill me for this!"

Trembling with cold and fear, he crawled stiffly from the tent. It was early morning; a chilly sun hung in the pale blue sky. He dashed to Jack's tent and yanked back the flaps, already composing an apology.

The tent was empty. The sleeping bag, *his* bag, lay dark and swollen on the floor. There seemed to be no one inside.

Or almost no one; for emerging from the top was what appeared to be a deflated basketball—only this one had red hair and a human face.

# WELL-CONNECTED

His first mistake, Philip later realized, had been in choosing a room without a bath. Years before, honeymooning in England while still on a junior law clerk's salary, he and his first wife had had great luck with such rooms, readily agreeing to "a bathroom down the hall" whenever the option was offered; they'd gotten unusual bargains that way, often finding themselves in the oldest, largest, and most charming room in the hotel for a third less than other guests were paying. Now, even though saving money was no longer an issue, some youthful habit had made him ask for just such a room, here in this rambling New England guesthouse. Or maybe his choice had been meant as a kind of test, one that might help determine if the young woman he'd brought with him this weekend was too intent on a luxury-class ride with him, or if she was the sort of person who remained unfazed by life's small inconveniences—the sort who might become, in the end, his second wife.

This time, however, it seemed he had guessed wrong; for here at The Birches, the rooms without a bath faced the front lawn, still pitted from last winter's snows, a smooth expanse of newly tarred road that ended in a parking lot behind a line of shrubs, and a large, rather charmless white sign proclaiming VACANCY and SINCE 1810, beside which stood the woebegone little clump of birch trees that, presumably, had given the place its name—while it was the bigger, more expensive rooms just across the hall that looked out upon the wooded slopes of Romney Mountain, rising like a massive green wall somewhere beyond the back garden. Disappointingly, too, while their room boasted such amenities as genuine oak beams and a working fireplace, it had no telephone, at a time when, with young Tony precariously installed at a private school near Hanover less than thirty miles away, he'd have liked one handy. He envied whichever guest was staying in the room opposite theirs; when he and Carol had passed it last night as they'd brought their bags upstairs, they'd heard its unseen occupant talking animatedly on the phone, embroiled in some urgent conversation.

It was the off-season, too late for even the most dedicated of skiers, too early for the annual onslaught of hikers, and the inn, from all appearances, was barely half full. It would have been a simple thing to request a different room. Still, some perverse sense of obligation to his youthful self kept Philip from speaking up. He had made his choice, and, vacancies or not, he was not about to pack up and move elsewhere. Anyway, it was only for two more nights.

Today was Friday, the first Friday all year that he'd taken off, though when he'd quit the firm last summer to set up his own practice, he'd vowed there'd be many such weekends. Maybe now, with Carol, there would be. The two of them had driven from Boston last night, speeding up Route 93 past the brightly lit ring roads curving round the city like lines of defense, through the lowlands of southeastern New Hampshire, and finally, long after darkness had fallen, past the dim shapes of starlit hills and a range of distant mountains, Sunapee and Monadnock looming far to the southwest. Their destination lay twelve miles off the highway, down a series of roads of ever-diminishing width, in a part of the state more settled a century ago than it was today, when men no longer worked the land and once-prosperous farms had been reclaimed by forest. The region around Romney Mountain, with its caves and scenic gorges, had known even grander days, having seen, in the century's opening decades, the construction of at least two lavish hotels, a scattering of summer homes for the well-to-do of Boston, and, it was said, even one clandestine casino. The hotels and casino were long gone, and only recently had the effects of the postwar real estate boom been felt here. The glistening black road that wound through the valley to The Birches had been dirt less than a year ago.

They had spent most of the morning in the king-size four-poster that dominated their little room, snuggled under a patchwork quilt that made up in atmosphere what it lacked in warmth, and didn't come down to the dining room till long after the tables had been cleared. Fortunately the proprietress, Mrs. Hartley, still had enough Westchester in her soul to sympathize with late risers, and she'd kept a pot of coffee warm for them, along with extra helpings of that morning's blueberry pancakes. She and her husband had purchased The Birches only last spring. Before that her only connection to hotelkeeping had been as a part-time pastry chef, and his as a salesman of advertising space to an occasional resort. It was obvious from the look of the place that, with more zeal than knowledge, the Hartleys were trying to restore the inn to something approximating its original appearance, or, failing that, to something approximating a house out of Currier and Ives—a row of whose prints, in matched maple frames, decorated the dining room wall.

While Carol slipped back upstairs to change, Philip checked the time; Tony would already be finished with his morning classes. In the alcove off the bar he found an old-fashioned wall phone and, through the unit in the office, obtained an outside line. He dialed Tony's school.

Summoned from lunch, the boy sounded distracted. "I didn't think you'd call until tomorrow," he said, breathless as if from running. "Braddon's giving us a multiple-choice quiz in half an hour, and then I've got to try out for the play."

Philip wished him good luck, pleased that the boy was keeping so busy, and asked what time tomorrow would be best to visit. Spending a day with his son was the primary purpose of his trip; relations between them had been strained these past years.

"Is somebody coming with you?" asked Tony warily.

"You know very well I'm here with Carol," said Philip. "I thought I explained all that in my letter." He immediately regretted the impatience in his voice. "Look, son, if you'd rather I came alone, I'm sure she can find something to do for an hour or two."

"Tomorrow's no good anyway," said Tony, having maneuvered his father into this concession. "We're supposed to have a track meet with Cobb Hill, and it's away. They told us last week, but I forgot." He added, apologetically, "They'll really be mad if I miss it. I'm one of the two best in the relay."

"How would Sunday be, then?" asked Philip. "I'd have to leave by three."

"Sunday'd be great. You could take me into Hanover for a decent meal. And Dad..."

Philip waited. "Yes?"

"Do you think you'd have time to tell me a story?"

Philip felt an unexpected rush of affection so strong it embarrassed him. "Of course," he said. "I'll always have time for that." It had been years since Tony had asked for a story; once it had been their favorite pastime.

The day passed quickly. It was too cold for swimming—the new semicircular pool at the end of the garden stood empty, in fact—but Carol, it turned out, was a nature enthusiast, and one thing The Birches had aplenty was nature trails. It was all Philip could do to keep up with her. Still, this Girl Scout aspect appealed to him; till now he'd only seen Carol's urban side, the tall, studious-looking girl he'd secretly lusted after at his former office, and who'd seemed far too smart for the routine secretarial tasks required of her. Clutching glossy new guidebooks provided by the Hartleys, the two of them trudged along the base of the mountain, dutifully peering at fungi in their various disquieting shapes, admiring the newly blooming wildflowers, and searching—in vain, as it turned out—for identifiable animal tracks, all the while snacking on the sausage, bread, and cheese that Mrs. Hartley had packed for them. They discovered, nonetheless, that by dinner time their appetites were quite unimpaired; they shared a bottle of cabernet with their meal, chosen from the inn's small but adequate wine list, and still found room for dessert. Glowing rosily, as much from the wine as from the bayberry candles that flickered at each table, they staggered into the lounge.

The room, high-ceilinged and handsome, was already occupied by several guests, who themselves were occupied over after-dinner drinks and conversation. Flames danced and sizzled in the obligatory fieldstone fireplace covering most of one wall. Before it, taking up more than his share of a bench by the fire, sat a large, barrel-shaped man, his bald head gleaming in the firelight, eyes sunken in wrinkles like an elephant's. He was wearing loose-fitting white pants and a somewhat threadbare cardigan. They had seen him in the other room, devouring Mrs. Hartley's rack of lamb with considerable gusto. Aside from one wizened old lady who, from her own table, had stared at him throughout the meal with apparent fascination, he was the only guest who'd dined alone. It was impossible to tell his age.

"Am I blocking you from the fire?" he asked. He flashed a smile at Carol. "Here, you young people, have a seat! April nights are chilly in this part of the world." There was a trace of accent in his voice, a hint of Old World frost-fires and battlements. He eased himself sideways and patted the bench beside him. Carol politely sat; Philip, with no room for himself, pulled up a wooden chair.

"I trust that you two are enjoying your stay." He spoke as one who expected an answer.

"So far," said Philip. "Actually, we came up to visit my son. He's at prep school a bit north of here."

"And, of course, to relax," Carol added.

"Of course!" The man grinned again. His teeth were long and widely spaced, like tree roots blanched by water. "And have you found your relaxation?"

Philip nodded. "Of a sort. Today we took a hike around the base of the mountain, and tomorrow we may go for a drive, maybe look for some antiques."

"Ah, a fellow antique-lover!" He turned to Carol. "And you?"

"I'm more of a swimmer myself. Unfortunately, this isn't the weather for it."

The other cocked his head and seemed to study her a moment. "Odd you should say that, because I happen to know where there's an excellent heated pool not half an hour's stroll from here. All indoors, with antique brass steps in each corner and a well-stocked bar right beside it, so close you can reach for your wine while standing in the water. The bar stools are covered in leather from, if the lady will pardon me—" He regarded her almost coyly for a moment. "—the testicles of a sperm whale." Philip and Carol exchanged a wary glance, then a smile. "It's true," the older man was saying, "I assure you! No expense was spared. The pool has its own underground oil tank which keeps it at exactly seventy degrees. You'll find a painting of Bacchus on the ceiling, best appreciated while floating on your back, and heart-shaped tiles on the floor shipped specially from Florence."

"I've never heard of such a place," said Philip. "There's certainly nothing like it listed in the guidebooks."

"Oh, you won't find it in a guidebook, my friend. It isn't open to the public." His voice was low, conspiratorial. "It's in the private home of a certain Mr. Hagendorn, on the other side of the mountain."

"Sounds like he must be worth a fortune."

The other shrugged. "You've heard of the Great Northern Railroad? One of Mr. Hagendorn's ancestors owned nine million shares. So as you might imagine, Mr. Hagendorn has always been accustomed to getting what he wants. The bed he sleeps in once belonged to an Italian prince, and the house itself is modeled on a Tuscan villa. It has its own greenhouse, a billiard room with four imported stained glass windows, and a sun porch with a magnificent view of the gorge."

"You seem to know the place pretty well," said Philip.

A shadow crossed the other's face. "I used to live there," he said softly.

"You mean you once owned it?"

"No, not at all. I merely worked there. I was young when I started, and new to this area, but by the time I was twenty I was Mr. Hagendorn's personal aide. Wine for the cellar, an antique painting, a new maid—whatever he required, I obtained. I served him well for many years, and we remain in close touch. He asks me often to his home. I'm always welcome there." He sighed. "So while I'm not a rich man, I suppose you'd have to say I'm well-connected."

"It sounds," said Carol, "like a fabulous place."

The man brightened. "Would you care to see it? I'm sure Mr. Hagendorn would love to have you as his guests. You could come for a swim, say tomorrow afternoon. Stay for an early dinner, and I'd have you back here just after dark. I know the trail by heart." Leaning toward them as if afraid the other guests would hear, he added, "You've never had dinner till you've had it in the great hall, overlooking the valley. The new people who've taken over this place—" His hand swept the room. "—they cook a meal fit for a peasant like me. But Mr. Hagendorn has employed the finest chefs in Europe."

"But why," said Philip, "would this fellow want to put himself out for two complete strangers?"

"The truth is, my friend, he's somewhat lonely. He doesn't get many visitors these days, and I know he'd want to make the acquaintance of two young people like you."

"But we didn't bring bathing suits," said Philip, hoping, somehow, that the matter might rest there.

"Speak for yourself," said Carol brightly. "I brought mine."

The old man turned to Philip with what looked disconcertingly like a wink, but it may just have been smoke in his eyes. "I assure you Mr. Hagendorn has plenty—for men, women, boys, girls. Though you may find them a little out of style."

Carol clasped her hands. "Oh, I love old-fashioned things. It sounds like fun." She turned to Philip. "Can we go, honey?"

He swallowed. "Well, I still don't like just barging in on the guy. I mean, what if he's not in the mood for visitors?"

The man stood, a surprisingly rapid movement for one so large and so seemingly advanced in years. "No need to worry," he said. "I'll simply ask him. I'll be speaking with him tonight anyway." Excusing himself with a courtly bow, he made his way from the room, picking his way among the other guests.

It was only after he'd left that Philip realized they had failed to exchange names, and that their entire conversation had been watched—with, it appeared, an almost indecent curiosity—by the wizened old lady of the dining room, who now sat regarding him and Carol from the depths of a wingback chair in the corner, dark eyes glittering.

"Maybe she's just got a crush on him," said Carol later, as they moved about the little room preparing for bed. "He looks like he's nearly as old as she is, and men that age are scarce."

"I'll bet that by tomorrow he changes his mind about the pool," said Philip, with a curious feeling of hope. "I'll bet he was talking through his hat about how chummy he is with his boss. He probably won't even bother to phone the guy."

But shortly afterward, when Carol returned from the bathroom at the end of the hall, she closed the door behind her and whispered, "You're wrong, honey. He's telling him about us right now—about how he met us in the lounge tonight."

"How do you know?"

"I heard him," said Carol. "He has the room across from us."

Gathering his toothbrush and towel, Philip stepped gingerly into the hall. Sure enough, he could hear a man's low voice coming from the room opposite theirs, and recognized it now as belonging to their companion from the lounge. Keeping himself half turned toward the bathroom as if that innocent goal were all he had in mind, he tiptoed closer.

"Yes, they're both coming… What's that?" There was a pause. "No, not at all. They both seem quite well-bred… Yes, she's charming. You're going to like her." Another pause. "It's agreed, then. Tomorrow, by three."

A door rattled somewhere down the hall. Philip whirled and hurried to the bathroom. By the time he emerged, the hall was silent. He thought he could hear, faintly, a snoring from the old man's room.

Carol was already in bed when he returned. She looked up expectantly. "So? Hear anything?"

He planted a kiss on her lips. "He says you're charming."

She laughed and pulled him down beside her. "How in the world did he find out?"

Later, as they lay beside one another in the darkness, she stirred and said sleepily, "I hope I don't dream again tonight."

"Had a bad one last night? You didn't tell me."

"I can't remember it." She pressed her face deeper into the pillow. "All I know is, it was scary. Leave your arm around me, will you?"

"It'll fall asleep in three minutes."

"Leave it around me for three minutes."

He himself was asleep in less than that. Some time later—it must have been near dawn, for beyond the lace curtains the sky had grown pale—he felt himself awakened by a tugging at his arm, and heard Carol whisper his name.

"Whatsamatter?" he mumbled.

"Is it really you?"

The idiocy of her question seemed, to his sleep-befogged brain, too enormous to contemplate. "Yes," he said, "it is." In a moment he was once again asleep.

"I got frightened," she explained the next morning, sunlight flooding the room. "I somehow got it into my head that there was someone else in bed with us."

"You mean, like threesies?"

"Like another man lying between us, pressing up against us both. And you know, I think he was black—a little black man."

"Maybe it was that guy from the mailroom."

She seemed not to hear. "What's so weird is, I'm sure it's the same dream I had the night before."

Philip yawned and rubbed his eyes. "Well, you know what they say about dreams. Wish fulfillment."

She poked him in the ribs. "Honestly, Philip, you're so trite!" Frowning, she looked about the room—the cloud pattern in the wallpaper, a spider-like crack in the ceiling, a row of dark pines in the painting above the dresser. "You don't suppose this place is haunted, do you?"

"Talk about trite…"

"I mean," she went on, "inns *have* been known to be haunted."

"Sure," he said, "they all are. Or claim to be. The ghost of some long-lost sea captain comes back every hundred and twelve years, or a serving wench who hanged herself appears at each full moon. Here it's probably Daniel Webster's brother-in-law. All part of the charm."

"Just the same, will you ask the Hartleys? Ask them if there's a ghost."

"Why don't you?"

"I'm too embarrassed."

Embarrassed himself, Philip asked Mr. Hartley in the office downstairs while Carol finished getting dressed.

"No ghosts that I know of," the man said, scratching his thinning hair. Suddenly he grinned. "But golly, I sure would like to have one. It'd help business."

Their stout companion was waiting for them in the lounge by the time they had finished breakfast. "It's all agreed," he said genially. "Mr. Hagendorn would love to meet you both."

"It certainly looks like a beautiful day," said Carol.

He nodded, beaming. "Magnificent. You'll be able to see clear to Monadnock." He seemed, on this sunny morning, the soul of jollity. "By the way, I didn't introduce myself last night. My name is Marius." His grip was like iron as they shook hands and arranged to leave after lunch.

When lunchtime arrived, however, a call came for Philip on the phone by the bar. "Sorry, Dad," said Tony, with a babble of youthful voices in the background. "I got it wrong. The track meet's tomorrow. Can you come see me today?"

"Hell," said Philip, "we've already made plans. I can't just—" He caught himself. "Yeah, sure, I guess. No problem. What time's good?"

"That's just it. I don't know yet. Jimmy and I are getting a lift into town, and we need you to pick us up." There followed a dismayingly complicated series of adolescent proposals and provisos, the upshot of which was that Philip was to wait for Tony's call "sometime in the early afternoon," whereupon further directions would be supplied.

Dinner with the reclusive Mr. Hagendorn was clearly out of the question. Marius, waiting for them at the bottom of the garden where the trail began, agreed to take Carol up to the villa for a swim alone and promised he would have her back by nightfall, in time for Philip's return. Far from being put out, he seemed to take the last-minute change of plans with surprising nonchalance.

"Mr. Hagendorn will of course be disappointed," he said. "He told me how much he looked forward to meeting you both. But at least I am bringing the young lady."

He was dressed in the same loose-fitting white pants, like some ancient man of medicine—they even had a drawstring, Philip noticed—but he'd added, over his white shirt, a warm alpine jacket, and his bald head was covered by an old-fashioned homburg. Far from being unfit for a protracted uphill walk, he looked younger and more powerful than he had by the fireside last night. It was clear he belonged on the mountain.

Carol carried her bathing suit wrapped in a towel. A camera dangled from a strap around her neck. "I'll bet the view's wonderful from up there," she said, kissing Philip goodbye. She blew him a second goodbye kiss as she and Marius started gaily up the trail.

The air had grown chillier as they climbed, but their exertions kept them warm. The walk was proving more arduous than Carol had expected. "How in the world did your boss ever manage to build a house up here?" she had asked half an hour ago, as they'd pushed their way up a steep section of path near the foot of the mountain.

"There's a narrow road that winds around the other side," Marius had said, pausing to tilt back his hat and wipe the sweat from his bald head. "We're going up the back way. You'll find, however, that it's faster."

He had sounded amiable enough, but since then they'd exchanged barely a word. As the day had grown colder, so had his mood; he'd become silent, preoccupied, as if listening for voices from the mountain, and when she'd asked him how much farther it was, he'd simply nodded toward the north and said, "Soon."

They had been on the trail for nearly an hour, following a zigzag course up the densely wooded slope. It was plain that Marius had misled her—or perhaps he had misled himself as well; though he continued, even now, to walk steadily and purposefully, with no sign of hesitation, she was beginning to wonder if he really knew the way as well as he'd claimed.

By the time the trail grew level, the trees had begun to thin out, and when she turned to look behind her she could see, in the spaces between them, the distance they had come. Below them spread the undulating green of the valley, though the inn and its grounds were lost from sight around the other side of the mountain. They were midway up the slope now, following a circular route toward the northern face. Ahead of her Marius paused, staring uphill past a faraway outcropping of rocks, and said, "We're nearly there. It's just past that curve of land."

Shielding her eyes, she searched the horizon for a glimpse of rooftops. Suddenly she squinted. "Who's that?"

"Where?"

"Up among those rocks." She pointed, then felt foolish; for a second she'd thought she'd seen a small black figure merge with the shadow of a boulder as it fell upon the uneven ground. But now, as she looked more closely, she could see that the ground lay covered in ragged clumps of undergrowth and that it was this, tossed by the wind, that had moved.

"Come," said Marius, "the house is just ahead, and we will want to be back down before dark."

Philip sat impatiently on the back porch, leafing through one of the previous winter's ski magazines while waiting for the phone inside to ring. The potted geraniums blew softly in the breeze from off the mountain. He found it absurdly unnecessary to keep assuring himself that Carol would be all right with Marius, but he continued to assure himself of that just the same.

He looked up to find himself no longer alone. The elderly woman from last night had seated herself in a chair nearby and had taken out some knitting. She nodded to him. "First time here?"

"Yes," he said, automatically raising his voice on the assumption that she might be slightly deaf. "Just a weekend vacation."

"I've been coming here for more than fifty years," she said. "My husband and I first came here in the summer of 1935. He passed on in '64, but I keep coming back. I've seen this inn change hands seven times." She gave a little cackle. "Seven times!"

Philip laid aside the magazine. "And does the place look different now?" he asked politely.

"The inn, no. The area is different. There've been a lot of new people coming in, and a lot of the old ones gone." She looked as if she were about to enumerate them, but at that moment the screen door opened and Mrs. Hartley emerged, an account book in her hand. She saw Philip and smiled.

"Still waiting for your call?"

"Yes," he said. "I don't know what's keeping that kid. I'll hear the phone out here, won't I?"

"Sure, but somebody's on it now, and it looks like they may take a while. I'll try to hurry 'em up."

Philip frowned. "How about the phone in the office?"

"Well, my husband's using it right now. He's going over the orders with our supplier down in Concord. But don't worry, it won't take long."

"The problem is," said Philip, with growing impatience, "my son may be trying to reach me at this very moment. Couldn't you transfer his call to a phone upstairs? I could wait in one of the vacant rooms."

She shook her head. "There aren't any phones up there. The two down here are the only ones we've got."

"But that's impossible," said Philip. He could feel his heart beginning to beat faster. "*Impossible! * That big fellow, Marius, has a phone in his room. I heard him just last night, and the night before. He was talking with someone named Hagendorn. I *heard* him." Yet even as the words rushed from his lips, he knew that what he'd said was false; that it was not impossible at all; that the only voice he'd heard had been Marius's. For all he knew, the man might have been speaking to the walls, the air, the empty room.

They had a word for people like that, people who talked to themselves. Psychos.

"*That's* where I know him from!" the old woman was saying. "He was Hagendorn's man. I knew I recognized him." She turned to Philip. "The person you were talking to last night, he used to be a kind of—oh, I don't know what you'd call him. A kind of valet. He worked for some dreadful man who lived up on the mountain. Bringing women up there for him, and I don't know what else. There were all kinds of stories."

"That's right," said Philip, eagerly grasping at any confirmation of the facts, however unsavory. "This guy Hagendorn. He's apparently got some sort of opulent villa up there."

The woman's eyes widened. "But that house burned down in 1939. I remember it—some kind of terrible explosion. Something to do with an oil tank. That man Hagendorn was burned to death, I remember distinctly, and everyone said it was just as well." She shook her head. "There's nothing up there now. There hasn't been a house there for years."


"Honestly, Marius," called Carol, "are you sure we haven't come too far? This can't be the way."

They had passed the outcropping of rocks and had wandered out onto a narrow tableland overgrown by scrub pine and weeds. Ahead of them, curving against the mountain's face, stood what looked like a low broken-down stone wall half concealed by vegetation. Beyond it the pines appeared to be anchored in nothing but blue sky, for at their base the land dropped away into a haphazard tumble of boulders a thousand feet below, as if giant hands had sheared away part of the mountain.

Marius was well in front of her, his pace grown more eager, while she, fearful of the drop, walked slowly now, eyes wary. With an impatient wave of his hand he motioned for her to join him.

"Marius," she said breathlessly, as she caught up with him, "where *are* we? Where is Mr. Hagendorn's house?"

"What's that? The house?" He pursed his lips and looked blank for a moment. Absently he gazed around him, like one seeing the place for the first time. Suddenly his gaze grew fixed; she noticed that he was staring past her feet. "Why, here's the house," he said in a small voice, as if explaining to a child. "It's right here."

She followed his gaze. He was pointing directly into the gorge.

She stepped back in confusion. *He's only joking*, she told herself, but her stomach refused to believe her. She felt his hand fall lightly on her shoulder.

"I suppose," he said, "that first you'll want to see the pool."

"Oh, yes," she said, trying vainly to twist away. "Yes, show me the pool, Marius."

For a moment his arm dropped from her shoulder and she was free; but already he had seized her hand and was dragging her implacably forward.

"Come," he said. "There's so much to see." Smiling, he gestured at what lay before them, a vast cavity in the rock, deep as a pit, cut sharply as the lip of a monstrous pitcher into the precipice's edge. Marius tugged her closer. With a gasp she realized that its three stony sides were squared off, as regular as the walls of some enormous dungeon, but cracked and weathered now, patchworked with lichen and moss—ancient. The bottom was a mass of weed-grown rubble opening onto the sky.

"And here," he said, "we have the pool."

Her wrist ached as he urged her to its brink. The ground seemed to shift beneath her as an edge of cloud swept past the sun. She took an unsteady step backward.

"No," he said in a chiding voice, "you can't leave now. You'll have to stay the night."

Drawn forward, she peered into the shadowy depths. Within them, as the light changed, something stirred, black as soot, like a stick of charred wood.

"The tiles are imported," he was saying. "No expense was spared."

She felt his free hand close tightly on her shoulder. The ground was spinning beneath her feet, the shadows rising to claim her.

"And now," he said, "it is time to meet Mr. Hagendorn."

Neither of the Hartleys had been of any help, beyond locating, in one of their local guidebooks, a map of the hiking trails that crisscrossed the mountain; but the old lady, lips quivering with concentration, had been able to make an educated guess where the villa had stood, just above a jagged grey line identified on the map as Romney Gorge. Judging by the map, it seemed, despite Marius's claim, the climb of at least an hour; but Philip made it in half that—in time to see a burly figure in hospital whites struggling with a young woman at the top of the trail, by the edge of a cleft cut deep into the rock and opening onto the sky.

He raced toward them with what little strength remained, knowing that, days later and far away, he'd be able to tell his son the story of how one of the pair was snatched back from the abyss while the other went to meet his master alone.

# CAMERA SHY

"Why would anyone take a picture of an empty chair?"

The front door slammed; he was back early today. In silence Mrs. Melnick worked her pudgy fingers through the dough, a cookbook propped open before her. Jennifer and Laszlo would be coming home later this evening, and she wanted to have the cake ready in time for their arrival. Only yesterday, it seemed, she had waved goodbye to them as they'd marched up the steps of the airplane; later she had watched the plane's winking yellow tail-lights disappear into the eastern sky. Yet soon—in a matter of hours—the two would be returning to the States, their honeymoon behind them. *Imagine,* she thought, *married one whole month...*

"I swear to God," called Mr. Melnick from the living room, "it's nothing but a goddamned empty chair!" The closet door banged open as he hung up his coat. "I *told* you not to hire that photographer!"

Mrs. Melnick stopped what she was doing. "What photographer?"

"The one who took the wedding pictures."

"You mean they're here?" She hurried from the kitchen, wiping her hands on her apron. "So don't keep me in suspense. How did they come out?"

"Terrific—if you like pictures of furniture!" He was sitting *Penseur*-like upon the edge of the couch, gloomily examining the photo in his hand. Others lay before him on the coffee table, piled atop a large manila envelope. He looked up as she came in.

"I found them in the mail just now. God knows what to make of this one." He held up the photo for her inspection. "See? If you ask me, it's a waste of perfectly good film."

Mrs. Melnick glanced at it and shrugged. "Just practice, I guess. Come on, let's see the others." Seating herself heavily beside him, she reached for the pile, then drew back her hand. "Go ahead. I don't want to get them sticky."

The photo on top showed the same empty chair from a slightly different angle, but the one beneath it was an ordinary snapshot in which wedding guests stood stiffly round a punch bowl. Behind them a trio of musicians were setting up their instruments, perspiration gleaming on their faces. The reception had been held at a local country club, early on a warm September evening. The sky, she recalled, had been brilliantly flooded with moonlight, yet in the photograph—due, no doubt, to some trick of the flashbulb—a row of windows in the background appeared to look out on a world of impenetrable darkness.

Her husband turned over the next photo, and the next. Smiling pink faces passed glossily in review. "A nice shot of Aunt Ida," he said, apparently surprised, "and this one of you and Jennifer is decent enough."

The sight made her wince. "God," she moaned, "I look so *fat!* And so does Jennifer. I only hope she's had the sense to keep her weight down over there, with all that Continental cooking." She thought briefly, guiltily, of the cake she'd been preparing for Jennifer's return, and of the letters they'd received from her this past month: ecstatic reports of the Alhambra by moonlight, Paris after dark, the best night-spots in Rome, dining by candlelight in Vienna—and then that odd, half-scrawled postcard from Laszlo's native village outside Budapest...

"Jennifer's not fat," Mr. Melnick was saying. "She's just a little on the zaftig side. And better zaftig than *this*." He pointed grimly to the next photo in the stack.

Turning to it, Mrs. Melnick sighed and shook her head. "Poor Pamela," she said. "Such a tragedy. Jennifer will be so upset when she finds out."

Pamela Lebow had been the bridesmaid. She'd been ill at the time of the wedding, but she nonetheless managed to attend, rising from her sickbed to join, albeit lethargically, in the nuptial rites. Afterward, however, as if exhausted from the strain, she had taken once more to her bed. While the bride and groom were winging majestically toward Europe, she had sunk into the all-embracing darkness of a coma. Less than a week later, she was dead. The doctors had blamed an obscure form of anemia, and checked to see that their malpractice insurance was paid up.

"She looks so *happy,* somehow," observed Mrs. Melnick. "As if she knew she hadn't long to live and didn't really care."

Mr. Melnick nodded. "Sad, very sad." He avoided mentioning to his wife that, with her deathlike face and shadow-haunted eyes, the young lady had in fact given him the creeps. In the photograph the two Melnick women, mother and daughter, were beaming at the camera like a pair of Bruegel peasants, shoulders broad and foreheads shining rosily, while Pamela stood beside them looking pale and oddly distracted. She was smiling a wan Mona Lisa smile and seemed to be staring at someone just beyond the edge of the picture.

Perhaps she was looking at Laszlo. The two of them had dated for a while, shortly before he'd met Jennifer, and they'd remained close even during Laszlo's engagement. Pamela had proved a good friend to them both; she had never shown an ounce of jealousy.

"The poor thing," said Mrs. Melnick. "It meant so much to her to come to the wedding." She handed the photo back to her husband. "We'll have to send a copy to her parents. You really must admit, dear, the photographer did a very fine job."

He grunted noncommittally, already peering at the next one in the pile. "Well, this shot of the three of us is okay, I guess, except my goddamned tie is crooked."

"Of course it is, silly! That's what I kept *telling* you."

"And look, here's one of that woman Seymour brought, who drank so much—"

"Ugh! Don't remind me!"

"—and who made that awful scene outside the ladies' room." He flipped through several more. "This one of Cousin Oliver's not bad"— Oliver had doubled as Laszlo's best man, since Laszlo's friends and family were, all of them, in Hungary—"but I still say I've taken better pictures myself, and for a hell of a lot less money." He reached for another. "The trouble with these so-called 'professionals' is that they don't know the first thing about— Hmm. Now *this* is strange."

Mr. Melnick squinted at the photo in his hand. His own plump face grinned back at him above a crooked tie. He was standing by the doorway of the reception room, one arm thrust awkwardly in the air. There was something terribly unnatural about the pose, something in the placement of the arm. He felt a tiny chill.

His wife leaned forward to study the photo more closely. A smile crossed her face. "He's certainly caught you at an odd moment," she said. "You look just like a lamppost!"

*Or a gallows,* he thought. He searched his memory, then gave up. "I can't understand it," he said. "I'm sure I never posed this way for anyone. Believe me, I'd remember if I did. The closest thing was... Well, you remember, don't you? That photographer asked me and Laszlo to get together for a close-up, and Laszlo didn't seem to want to, and I made a joke about how maybe he was afraid to have his picture taken alongside a handsome guy like me. In the end, of course, he agreed, and we posed together by the doorway—me and Laszlo, standing arm in arm..."

He fell silent.

"Well," his wife said at last, "Laszlo certainly isn't in *this* one."

Mr. Melnick frowned. "The odd thing is..." He cleared his throat. "The odd thing is, he doesn't seem to be in *any* of them."

Indeed, he was not. What's more, the photographs looked terribly strange without him. Cousin Oliver turned up in another close-up, but from his position at the left half of the picture it was clear that a second figure was supposed to have been standing by his side. Jennifer, in a later photo, was shown feeding a slice of wedding cake to thin air while a ring of smiling faces looked on. In still another, the young woman appeared to be dancing with herself, while poor Pamela gazed longingly at the place where Laszlo should have been.

"Why, it's the silliest thing I've ever heard of," sniffed Mrs. Melnick. "Laszlo's been completely left out! Do you suppose they misplaced his pictures?"

"Maybe," said Mr. Melnick. "Or someone's playing a rather elaborate joke on us." He reached for the phone book. "What was the name of that agency?"

"Celebrity Associates," said his wife. "Aunt Ida recommended them, remember? She said that since Laszlo had aristocratic blood and all, he was practically a celebrity, and so I thought—" But her husband was already dialing the phone.

The man on the other end was soft-spoken and cordial, but the cordiality receded as the nature of Mr. Melnick's call became clear. "No groom?" he cried. "Impossible! Our guys follow a routine, it's the same at every wedding: bride with bridesmaid, bride with groom, bride with father and mother, father of bride with groom—"

"There *is* no groom!" It was hard to keep from screaming. "And I'll be damned if I pay good money for someone who's not there. Your man was hired to take wedding pictures—that means pictures of a *couple*, a *pair*. If I'd wanted just my daughter I'd have taken them myself."

"Okay, mister, okay. Maybe there was some kind of screw-up. Do you happen to remember the photographer's name?"

"Jerry something, I think. I'd like to ask him if—"

But the voice had disappeared, to be replaced by silence.

No, not silence. Echoes—echoes just beyond the edge of comprehension. Mr. Melnick pressed the phone to his ear and strained to make sense of them. He half fancied he heard wails, a hissing, laughter, the chattering of a hundred demons skipping rope amid the phone wires.

"Mr. Melnick?"

He jerked back, startled. The voice had returned.

"Listen, I just spoke to Jerry. He says—"

"I'd like to speak to him myself."

"Uh-uh, we've got him down in the darkroom today. He can't come to the phone. But he told me he remembers the wedding, and that he had a lot of trouble with the groom. He says it was very hard to get the guy to sit still and have his picture taken. You know how it is, some people are just camera shy. Jerry says he got him, though, in all the standard shots. Bride with bridesmaid, bride with groom—"

"He isn't *there*, I tell you!"

The man gave an exasperated sigh. "Okay," he said wearily, "here's what you do. Send us back the negatives so we can look them over, and I'll see to it you don't get charged. Of course—" His voice was all business again. "—if you order extra prints, you're gonna have to pay for them just like everyone else."

Mr. Melnick was grumbling as he got off the phone, and continued to do so all evening—especially when, shortly after midnight, with still no sign of Jennifer and Laszlo, he telephoned the airline and learned that their flight was three hours late.

"That's it for me," said his wife. "You can wait up if you want to, but I'm going to bed." Yawning, she moved toward the stairs. "And for heaven's sake, stop worrying about Laszlo. If you absolutely *have* to have his picture, you can take it yourself in just a few hours, when he and Jennifer come home." She paused at the landing. "And be sure to wake me when they do."

The house, once she'd gone up, seemed unnaturally empty, a stage set with the props all in place but with the performers yet to appear. Entering the kitchen, Mr. Melnick nearly failed to recognize the face that scowled and peered at him through the windows near the sink; it was his own face reflected in the glossy blackness of the panes, yet subtly altered, imbued now with an almost spectral pallor caused, no doubt, by the glare from the fluorescent bulb. Upstairs he heard the sounds of washing, the snapping off of lights, the creaking of floorboards and bedsprings as his wife made ready for sleep. Pouring himself a cup of coffee in the kitchen (fortified with a shot of Jack Daniel's), he returned to the living room and settled back on the couch with a half-completed crossword puzzle from that morning's *Times* which, as usual, his wife had tried and then abandoned. He stared at the puzzle for a moment, thinking of what she'd said earlier. Perhaps, some time tomorrow, he *would* ask Laszlo to pose for a picture or two, just to have something to include among the wedding photos.

The air outside was growing colder. Around him, like a sleeper, the old house shifted and groaned, drawing itself closer for the night.

Odd, come to think of it—he didn't have a single picture of Laszlo. Not a one. Even though he'd always been something of a camera buff, he had never managed to include Laszlo in a shot; the fellow always had some excuse for staying out of range. "Camera shy," the man at the agency had said.

Not that Laszlo had anything to be ashamed of. He was a decent-looking young man with what Jennifer liked to call "dark European good looks," albeit a bit sallow of complexion. But then, what could you expect from someone who kept such ridiculous hours? "I guess I am just—how you say?—a 'night person,' " he'd explained with an apologetic smile.

Well, habits like that were easy to break; Jennifer would soon set him right. She was a trifle on the heavy side, perhaps (she took after her mother), but she'd always been a strong, healthy girl of formidable enthusiasm and energy. Some of this was bound to rub off on Laszlo. Ideally their honeymoon together had put a little color in his cheeks.

Yet what if, in fact, the opposite had occurred? What if Laszlo and his ways had proved the stronger? The Old World, he knew, had a certain allure, especially to an impressionable young woman seeing it for the first time. He remembered that last, hurried postcard of Jennifer's, written just after meeting Laszlo's family. *"Dear Mom and Dad,"* it had said, *"Laszlo has shown me a whole new way of life. Can't wait to let you both in on it."*

Somewhere in his stomach he felt a tiny, hard knot of unease. The feeling seemed distinctly inappropriate so near to his daughter's return. He got up to make himself another drink, this time omitting the coffee.

Outside, there was movement. A chill October wind had risen from the east, scattering the dead leaves in the yard and stripping the branches of the trees. The old house stirred. In the kitchen, with a terrible suddenness, the refrigerator fell silent. Its noisy little motor had been churning steadily all evening, but until this moment he hadn't really been aware of it. Now the sound was, in that familiar phrase, conspicuous by its absence.

*Just like Laszlo.* The thought had come unbidden to his mind. Setting down his drink, he opened the manila envelope and looked once again at the photos.

They still made no sense. Here young Laszlo should have been beside him, son-in-law and father-in-law standing arm in arm. Here his daughter, in the dance, appeared to have her arms around a phantom, yet one that she apparently could see. Even Pamela—poor Pamela!—was staring, it seemed, in Laszlo's direction.

Holding the photos to the light, studying the faces of the wedding guests, Mr. Melnick frowned. Laszlo, for all his non-appearance, seemed curiously *present* in scene after scene, visible to all but the camera—as if the very chemicals in the film had balked at recording his image.

The notion, of course, was absurd. It contradicted all the laws of physics; though on a fairy-tale level it seemed reasonable enough—like that legend, half-remembered from his childhood, about vampires casting no reflections. Dimly he recalled a scene from a long-ago Sunday matinee, Lugosi lunging for someone's pocket mirror and smashing it to the floor, preserving till another hour his dreadful secret.

Silly, he thought. Yet if such beings passed unseen before the silver in a looking glass, might they not have the same problem with—what was it again?—the silver nitrate in a roll of film?

He forced himself to stop. One didn't apply logic to patently illogical concerns. Laying aside the photographs, he turned back to the puzzle. *Seventeen across, Rhode Island river; twenty-two down, author of "Casting the Runes"...*

But illogical concerns kept crowding at his mind. His wandering gaze, in search of other puzzles, settled on the topmost picture in the stack: the photo of his wife and daughter standing beside Pamela Lebow. *Poor Pamela!* he thought automatically. *To die so young!* He remembered her funeral, and before that, her illness...

And before that, her brief romance with Laszlo.

Taking a gulp of his drink, he scrutinized the image of her face. She looked drawn, pallid, drained of life. Was she pining away for Laszlo, perhaps? Or merely ill?

Or was she, in fact—

Outside, the night-breeze moaned softly. Dead leaves sprang into the air as if on tiny wings and hurled themselves against the windows. His thoughts, like driven things, rushed on ahead. What if—just for the sake of argument, of course—what if Laszlo *were* that sort of improbable being, and Pamela, in fact, his first victim?

This late at night, with the house creaking and shuddering around him, the idea didn't seem so outlandish. Maybe it was just the Jack Daniel's, but it seemed to make a queer, uneasy kind of sense.

Still absorbed in Pamela's picture, his gaze dropped to her neck. He half imagined he could make out, concealed behind the collar, two telltale reddish marks. If Pamela were the first victim, it suddenly occurred to him, then his daughter would be next.

His wife's suggestion came back to him again. "If you absolutely *have* to have his picture, you can take it yourself."

Well, yes, perhaps he would. Just to put his mind at ease.

Rising, with an effort, to his feet, he moved unsteadily to the closet and hauled down the small black Polaroid she'd bought him last winter. Carefully he loaded the film pack and attached the flash, then returned to the couch and settled back to wait, the camera in his lap. Jennifer and Laszlo would be along soon. Right now they'd be nearing the airport, perhaps, their jet circling somewhere overhead. He could almost see it in the sky, a great predatory birdlike thing, pale against the night. It was spiraling inexorably toward him, ravenous for life, and the darkness echoed with its roaring...

He awoke with the camera still cradled in his lap. The roaring was the sound of a taxi pulling up before the house.

Hurriedly he jumped to his feet and switched off the table lamp beside him. Clutching the camera like a weapon, he retreated into the shadows behind the stairs. From outside he could hear the sound of voices, the slamming of a car door and a trunk. With a rumble of its engine the taxi pulled away, disappearing somewhere up the block, and in the returning silence he heard footsteps advance across the porch, the jingle of a key-ring, the click of a key in the lock. *Why am I doing this?* he wondered, but it was too late to change his mind; the front door was already opening, and a hand was groping for the hall light.

He burst into the hall, camera raised, just as the light snapped on. Two figures were standing in the doorway, their baggage at their side. Behind them, past where light fell on the porch, yawned the night. His thumb found the button; the flash went off in their startled faces.

"Surprise!" he said. He brought the camera down, the photograph already emerging from its base.

The two regarded him in silence.

"Welcome home," he added nervously. He forced a smile. "Forgive my little experiment, I just—"

"You shouldn't have done that, Mr. Melnick," said Laszlo. He stared down at the camera, shaking his head. "You shouldn't have wasted good film on *us*."

"I think he deserves a kiss," said Jennifer. She stepped into the light. He saw, as she came toward him, that she had lost weight. Her face looked alarmingly pale. "Come on, Daddy. Let me give you a kiss."

Laszlo was still staring at the camera. There was a kind of sadness in his eyes. Glancing down, Mr. Melnick saw the photograph and drew it forth. Somehow it hadn't yet developed; the hallway was an empty pool of light, with a black sky stretching endlessly behind it.

Jennifer was by his side now; he bent down for her kiss, but his gaze remained fixed on the photograph. As he felt his daughter's lips brush his cheek and move gently to his throat, he watched the pool of light, waiting in vain for the figures to appear.

# LADDER

"When asked to identify the mood of our times, she answered, 'A desperate search for a pattern.' "
                                        —Prof. Huston Smith on Rebecca West

Birth, I see now, was merely a rung on the ladder. Rather deflating, when you think about it; you live, you struggle, you learn and grow and suffer, and you realize, after nearly seventy years of searching, that your life has been nothing but a metaphor. It's not the sort of thing you see while you're living it, of course. It's like that Greek said, the one they used to teach in school: you can't judge whether your life is a success or a failure until its final moments. Though my memory's not so keen as it once was, I remember that remark; I suppose it must have stuck in my mind because, even as a very young boy, I was consumed with curiosity. How would my own life turn out? What would *I* judge it to have been, as I lay dying? But now the question of its success or failure seems sadly beside the point—less important, anyhow, than the one raised by Dame Rebecca. The answer to that, too, has to wait until the end; you can't see the pattern while you're living it. And you certainly can't see it while you're busy being born, dragging that first chilly air into your lungs, already exiled, forlorn in the sunlight of a winter's morning, the damnable game already begun. Though I have no memory of the time, the first thing my eyes beheld was probably the heath, with the icy waters shimmering behind it... And it will likely be the last.

The Firth of Lorne, that was the waters' name; can you think of a starting place more fitting? It was fit, at least, for me, who have never married, never fathered children, never stayed in one place long enough to make a lasting friend (except the holy man), never owned any property but the tiny bungalow where, lying on my cot, an old Navy pillow propped behind my back, I'm now scratching out this memoir. The Lords of Lorne once owned a third of Scotland; now the estuary that bears their name borders a region of deserted forts, ruined castles, and roofless crofts, their stone portals tumbled down and half concealed by meadow grass, the families that built them long since scattered to England or America or the other side of the world. Any of these houses, in their years of habitation, might have passed for the one where I was born, near the coast between Kilbride and Kilninver. Its low ceiling, heavy beams, and whitewashed plaster walls afforded barely space enough for the three of us, but as the beloved only child of two elderly parents, I was happy there. My father was a minister's son from Glasgow, my mother a MacDougall, of the clan whose ancient stronghold, now little more than rubble, stands on the island of Kerrera in Oban Bay. From the esplanade at Oban, the region's largest port, you can still make out the ruins; as a child I liked to think of them as my ancestral castle. Beyond Kerrera lay the headwaters of the firth and, looming in the distance, the mountains of Mull. Steamers—they were called "puffers" in those days—plied among the islands, from Mull to Lismore, Colonsay, Coll, and the Outer Hebrides. Other boys dreamed of sailing on them, to see more of the world before they died; I was content where I was. I planned, in fact, to continue sheep raising like my father; we had a flock of black-faced Argyllshires whose regular comings and goings from pasture to fold, daybreak to dusk, season to season, filled me with a sense of peace. Though we owned a car, our lives, by the standards of today, seem almost medieval in their simplicity. I remember doing schoolwork by lantern light, a single lantern for all three of us, and how we'd try to keep one coal glowing all night in the stove to light the fire again the next morning. (It never occurred to me that the sight of glowing coals could ever be anything but precious.) I loved the way the heath would change from green in spring to purple and gold in the fall, and how it gleamed like crystal in winter. I would gaze across it every day as the rattling old bus, its windows leaking draughts of icy air, drove us children to Church School in Kilninver. Over the doorway, I recall, carved into the granite, were foot-high letters spelling out the opening line of Saint John: *In the Beginning Was the Word.* I wasn't a clever student—I had trouble seeing the connections between things, even then—but I worked hard at pleasing my teachers. My parents were pious people, and I trusted in a strict but fair Creator who, as they did, hid His kindly intentions behind a stern exterior. I remember how comforting it was to think of the Lord as a shepherd, and we His sheep... But then, one rainy night on the very eve of my graduation, just as my parents were returning from Oban in their car after buying me a new wool coat, a suit, and a bound set of *Youth's Companion*, they were swept off the road by a freak storm; or perhaps it was the fault of a rain-smeared windscreen. The car, with their bodies, was discovered at the bottom of a glen. The coroner described it as "an act of God." Immediately my world changed forever. I was alone now. My father, I discovered, had not been as prudent as I'd grown up believing; he'd borrowed over the years from a neighboring family of landowners and had left me in debt. I had to sell the farm to them—the house, the flock, the pastures. They offered to let me stay on, but I knew it was time for me to go. God, I told myself, had done this for a reason; He had plans for me. Sensing that I'd been thrust out into the world like a sheep from the fold, I packed my things, ready to submit to His will.

Forth I went, my new suit in a satchel beneath my arm, to seek what I thought was my destiny. I had already sold my coat. My *Youth's Companion*s lay unopened amid the pile of books I was leaving behind; my youth was over. I would have to make my own way now, settle in a town, and learn a trade. I did know something about wool; I knew its grades, how to unkink it, how to make it take the dye. I was not, I told myself, entirely unprepared. Unlike my fellows, who dreamt of America, I had an idea that the course of my life—the pattern, if you will—lay toward the east; something, I see now, was calling me in that direction, toward my eventual encounter with the holy man and the secret he revealed. Into the Lorne flows the River Awe, cutting through the Pass of Brander from the Falls of Cruachan, and it was toward these magical names that I turned my steps. The heath was swimming in wildflowers, like foam on a choppy sea, as I walked to the highway and waited for a ride, wondering if I'd ever be coming back. Glen Mor, the Great Glen, lay ahead of me, sixty miles of waterway cutting across the highlands, from the Lynn of Lorne beside me in the west to Inverness in the east, where Loch Ness meets the Moray Firth and flows into the North Sea. The region that I passed through was as picturesque as I'd once been told, with menacing crags and pine-shadowed valleys, ghostly waterfalls and scenes of ancient slaughter. The land here had seen its share of blood; but beyond it, I knew, lay the wide world.

Forts William (named for William III) and Augustus (for the Duke of Cumberland) stand guard on either side of the glen, their broad streets sloping toward the great Caledonian Canal. Fort William, the first I reached, was noisy, traffic-clogged, and, I thought then, irresistibly exciting; it was the largest town I'd ever seen, with handsome white houses, hotels crowded with vacationers, and the grey granite mass of Ben Nevis rising up behind it, its top obscured by clouds. One look at the women in the shops, all of whom seemed beautiful, and I resolved to go no farther; I would settle here. And I did—for a time. I put up at a cheap boarding house near the edge of town and found work in a tailor's shop, fitting hikers with tweed suits—in those days one dressed up to hike—and mending worn collars. I'd been employed there less than a month, however, when one morning I arrived to find the street filled with shouting firemen and the shop a smoking ruin. I don't know if they ever found the cause. At the time I suspected the landlord's younger son, who'd had a dispute with the tailor; now I suspect God, who has lightning at His command. It was clear to me, at any rate, that I had to move on. I continued eastward, to Fort Augustus, at the foot of Loch Ness, where anglers stalk salmon and Americans search for monsters. The King's Own Highlanders were garrisoned at the fort there, and I soon found myself a job helping keep the books for a firm that made uniforms for these troops. And then I fell in love. I shan't write down her name; I haven't done so in half a century. Sometimes I manage to forget her; I think I prefer it that way. Suffice to say that I hoped to marry her, and plans were made, and then she got ill—she had a brother in the garrison, where a fever was raging—and finally God took her. No use protesting; He simply had other plans for me, and the girl had gotten in the way. I see that now; it's why I'm writing this, so I'll see it all for what it was before I go. I wasn't supposed to linger at Augustus; my destiny—the great destiny awaiting me—lay somewhere to the east. Pushing on to Inverness, I booked a passage for Edinburgh, where I found a ship to travel on, the *Saracen*. She was a rusted old tramp steamer, her twin smokestacks stained with grime, but they needed a purser on her and were willing to hire me. Besides, I liked her name. I signed on board, eager to see what God had in store.

Ports all over the world welcomed me in my quest. We docked at Lisbon, the Canaries, and Capetown, then sailed north to the Maldives and Bombay. In succeeding years I transferred to other ships and added new names to my catalogue of places seen. In a single year I saw Athens and Adelaide, Singapore and San Francisco. In another I did nothing but sail back and forth between Manila and Hong Kong. I saw a temple in Java where they worshiped small green spiders, and a woman in Ceylon who gave herself to snakes. I visited the New Hebrides and New Caledonia off Australia, lured by the Scottishness of their names, and the great port of New York, a universe away from the tiny ruined hamlet of the same name near my birthplace, at the edge of the Inverliever Forest and Loch Awe, where anglers feast on salmon and trout. The world left its marks on me, but I welcomed them. In Shanghai my face was slashed during a robbery, but I found the scar handsome. In Montevideo my nose was broken in a waterfront brawl, but I decided I liked it better that way. I was aimless, for once; I enjoyed it. I fell in love with travel. For a while, in the early years, I worried that God had forgotten me; then I hoped He had. Throughout these years I found myself employed with increasing frequency by the Britannic East India Company. The work—the purchase of shipboard supplies, the keeping of books—came easily now, and the Company and its concerns were seldom in my thoughts. But it seemed I was in theirs, because when the director of agricultural development unexpectedly took sick and died, they made me his successor.

Posts in Gibraltar and, later, Bombay awaited me. Once again my life had changed drastically; after gallivanting across the globe, I was suddenly planted in an office. I missed my vagabond days, but didn't have the strength to refuse the raise in pay. My first post, in Gibraltar, lasted exactly seven weeks; I was supposed to expedite the transfer of olive trees from Rabat to Madrid, but a Moroccan revolution cut off our supply. In Bombay, I had barely unpacked my bags before I was placed in charge of a plan designed to introduce Welsh merino sheep into the south Indian state of Andhra Pradesh. The poor beasts had been wrenched from their homes and shipped halfway around the world; I felt a kinship with them. I set up a small office in the interior, in a dusty little village whose name I could never pronounce. It seemed as remote as another planet, though the wrinkled grey hides of the elephants passing on the streets reminded me of the slopes of Ben Nevis. Only after we'd gotten set up did I discover that I'd arrived at the hottest time of year, in one of the hottest years on record. For once I didn't work hard; I sat there in my shirtsleeves and perspired. One morning a little old man, his face as brown and wrinkled as a walnut, strolled unannounced into my office. He was Mr. Nath, he told me in a shrill singsong voice, "a holy man." His forthrightness amused me, and I offered him a chair. He'd come, he said, because the locals were complaining that I'd brought the heat wave with me. They feared that I was cursed. "Well," I said, not entirely joking, "perhaps I am"—and I proceeded to sketch the particulars of my life. "I feel," I said, "a little like a pawn, constantly being shunted from one scene to another at someone else's whim. I still believe there's a design to it all, but damned if I know what it is." Mr. Nath had been listening intently, nodding as I spoke. "All lives have a pattern," he said, "that we see in their beauty and completion only at the end. One man is the second son, and will be second in all things. One will forever be doomed to arrive too late. One will go from rich to poor and back again several times in his life. Another will always take wrong advice. Another will win only one race, at the start, and thereafter will know nothing but defeat. One will make a miserable first marriage, and then a second wife will bring him only bliss. Another will rue every day but the last. Another's life will follow the pattern of a spiral, or a chess game, or the lines from a child's nursery song. But you, my friend—" Suddenly I saw his eyes widen. He was staring at a swarm of bugs that had just flown into the room, a seething little microcosm of darting energy and flashing wings hovering just above our heads, humming in the morning heat. They were, I don't know, gnats, mosquitoes, tiny flies… India has so many. Their presence in my office was unremarkable; the door to the other rooms had been open, and the cloth screens were riddled with holes. What unnerved me was the manner of their coming, the sheer *abruptness* of it, as if they'd been rushed onto the stage by some great unseen hand. The little man seemed more upset than I. "Bugs," I said, shrugging. He shook his head, eyes round with horror. "No," he whispered. *"Pests!"* I mistook this for a reference to the plague, and, thinking of my lost love, felt a stab of sadness. And at that moment, just as quickly as they came, the bugs vanished—simply melted into the air, as if that same great hand had wiped them off the board. The little man's eyes nearly popped from his head. He opened his mouth, made a strangled sound, and ran from the room. I was left staring at the place where the bugs had been, feeling more bemused than frightened. Those creatures didn't scare me, not then. But they scare me now. Because now I know what they were.

The costs of running the Bombay branch proved too high, that's what I was informed, and I found myself abruptly—and, I might add, high-handedly—relieved of my post. Blame it on the dreadful heat I'd brought with me (for I'm more than half convinced I did), and on the drought that followed. No one had ever seen such weather; the Company's coffee crops withered, the sheep sickened and died, and the survivors had to be shipped north at considerable expense. Blame it on the war then raging in Europe, which more than doubled the price of doing business. Blame it on an act of God. All I knew is that I was suddenly being uprooted again, another chapter closed behind me. As I stood on the Bombay dock, gazing at the ship I'd soon be boarding while, around me, workers with ropes and pulleys strained to hoist cargo into the hold, I thought of the stable world I'd known as a child; I seemed to be inhabiting an entirely different place now, pushed from one scene to the next. These gloomy reflections were cut short by the high-pitched voice of Mr. Nath, who had come to see me off. I'd become friends with him following the incident in my office; and though it was the one subject on which he'd refused to talk further, I'd relished his insights on other matters—so much so, in fact, that I'd hired him as my assistant. He had accompanied me back to Bombay; he, too, was now jobless, but seemed much less downcast than I, and was looking forward to returning to his village. As he walked me up the gangplank, he listened impatiently as I complained once more about the turns my life had taken. "Surely," I said, "God must be behind these huge changes." He gave a little sigh before he spoke, as if this were something he'd been hoping to avoid. "Yes," he said, "and no. The changes you speak of are *maya*, illusion." We had reached the deck now; he gripped my arm and stared at me with, for the first time, a hint of urgency. "In the things that matter," he said, "the Lord works very slowly and deliberately, with a hand far more subtle than you imagine. Don't you know how He changes a dog into a cat?" He paused, smiled when he saw my bewilderment, and seemed about to answer his own question, when suddenly I saw him look past me; his eyes widened with horror, the way I'd seen before—with horror and, I think now, a kind of terrible understanding. A shadow fell across the deck, and I looked up, half expecting to see a swarm of insects. But something else darkened the sky: a rope had snapped, and an enormous wooden crate destined for the hold was hurtling down upon us. I stumbled back in time; Mr. Nath was not so lucky. The crate caught him almost head-on, crushing him like a bug and bursting open on the deck, its puzzling contents spilling out and all but burying my friend.

Coats, that's what the crate had contained; the word, in fact, was stenciled on the side. Greatcoats, dress coats, army issues, fancy leather affairs with epaulets and brass buttons. They lay scattered across the deck, some of them dropping into the warm blue water. I even think I saw my old woolen coat from Oban disappear beneath the waves. None of this made sense. The weather was hot in this part of the world, preternaturally hot at the moment, the climate muggy even at its best; these garments were as out of place here as a pair of snowshoes. Now, of course, as I set this down and read it over, the whole thing is comically clear; I must have been blind not to see it. But at the time my friend's last words, and the contents of the crate that had killed him, were sufficiently enigmatic that I spent most of the voyage pondering them. It was a shorter voyage than anyone expected. The ship, the *Jane Guy*, traveled south, then eastward, then south again. We kept clear of Japanese waters—there was still a war going on—but in those days nowhere was truly safe. Passengers took turns on deck, searching the horizon for a sign of danger. As I stood my watch one moonless night, preoccupied by thoughts of God and death, the ship gave a lurch, and somewhere metal echoed upon metal. Later a survivor would theorize about Japanese torpedoes, but it seemed to me that a piece of the ocean floor had simply risen up and speared us. However, there was no time for speculation. We were sinking.

Boats were lowered over the side, passengers and crew having scrambled aboard, and those of us who could lay our hands on oars paddled madly away from the ship. My boat lost the others in the darkness. We heard the sound of distant screams and a great rushing of water, but when the sun rose we found ourselves alone. Several of us unfurled the single sail, but the canvas hung limp; there was no wind. The sun's gaze was as blank and pitiless as poets have warned. There were thirteen of us in the boat—we joked about it, of course—and it wasn't many days before the other twelve were dead. Half-starving and delirious, I shoved their bodies over the side to thwart temptation, and looked forward to dying myself. I felt like Ishmael or the Ancient Mariner; I couldn't understand why I'd been spared. That I *had* been immediately became clear, for no sooner did the last body hit the water than a sudden wind sprang up and filled the sail. The boat began to move. I can see God's hand in that wind now, and in the calm that preceded it as well. It is not a kindly hand; I wish now I'd had the courage to leap over the side and defy it. But all I could do at the time was lie back, mumble a prayer of thanks, and let the boat carry me where it would. I no longer questioned the plans He had for me, though I must have lapsed into a sun-dazzled reverie of some sort: boyhood memories, faces, questions, words. But suddenly those thoughts were interrupted by a rhythmic thumping...

Beats of a drum were echoing across the water, above the pounding surf. I raised my head. Before me, in the distance, lay an island: coconut palms, thatched huts, and a row of natives waiting for my boat to wash ashore. They reminded me, as the boat drew nearer, of the black-faced sheep of my childhood—only sheep had never worn bones in their noses, nor gazed at me so hungrily. I can see even now, as in a fever dream, the group of them come toward me, dragging my boat onto the beach. In the background women are tending a fire; the glowing coals remind me of my boyhood. The largest of the men lifts me from the boat. He ties my hands; he anoints my face; he drags me forward...

And heats a pot that's large enough to be my coffin. Wearily I whisper a final prayer... till at that moment, borne before a huge unnatural gust of wind, a sailing ship appears on the horizon. The cartoon natives run away, and I am saved. The ship meets a steamer which returns me to Scotland; I set foot once more on my native soil. Still dazed and emaciated, a grey stick figure in cast-off Navy clothes, I sink to my knees and praise God for his goodness; I consider myself blessed. Later, as my weary legs carry me toward the house where I was born, I believe I finally see the pattern He's imposed on my life: a madman's full circle, clear around the globe.

The heath now stirs around me in the autumn wind. I have returned, like a piece of ancient driftwood, to the spot where I began—though not, in fact, to my parents' doorstep. Their cottage now stands empty like the others, roof rotten and fallen in, a picturesque ruin. Instead, I'm now living in a tiny bungalow just down the hill from it, on a small plot of what was once my parents' farm. The land is subdivided now, along with the land of our neighbors, and a company down in London is busy populating it with vacation homes. Tourists, hikers, and holidaymakers now roam the hills where once I tended my father's flocks. The old "puffers" have been replaced by diesel-powered vessels that take Americans to Jura and Islay; and the deserted forts, those still in decent repair, have now become museums. In one of them, devoted to local history and antiquities, I recently had the novel experience—novel but eerily disorienting—of finding a shelf of my own childhood books on display in a room labeled "Typical Crofter's Cottage, Early 20ᵗʰ Century." I felt a queer burst of homesickness, seeing them there in that reconstructed room; they looked as clean and well cared for as if my mother were still alive to dust them. Among them were the bound *Youth's Companions* that circumstance had robbed me of the chance to read. I removed one and sadly flipped through it. It fell open, as if by design, to a page entitled "Rainy Day Puzzles and Pastimes," below which my eye was caught by a familiar question: *"How do you change a Dog into a Cat?"* Heart pounding, I read on: *"By changing one letter at a time. This age-old game is called a 'Word Ladder,' for each change must make a new word. You can turn Dog into Cog, and Cog into Cot, and Cot into Cat—just three steps. Or you can do it in four, from Dog to Hog, to Hag, to Hat, to Cat. Or in five, from Dog to Bog, to Bag, to Bar, to Car, to Cat. In fact, the ladder may stretch as long as you like. The possibilities are endless!"* And, by God, they are—though at first I didn't understand; it's taken me this long to work it through. And now, at last, it's all laid out here in this memoir, the secret itinerary of my own career from "Birth" to "Firth," to "Forth," and on to "Forts"... and all for His amusement. All those deaths! The men of the *Jane Guy*, my father and mother, my friend Mr. Nath, the girl in Fort Augustus... Was it really for *this* that she had to die? To move me one rung down, from "Forts" to "Ports"? Couldn't He have spared her? Couldn't He have set me on a different course? I might have gone instead from "Forts" to "Forks," "Folks," "Folds," "Golds," "Gelds," "Melds," "Meads," "Meats," "Heats," and "Heath"... Or in an even more roundabout journey, from the "Posts" I once held, to "Poses," "Roses," "Ropes," "Rapes," "Races," "Faces," "Facts," "Fasts," "Fests," "Tests," "Tents," "Dents," "Depts.," and "Depth" (assuming the old cheat would allow Himself the use of an abbreviation near the end). But in my case He seems simply to have plumped for the easiest and most direct route—except, I now realize, for a single false step. The holy man must have noticed it at once. "Pests!" he'd cried. Not "Bugs!" but "Pests!"—a chapter that, in someone else's life, might well have followed "Posts." Those creatures, had they been permitted to remain, would likely have led me on an alternate route to "Tests," "Bests," "Beats," and "Heats," arriving precisely where I am today. Instead, God must have changed His mind—

and erased that swarm of pests from the game so hurriedly that my friend saw what it meant. Perhaps, in the end, He simply found it easier to move from "Posts" to "Costs," and to drag in that dreadful crate of coats... Well, I always knew I was destined for something; I just never thought it would be this. Saint John had it right, I see that now: In the Beginning Was the Word. Unfortunately for me, the word was "Birth," and it was all downhill from there. Below me now lies one more rung—the bottom rung, the one that follows "Heath." I'd rather cling to this one for a while, but I know that, like any true gamesman, God's going to have the last word.

# RENAISSANCE MAN

Everyone cheered when the little man told them he was a scientist.

Theoretical physicists danced beside their computers; electronics technicians whooped and hollered, abandoning their instrument panels. The huge laboratory rang with the applause of the assembled journalists, and Salganik of the *Herald* was moved to describe the scene as "reminiscent of the jubilation NASA workers demonstrated years ago during the Apollo space shots."

"Thank God!" said Dr. Bazza, an Italian biochemist. "Thank God he's not a janitor!"

The reporter looked up from his notes. "Pardon me, sir. You were saying?"

"Thank God we pulled back a man who'll be able to tell us something."

"Was there really that much doubt?" asked Salganik, his pencil poised, prepared to take it all down.

"But of course there was," replied the Italian. "We knew we'd pull back someone from the Harvard Physics Department, because we're here in the building right now. But it could have been just *anyone*. We might have found ourselves questioning a college freshman…or a scrubwoman…or even a tourist visiting the lab. We couldn't be sure exactly where our ATV would appear—"

"ATV," said the reporter, feverishly writing in his notebook. "That's 'area of temporal vacuity,' of course?"

"Correct. Rather like those devices you Americans used back in the '70s, on your interplanetary probes, to collect random samplings of soil. Only this time we've scooped up a living human being, and from our own world. The man is simply—how shall I say it—a random sampling."

"But not *completely* random, I hope."

"Oh, no, of course not. We knew our ATV would appear somewhere in the vicinity of this physics lab; we assumed it would remain a site for advanced research for years to come. But our notion of locality was really quite vague—just a building. And as for time, we simply knew that our visitor—" He gestured toward the little man, who was smiling and appeared to be shaking his head in wonder. "—would come from somewhere three to four hundred years in the future."

Salganik stared across the room at the new celebrity, now surrounded by cameras and lights. He could have gotten a better view, of course, by watching the television screen on the wall nearby—for the scientist's six-hour sojourn in the present was being televised, in its entirety, around the world—but he preferred to watch the little man with his own eyes. *I was there*, he'd be able to tell his grandchildren. *I was right there in the room when we plucked a man out of the future.*

Some idiot journalist had yelled out the traditional "how does it feel?" question ("How does it feel to be the first man on the moon?" they used to ask. "How does it feel to win seven gold medals? How does it feel to know that your wife and family have been wiped out by a meteor? How does it feel to be elected president?"), and the little man was attempting a reply.

"Well," he was saying, blinking at the lights, "it was all pretty unexpected, this happening to me and all. I mean, I've never won anything in my life, and I never could have imagined that *I*, of all people, would be the one to, um…you know…be here like this. And I want to say that it's certainly a great *honor* and all, and that I'm certainly as proud as can be to find myself here with you, even if it's only for so short a time… Umm…" He bit his lip, blinking at the lights. "I'm happy to say that my era is a really, um, *advanced* one—at least *we* think it is!" He laughed. " 'A Third Renaissance of Learning and Scientific Achievement,' that's the motto of the World's Fair over in Addis Ababa—a renaissance rivaling the one in the early 2200s… But of course you wouldn't know about that, would you? Hmmm… I'm not really a very good speaker, you see, but, um…I sure hope I'll be able to provide you with knowledge that will maybe interest you and, um, *help* a bit, maybe?"

He smiled bashfully.

"It's remarkable!" muttered Dr. Bazza. "You'd think the language might have changed over the centuries, but this man speaks English better than I do! Perhaps it was cinema that stabilized the language."

"And a good thing, too," whispered Salganik. "If this project turned out to be a fiasco—if you guys had materialized a three-year-old baby, or some moron with nothing to say—the government would pull its money out so fast you'd get dizzy."

He remembered how hard NASA had tried to persuade Congress that the lunar explorers were carrying back valuable scientific information—that half a dozen bags of moon rubble were worth all those billions of dollars. In the end Congress had deemed the missions "impractical" and had discontinued them.

The men in this lab had been under the same kind of pressure. But it looked as if they'd made a lucky catch.

"Oh, yes," the man was saying, "I've been a professor of plasmic biophysics for almost… Let me see… Nearly twenty-eight years."

"Could you tell us what that means?" shouted one of the reporters who had crowded his way toward the front.

Immediately a storm of abuse broke over his head: *Hush! Please! Expel this man! Ssshh! We'll get to that later! Quiet!*

Reporters were supposed to remain silent, leaving all questions to a panel of scientists who, it was hoped, could make better use of the limited time, too much of which had been wasted already.

"Professor," asked Dr. Sklar, the Nobel Prize-winning pathologist, "let's start with the most vital issues first." He spoke solemnly, aware that the world was listening to every word. "I shall not even pause to ask you your name—"

"Modesto 14X Goodyear," interrupted the little man.

"—or to find out anything about yourself. Those of us gathered here are interested in solving some of our most pressing problems. To begin with—"

He paused portentously, allowing the drama to grow.

"—have men in your time found *a cure for cancer?*"

The visitor smiled. "Oh my *gosh,* yes," he replied. "We hardly even *talk* about cancer anymore. I mean, the only ones who come down with it these days are men in deep space, and—"

Sklar cut him off. "Can you explain to us how it is cured?" There was urgency in his voice.

"Whew!" said the little man, puffing out his cheeks and glancing toward the ceiling. "Hmmm, let's see. That *is* a toughie, I'm afraid." He looked blank for several seconds. "You see, I've never had that problem myself, and few people I know have… But if we got it, we'd ring for a physician, and he'd come and, um…"

"What would he do?"

"Well, he'd administer this drug, and then we'd just…sleep it off, I guess you'd say."

"This drug?" demanded Sklar.

"Yes, well, I'm afraid I only know the brand name—Gro-Go-Way, it's called. But I suppose that's not much help to you…"

Dr. Sklar looked disappointed.

"You see, that's not really my field," explained the visitor, with an embarrassed shrug.

"A moment ago you spoke of 'ringing for a physician,' " said another panelist, while Dr. Sklar busied himself writing down new questions. "I'm a communications engineer, and I wonder if you might tell us something about communications in your day."

"Delighted."

"For example, what exactly happens when you ring for the doctor?"

"Why, he comes immediately. Or at least he's *supposed* to. But I don't mind telling you, quite often you get *rude* and *shoddy* treatment, you'll be told he's too *busy* right now, and—"

"Please, sir! How does the thing work? Do you have instruments like this?" The engineer pointed toward a nearby table. "Telephones?"

"Oh, telephones! Yes, sure we have them, only they don't look like that. My, oh my, what an antique *that* would make... No, ours fit behind your ear." He reached back behind his own. "Oh, dear, I've left mine off today, otherwise I'd show you... But anyway, it's different when we ring for a physician. Then we press a red button in the bathroom, right by the bed, and we describe our— But you look confused."

"No, no, go on."

"We just say, in effect, 'I feel sick, send somebody over.' "

"And who's on the other end?"

"Well...*people*. And they hear me and send help." He paused, looking a little doubtful. "Of course, it takes a few minutes."

"And how does all this work? Explain the mechanism."

"Gee," said the scientist from the future, "I'm sure I don't know. I never really bothered to find out. I mean, it's always been there on the wall, and I just... I feel guilty as hell, but I mean, it's just not my field. I deal almost exclusively with a type of chromosomatic plant nodule, they're called Phillips' bodies, and... Well, let me say *this* about communications: those people on the other end of the line are by no means the most efficient in the world, believe me, the service is *atrocious* these days and they're forever going out on strike for one reason or another, so..."

"Weapons!" spoke up a general. "What are the most sophisticated weapons in your military's arsenal?"

"Well, we have no military *per se*, but... Oh, yes, we *do* have some horrible weapons at our disposal, oh *my* yes. There's one called a VRV— I'm not sure what the letters stand for—that can leave a fourteen-meter deep crater where a city used to be, and the neighboring towns won't even be touched. One was actually used—on San Juan, in fact."

"How does it work?"

"Hmmm... You've got me. I'm afraid I'm stumped." He paused, looking downcast—and then brightened. "You know, you want to talk to a nuclear engineer about that. Your best bet would be a fellow named Julio 6X Franklin, an old friend... Though of course that's impossible right now, isn't it? Hmmm... I *think* I read somewhere that it uses the same principle as the moon pulling on the tides—moon on the tides, does that sound right?—but I'm really not the man to see."

Salganik leaned toward his companion. "I hate to say it," he whispered, "but this guy doesn't know beans about anything. What gives?"

But Dr. Bazza only shook his head. He looked as if he were about to cry.

The little man was attempting to explain the construction of the anti-gravity belt his son wore when walking on lakes. "It broke down once and we had to have the repairman over. He... Let me see, he told me it had a battery, yes, and a triangular chunk of this spongy substance... Levia, I think it's called, but I don't know exactly what it's made of. Zinc, maybe? Or some sort of alloy?"

The scientists had already stopped taking notes.

Dr. Bazza turned to Salganik. "Listen," he pleaded, his voice edged with desperation, "how much do you think *you'd* know if you went back into the Dark Ages? Could you tell them how to build an airplane? Or perform an appendectomy? Or make nylon? What good would *you* be?"

Salganik shrugged. "I guess..." he ventured. "I guess that, even during the Renaissance, there weren't many Renaissance Men."

The cameras and tape-recorders continued to whir.

"I recall looking over the repairman's shoulder when he replaced the battery," the little man was saying, "and there was this tangle of wires..."

# CURTAINS FOR NAT CRUMLEY

He heard the creak of ancient floorboards, the scurrying of rats, and the squeak of hand-forged hinges as a massive oak door was slammed shut. From somewhere below came the crackle of flames and the clanking of metal on rock. Footfalls echoed from a monstrous stone staircase and reverberated through the gloomy halls.

Which was odd, on the face of it, since he was living in a small one-bedroom apartment.

All journeys, it is said, start with a single step. This one had started when Nathan "Nat" Crumley stepped unsteadily out of his bathtub, wearing nothing but a frown.

It was October in the city, and just beginning to grow dark. Crumley, raised on the principle of a clean mind in a clean body and still a believer in the latter, had been taking a long, luxuriant shower.

It was an unusual time for a shower, a time when most of his neighbors in the building had either just returned from work, had settled down to dinner, or had already parked themselves in front of the TV; but Nat Crumley knew from nearly thirty years' experience that it was the best time to bathe. The building was an old one, just six stories high, and the water heater in the basement was in frequent need of repair; if you waited until bedtime, or chose to shower in the morning when tenants in the other apartments were preparing for work, you might well find yourself without hot water.

But he had a more important reason for showering now. He was planning to drop over to the Social Center this evening—its full name, the West Side Seniors' Resource Center, sounded too depressingly geriatric—and he wanted to look his best, especially because a curvaceous blond widow named Estelle Gitlitz might be there, playing canasta with her friends.

He had seen Estelle just last night, for a pair of mocha decafs at one of the many small coffee bars that had sprung up in the neighborhood. It had taken him months to work up the courage to ask her out. Their date had not gone well—Estelle had not seemed entertained by his reminiscences of thirty years in the collection department of a local printing plant, where he'd methodically arranged payment schedules for small impoverished publishers who would otherwise have faced legal action—and after half an hour she had excused herself and left; she hadn't even asked him to walk her home. But maybe she would call. He hoped she would.

Or maybe she'd be at the Social Center tonight. It was the only place he had for meeting women lately, now that he'd stopped working; it was damned near the only place he could afford. There'd been women at the office that he'd flirted with, some he had dated, and two he'd even slept with, briefly. But all that was behind him; he hadn't set foot in the office for nearly a year. Ever since he'd accepted early retirement, electing to live frugally on his pension and his buyout money (for he was still too young for Social Security, thank God), he had looked to the Center for female companionship.

Running a hand over his chin, as he stood there in the tub with the water coursing down his sparse hair, bony shoulders, and legs that might normally be called spindly (except that spindles were more graceful and sturdy), Crumley realized that he needed a shave. He was meticulous about being clean-shaven and well-groomed—so meticulous that he tended to spend more time preparing for a date than on the date itself.

In fact, he was meticulous in all things, maybe too much so; he'd been told more than once that he was not an easy man to live with. He was quick to find fault with other people's work, behavior, and appearance, though equally quick to apologize. He was prone to tiny, unexpected bursts of rage—unexpected even to him—though never directed at anything other than typewriters, toasters, and other inanimate objects. His wife had divorced him decades ago, after just three years of marriage; his grown-up daughter had moved across the country and telephoned only on holidays.

He reached for the razor, a throwaway plastic thing, in its customary place on a corner of the flat rim of the tub. It wasn't there. For one confused moment he was startled, then frightened, then actually furious at the loss—he was, above all else, a creature of habit—but suddenly he remembered: he had put it away yesterday in the medicine cabinet. He had hoped, at the time, that Estelle might possibly come over, after their coffee date, for some late-night TV and maybe something more. Just in case, he'd spent an hour cleaning the apartment. It had not been an unpleasant task; he liked cleaning up, and he believed that he liked playing host, rare though it was that he had guests. It had turned out, this time, that he'd cleaned up for no one but himself.

The tub in which he stood took up one wall, end to end, of the tiny windowless bathroom. The medicine cabinet, concealed behind a large hinged mirror, was attached to the same wall as the shower head, with the bathroom sink projecting just below it. Because of the sink's bulk and its closeness to the bathtub, one was all but prevented from stepping in or out of the tub at that end. Invariably, therefore, Crumley would open the shower curtain from the opposite end, farthest from the spray of water. The curtain itself was of faded cream-colored plastic with vertical yellow stripes, like the bars of an old-fashioned jail cell; he left it spread wide and unwrinkled even when he wasn't showering, in an effort to keep mildew at bay. He was conscientious about things like that.

This October evening, with a touch of cold in the air, Crumley broke with habit; he needed the razor, and wasn't about to step dripping from the tub to retrieve it. Directing the flow of water so that it wouldn't spray on the floor, he pulled back the curtain from the shower-head side, the side that normally remained closed. All too aware that half of all household accidents happen in bathrooms, he grasped the end of the round metal curtain rod with one hand where it was attached by screws to the wall, then placed a foot cautiously onto the edge of the tub. With his other foot still inside the tub, up to its ankle in warm water, he stretched precariously toward the medicine cabinet with his free hand and slowly swung its mirrored door toward him. Reaching beneath it, he groped blindly along the cabinet's bottom shelf, fingers searching for the razor among bottles of tranquilizers and vitamin pills.

It occurred to him, as he gazed idly into the mirror, that this was an unusual position to find himself in. Indeed, he had probably not assumed this particular position, foot planted firmly on this particular spot, facing the mirror at this particular angle, in all the thirty years he'd lived in the apartment.

He paused for a moment, puzzled. Something didn't look quite right. There was something odd about the reflection in the mirror.

As he always did except in the chilliest weather, he had left the bathroom door half open; otherwise the airless little room became too steamy, and the dampness was bad for the paint. Even now, the mirror was slightly fogged, but he could still see himself in it. Behind him he could see the open doorway and, beyond it, the hall, most of it dark now because of the advancing night and, in contrast to the brightly lit bathroom, all the darker; he was not the sort of man to waste electricity by leaving lights burning in other rooms.

Directly outside the doorway, however, a portion of the hall was illuminated by the light spilling from the bathroom. And in this parallelogram of light, the hall looked…different.

While his fingers resumed their search for the razor, he studied the view in the mirror. Seen from this unfamiliar angle, the hall looked somehow wider. In truth it was barely wide enough for even a skinny man like Nat Crumley to walk through without brushing against the sides, especially since he'd fitted a small shallow bookcase against one of the walls. Now, outside the doorway, the hall appeared spacious, almost cavernous; and where once the bookshelves had displayed a ragged collection of cartoon books, crossword puzzle books, and other cheap paperbacks, now the shelves had taken on a more substantial look—at least the narrow section that was visible—and seemed to support more substantial-looking books of uniform size and uniform dark binding; or so they appeared, however indistinctly, in the mirror.

And it was the mirror, no doubt, that was the source of this illusion. His brain clung to that certainty, even as his eyes noticed something else. Above the bookshelves, in the circumscribed area of light, he could make out the bottom corner of a painting that had been hanging in the hall for the past thirty years. It was a painting he knew well, one that he'd completed as a boy of twelve, a paint-by-numbers picture of ducks sitting placidly in a pond. It was the first such painting he'd ever gotten right; he knew every furry cattail, every cloud. He remembered how, in his awkward fingers, his paintbrush had strayed outside the lines on several earlier attempts—a picture of sailboats, one of the Alps, another of Old Mexico—and how he'd torn up those paintings in a rage.

Yet tonight, unless his eyes were deceiving him, the painting looked larger than he'd remembered. And though most of the scene lay in shadow, it appeared to him as if the little duck pond had been replaced by something darker, and that the crabbed, meticulous style of his youth had given way to one looser, cruder, and more disordered.

Had the painting, the books, really changed? No, it simply did not compute. "There ain't no such animal," he heard himself say, unconsciously quoting what the New Jersey farmer had said upon seeing a camel for the first time.

Yielding, nonetheless, to a certain curiosity, he was about to look over his shoulder to examine the doorway directly—a maneuver that, in his present position, would have meant twisting his head and upper body to an uncomfortable degree while keeping his feet planted where they were—but at that moment his fingers encountered the plastic handle of the razor. Reflexively he shut the medicine-cabinet door and withdrew back into the shower, closing the curtain again.

As he lathered his face and stood shaving—ordinary bath soap, he believed, was as good as shaving cream and far more economical—he tried to make sense of what he'd seen. He'd been the victim of an optical illusion, a trick of the shadows, a freak of perspective; of this he was sure. Blame it on the unfamiliar angle of the mirror, or on the steam from the shower that, even now, was rising in clouds around him.

The other possibility, of course, was that, just beyond the shower curtain, something very weird had just happened. It was a possibility so far removed from his normal experience that he hardly knew how to get a grip on it.

Finished shaving, Crumley placed the razor back in its usual spot on the rim of the tub. He reached once again for the soap, but a tiny worm of uncertainty now gnawed at him: What if, out there, the world had somehow changed? What if he was, in effect, an unwilling traveler, lost and far from home?

It was a childish fear, and not a terribly real one, but he couldn't resist, just for a moment, sliding back the shower curtain from the usual end, the end farthest from the faucets. Gripping the towel rack and leaning outward, hair dripping onto the bathroom rug, he peered through the steam at the medicine-cabinet mirror—and, to his relief, was able to make out the familiar hallway, a cozy place of crossword puzzle books and paddling ducks.

He closed the curtain and stepped back beneath the shower, his mind once more at ease, but already playing with a new idea. What if that more spacious hallway, with its darker books and cruder art, was just as real as the one he knew lay outside the door; but what if it could only be glimpsed from the other end of the tub?

It would be a little thing, he realized, the smallest of inconsistencies—and yet momentous. You stuck your head out of one end of the shower and you were one place; you peered out of the other end and you were somewhere else. Somewhere very similar, maybe, but different enough to set the universe on its ear.

And that's just what it would do; that's all it would take to shred the laws of logic. A Cheerio rising slowly out of your cereal bowl was as monstrous an affront to the known universe as a flying saucer twice as big as Texas.

Idly he wondered, if such a thing were true, who'd be the most appropriate one to call. A friend? A physicist? The *Enquirer*? The police?

Impulsively he drew back the curtain from the end by the shower head—letting in, as he did so, a wave of cold air—and stood looking out at the world. The mirror, by now, was too fogged to reveal anything, and the hall outside, from where he stood, was lost in shadow. Carefully he turned the shower head to avoid wetting the floor; then, holding on to the sink to keep his balance, his back to the doorway, he stepped out of the tub and onto the bathroom rug.

Even before he had the chance to turn around, he heard the ringing of the telephone. It came from his bedroom a few feet down the hall. For a second it occurred to him that perhaps the sound was a touch deeper than the sound his phone normally made; but then, he was so prone to losing his temper, smashing telephones and having to buy new ones—all of them flimsy plastic affairs—that he was hard-pressed to remember exactly what the latest phone sounded like.

At the second ring, all thought fled. After the third, he knew, his current phone machine would answer (unless he'd smashed that one as well; he couldn't remember), at which point, many a caller—who knows, maybe even Estelle Gitlitz—might well hang up. Crumley had trained himself to get to the phone before that third ring.

Galvanized into action, he snatched a towel from the rack, and, with the shower still running, he hurried down the darkened hall toward the bedroom. That the doorway to it seemed a few steps farther away than usual was not something he had time to notice; nor did he so much as glance at the picture on the wall.

The bedroom was dark, but his hand found the phone as it commenced its third ring. He picked it up before the sound had died.

"Hello?"

From the other end came the rumble of traffic. Someone was calling from a pay phone on the street, or maybe from the subway.

"Hi," shouted a woman's voice, above the din. "This is Marcy Wykoff. We're running a little late."

"Who'd you say it was?" asked Crumley. He knew no Marcy Wykoff.

"I can barely hear you," she shouted. "Brad and I took a wrong turn up one of your winding country roads—"

"Are you sure you've got the right number?"

"—but it's okay, we're back on the highway now."

As if to prove the veracity of what she said, her words were drowned out by the thunder of what sounded like the Cannonball Express. By the time it had passed, to be replaced by a series of blasts on the sort of horn he associated with little English sports cars, the woman was saying:

"—following your map, so we should be there in half an hour, maybe forty-five minutes. Oops, Brad's honking, gotta go. Bye."

He stood there dripping in the darkness, the towel in one hand, the dead phone in the other. It felt, he now noticed, oddly heavy. And the floor felt cold beneath his feet; wasn't there supposed to be a rug here? In the sudden silence, he found himself gazing at the window across the room. The sun had set, and the first few stars were beginning to appear.

It was several seconds before he registered exactly what he was looking at. He was looking at the sky. The night sky. Complete with stars.

But the sky was not visible from this window—at least it hadn't been until this moment. Except for a narrow strip at the top, it was blocked by the buildings just across the street.

Now, however the only things blocking the sky were—he swallowed hard—trees.

Where the hell was he? Breathless with panic, he dropped the phone and looked wildly around the darkened room. His fingers found a wall switch, and the room was flooded with light, revealing ancient-looking paneling, a high ceiling, a foot-worn plank floor, shelves of books, a rumpled bed.

This was not his room.

The realization hit him with the force of a nightmare, one of those nightmares in which we find ourselves wandering naked through a classroom or a cocktail party. He felt suddenly very vulnerable. Hurriedly he wrapped the towel around his pale midriff.

The first thing that occurred to him, though it made no sense at all, was that somehow, crazily, he had wandered by accident into someone else's apartment, someone who wasn't home right now; that he had taken a shower in someone else's bathroom; and that he must get back to his own apartment at all costs.

What do you do when you step out of the shower and find yourself in someone else's home? You step back in the shower. It was crazy, all right—as senseless as a horse or a child running back into a burning building—but at the moment, its fairy-tale logic appealed to him. I'll dash back into the shower, he told himself. (The shower was still going; he could hear it down the hall.) Once I'm back under the hot water, I'll be safe. All this will be gone; all will be well again...

He had replaced the phone (beside an answering machine that definitely wasn't his) and was about to sneak back into the hall to the bathroom when, above the sound of the water, he heard the slamming of a door—a heavier, more solid door than had ever existed in a New York apartment. The thud of footfalls and the scrape of metal echoed through the corridor.

The sound was unmistakable; panic seized his heart like a fist. Someone huge and clumsy was dragging something up a stone staircase.

Yes, staircase. There was no sense kidding himself: this was no apartment. He wasn't even in the city. He was in an unknown house, he didn't know where; and at this very moment, its occupant was coming up the stairs.

He stood in the doorway, trembling with indecision. He could step into the hall right now and greet whoever was approaching; he could acknowledge he was trespassing, admit that he was lost, and throw himself upon the other's mercy. Maybe that was what he ought to do. At least, that way, there was a chance that maybe they could talk this whole thing over...

But maybe he didn't have to give himself up; maybe he could get away with it. Maybe he could hide right here in this room, wait for the right moment, and somehow escape—flee the house or slip back into the shower—without ever being discovered.

It was a gamble either way, presenting risks beyond calculation. He could step out into the hall and take the consequences, or he could hide right here and pray that maybe, just maybe, he'd get off scot-free.

The only problem with hiding was that, if he was caught—discovered here in someone else's bedroom dressed only in a towel, and sopping wet—the consequences would be much, much worse.

The footsteps came closer. They sounded huge.

He hid.

As he squeezed himself behind the open bedroom door, he realized, with dismay, that he should have remembered to turn off the light. Anyone entering the darkened hall would notice it immediately.

But it was already too late to turn it off; that, too, would be noticed. And anyway, the switch itself was on the opposite wall. There was no way he could reach it and remain concealed.

Down the hall, the footsteps paused. Several seconds passed. Then the silence was broken by what sounded like the opening of a door. The steps resumed, but softer now, and then seemed to recede, as if the newcomer—the occupant of the house, most likely—had disappeared into another room. From somewhere came the muffled clank of metal.

Crumley waited, listening. Whoever was out there remained nearby but busy with other things—at least for the moment. He felt chilled to the bone, standing here half naked with a puddle of cold water growing at his feet; he was shivering, as much from cold as from fear. But maybe if he hid here long enough and kept silent, the person out there would go away.

He stared at his new surroundings, which struck him, in his present predicament, as dangerously, almost obscenely, well lit. From where he stood, he could see an edge of rumpled bed and a section of expensive-looking bookcase—less than half the room, but enough to know that its occupant was a very different sort of person than he was. He felt a flash of anger at the bed, and perhaps a touch of envy; he'd never left his bed unmade, even as a boy, and had always been sure to put hospital corners on the blankets.

He scanned the contents of the bookcase. Instead of the familiar shelf of well-thumbed self-help books, biographies, and medieval histories that occupied one wall in his own room, the volumes here, most of them in dust jackets, looked newer; and judging from what he was able to read on their spines, they appeared to concern themselves with a single subject: crime and criminals.

Or rather, one criminal. He noted a few of the titles: *The Count Jugula Murders. The Jugula File. The Mind of Count Jugula* by Colin Wilson. *Down for the Count* by Ann Rule. *Jugula Exposed* by someone named Von Goeler.

Weird.

And even weirder: All in a row in the center of one shelf, resplendent in their glossy dust jackets, stood nine hardcover editions of something apparently written by the man himself, *Confessions of a Serial Killer* by Count Jugula.

Why in the world would anyone want so many copies of the same book?

The bottom shelf, he now noticed, held a mass of lurid red paperbacks bearing the very same more than a dozen in all—more than enough for even the most avid title, piled horizontally. There must have been collector. Why, Crumley wondered, would someone buy so many?

His eye was caught by light reflected from something mounted on the wall just beyond his head. He turned and saw that it was an inscribed photograph, carefully framed, of a plump Oriental woman; he recognized her, after a moment, as a newscaster he'd seen interviewing celebrities on network TV. Standing on tiptoe to cut down the glare, he read the inscription: *To Count Jugula—Thanks for a fascinating afternoon!*

It dawned on him what those multiple copies of *Confessions of a Serial Killer* were.

Author's copies.

A clank of metal echoed up the hall, followed by the sound of footsteps. Crumley's eyes widened; the steps were growing louder. He heard the floorboards creak as the occupant of the house—someone large and heavy—drew closer to where he was hiding.

The worst thing, he reasoned, with someone of that size, would be to jump out at him… No, the worst thing would be to do nothing. He should step into the hall right now; he should identify himself. It would go worse for him if he was discovered in here.

But he was paralyzed; his legs would not move. He stood frozen to the spot, watching with horror as a small stream of water from the puddle at his feet advanced slowly beneath the bedroom door.

Just beyond it, at the open doorway, the footsteps paused. Crumley, straining to listen, thought he heard the sound of breathing. It was barely audible—perhaps intentionally so. Not the thin, piercing sound of one who breathes through the nose, but the deeper sound of breathing through the mouth. Two long breaths. Three.

Then, with a hollow scrape of metal, the steps moved slowly on, advancing farther up the hall toward the bathroom.

Until this moment, above all thoughts of escape, Crumley had clung to a half-mad hope of dashing back into the safety of the shower. Now, however, with the author of *Confessions of a Serial Killer* headed in the very same direction, all such notions fled. The trick, he saw now, would be to get out of the damned house without getting caught.

And this would be the perfect chance.

Slipping around the door, Crumley peered warily into the hall. Outlined in the light streaming from the open bathroom doorway stood a wide, square-shouldered figure, partially enveloped by clouds of steam rising into the darkness. One hand held what looked like a barrel or a garbage can. Facing the light, with his broad back turned to Crumley, the man appeared to be staring into the little room, toward the shower.

Just as Crumley made his move, he noticed something else, something he wished he hadn't. On the wall opposite the bathroom hung the painting he'd glimpsed in the mirror. He could see it in its entirety now, illuminated by the bathroom light; and just as he'd feared, it depicted nothing resembling a duck pond. From what he could make out, the subject was more a sort of anatomical study—a human hand, large, burly, and imperfectly rendered, holding by the hair a woman's severed head.

But by this time he had crept into the hall and was tiptoeing swiftly in the other direction, toward the distant stairs, praying he was too light to make the floorboards creak—and if they did, that the shower would mask their sound.

Before he'd gone more than a few steps, the telephone rang again in the bedroom.

It was as loud and jarring as an alarm bell. He stopped dead; the game was up. He was old and skinny and wearing nothing but a towel; there was no way he'd escape the hulking creature behind him. He turned to face his antagonist, trying to say in one heartfelt expression, *I'm harmless, please don't kill me!*

Down the hall, the man by the bathroom hadn't moved. He continued to stare into the steamy little room.

The phone rang a second time—and still the man didn't move.

Neither did Crumley, the doomed smile now frozen on his face.

Seconds later, from the bedroom, came an audible click, then a whirring, and then a voice, sinister and insinuating:

"*Grrrreeeetings* to you. Thees ees Count Jugula's...*D and D!*" The speaker let out a screech of maniacal laughter that sounded as phony as the accent. "I'm tied up right now—or maybe tying up *someone else!* Eef you should leave your name and number, I'll be sure to get back to you. Eef you don't, I'll be sure to *get* you!"

Throughout the message, Crumley had stood rooted to the spot, and the man in the hall hadn't moved.

Now he did—away from Crumley. Farther down the hall. As if he hadn't heard.

Like the deaf.

Crumley watched as the other shuffled slowly into the darkness. Yet he didn't seize the chance to turn and run. He stood dazed as if poleaxed, trying to make sense of what had just happened.

Even as the machine in the bedroom emitted an electronic beep, followed by another voice—a woman's voice, requesting a brochure and leaving an address in Cleveland—Crumley didn't move. The woman's message was baffling, yet he was far more baffled by what had preceded it. It had left him stunned.

He'd gone through a lot of phone machines in his time, from cheesy and primitive to state-of-the-art; he knew how poorly they reproduced voices. But he recognized the voice he'd heard on this one, distorted though it was by the tape and the phony accent. It was his own.

In the shadows at the far end of the hall, he saw the hulking figure open another doorway, reach inside, flick on a light, and disappear into a room. It was clear that Crumley hadn't been noticed and that the phone had gone unheard.

Pushing all questions from his mind and willing himself to move, Crumley whirled and hurried toward the stairway, where the smooth wooden floorboards abruptly gave way to the roughness of stone. Chilly as the wood had been beneath his bare feet, the stone felt even colder as he padded down the stairs. Behind him he could hear the echo of hollow metal as the man he'd just escaped from—a mere servant, it now seemed—emptied garbage cans.

By the time he'd reached the bottom step, he was still in a daze, but his spirits, paradoxically, had begun to lift. He found himself beneath a high vaulted ceiling in what was obviously the front room of the house. Directly ahead, down a short, shadowed passage, lay the entrance.

He gazed at his surroundings with a growing sense of wonder and relief, like a tourist who, having just survived an air crash, regards the airport's souvenir shop and luggage carousel with the same astonishment he might normally have reserved for the Eiffel Tower or the Pyramids. His odyssey through the chambers of the house, from shower down to foyer, so nightmarish until just a few seconds ago, had now begun to take on the quality of a dream—and perhaps even a good one. He was starting to feel comfortable here.

Best of all, there was a spot here to warm his feet, before an imposing stone fireplace almost too grand for the room, where flames fizzed and crackled on freshly stacked logs that looked as if they'd last the rest of the evening. An antique candelabra flickered atmospherically overhead, while the two electric lamps that provided most of the room's light stood discreetly in the corners. Crumley was especially impressed by the tall grandfather clock, the sort he'd always wanted to own but had never had the space or money for, and by a grim-looking door near the foot of the stairs, adorned with iron bars and an improbably giant padlock, designed to look like the entrance to a dungeon but which was in fact, he decided, the doorway to a wine cellar, one that might well be worth a visit.

Now that he'd begun to get his bearings, he could see what this place actually was: an old stone house converted to an inn—in fact, it appeared, judging from the room and its furnishings, a sort of *theme* inn. There was even, by the door, a simple check-in counter, complete with oversize guest book and credit-card machine.

Determined to explore the house further—*the* house? he'd half begun to think of it as *his* house, for he sensed that the mystery was perhaps going to be solved in his favor—he wandered through another doorway into what appeared to be the main room. It was as deserted as the first, dimly lit, and dominated by an even larger fireplace, though at the moment it was bare. The only illumination came from a recessed light in the ceiling. Most of the floor was covered by a thin green carpet and, near the fireplace, by a slightly ratty bearskin rug; as he circled the room, the rug felt good against his feet. Along one wall a bay window revealed the dark shapes of trees and what may have been a lawn. Beyond the trees, the night looked almost impenetrable.

In the shadows against the farther wall, behind a row of high wooden chairs, stood a small but well-stocked bar. He crossed to it and, still in his damp towel, hoisted himself into one of the seats. The air here smelled pleasantly of liquor. On the bar top, just within the perimeter of light, lay a stack of printed cocktail napkins bearing a cartoon of a grinning ghoul in a cape with a high peaked collar. He noticed, with mingled relief and disappointment, that the ghoul's face was so crude as to be unrecognizable; after the shock of hearing his voice on the tape, he'd half expected that the face would be a caricature of his own. The creature was welcoming guests into a forbidding-looking mansion, cartoon-gothic in style, surrounded by a flock of cartoon bats. A sign in front read COUNT JUGULA'S DEAD & DREADFAST.

Appalled by the pun, he winced and looked away—and noticed, on the wall above the bar, a set of framed pictures; or rather, he could see now, framed articles. They were in shadow, however; he couldn't make out what they said. Snapping on a small clown-shaped novelty lamp, he got down from the chair and walked behind the bar to examine them.

The largest of them, an entire page from one of the supermarket tabloids, caught his eye first—not because of its size, but because it bore a muddy black-and-white photo of Crumley himself, or of a man who looked just like him, dressed in an expensive tie and jacket and standing, it appeared, before some sort of public building. He was grinning broadly; Crumley, though horrified at the context, was pleased to see how good he looked. The headline proclaimed PAROLED KILLER ALL SMILES NOW—BUT THE FANGS STILL SHOW.

Above it, and already slightly yellowed, hung a small newspaper editorial ("Blood Money") expressing outrage that "thanks to the liberal court's so-called 'Count Jugula' decision," a mass murderer could now become rich while serving time in prison for his crimes. It accused the Count of "cashing in on his notoriety."

And he'd apparently cashed in well, judging from the *Money* magazine article next to it: AN AUTHOR INVESTS PRUDENTLY—FROM HIS PRISON CELL. Nearby hung a photo, captioned *Jugula Spills All*, that looked as if it

came from a local pennysaver. It depicted the Count, or Crumley, flourishing a pen before an open volume at a book signing, presumably after his release.

The Count's picture appeared again, along with several others Crumley didn't recognize, on the cover of a true-crime monthly called *CrimeBeat*. The story, "Men Who Kill Women—and the Women Who Love Them," contained a display quote in large red type that sprang out from the page: THERE'S NEVER BEEN A MURDERER, NO MATTER HOW DEPRAVED, THAT DIDN'T HAVE HIS COTERIE OF FANS.

Beneath it hung an illustrated feature from a travel magazine (COUNT ON THIS INNKEEPER—FOR A VACATION OFF THE BEATEN TRACK), describing how, "mellowed and rehabilitated," the former convict now devoted himself to his so-called "D-and-D." He was, the article declared, "the most affable of hosts, his violence all behind him: 'I've gotten it out of my system,' he explains. 'I want to get on with my life.' " A photo showed him smiling genially as he greeted two female guests, while their bags were carried upstairs by the shambling creature Crumley had avoided earlier. "I like to call him Igor," the Count confided in the caption, "but his real name is Bruce!"

A final photo, a flattering full-face publicity shot, appeared to have been clipped from the TV section of a newspaper. The caption said it all: *Nathan "Count Jugula" Crumley tells the NBC audience that life outside prison has been good to him.*

He reached for the nearest bottle, opened it, and drank.

He drank a goodbye to Nat Crumley—goodbye to Nat, hello to the Count—and a toast to his peculiar good fortune. For more than half a century he'd led a life of restraint and strict routine, holding his demons in check, and all the while another man, the man he might have been, had been out in the world accomplishing great things. Instead of reading books on self-realization, Jugula had acted.

Now, thanks to the tiniest of breaks in that routine, with a single unwitting step out of character, he was that man.

Or almost. He certainly didn't feel very liberated. He was still an angry soul, a finicky misfit who smashed his possessions and forced himself to paint within the lines. Not like the genial Count Jugula.

But then, the Count was different; he had, so he claimed, gotten it all out of his system. Crumley had not. Not yet.

He was going to have to think about that.

Meanwhile, he had new responsibilities: the house to maintain, a reputation to uphold, a world full of enemies to occupy and obsess him. And right now there was cleaning up to do; in the second-floor bathroom the water was still running, and he was still damp. He would have to wipe up all the spots where he'd been dripping. Guests were on their way, that's what the woman had said. The Wykoffs, they were called. He would have to get things ready for them. Tightening the towel around his waist, he hurried upstairs to turn off the shower.

# Magic Carpet

The 747 was almost full; the final boarders were straggling down the aisle while muzak speakers piped "Up, Up, and Away." Cursing, McAllister checked his watch. They'd probably be at least half an hour late getting into Los Angeles, and he already had two appointments lined up for this evening.

He cursed again when, looking up, he saw the stewardess shepherding a small boy down the aisle. They were coming towards him; she'd spotted the empty seat to his right, next to the window, on which his attaché case and raincoat lay piled.

"This looks like a nice seat," the stewardess was saying, smiling at the boy with professional tenderness. "Right next to this nice man." She stood towering above McAllister, then leaned past him and snatched the raincoat from the seat. Her face, he saw, had become as empty of expression as a clock's. "I'm afraid we can't allow anything left on the seats, sir," she recited. "It interferes with flight safety regulations. I'll just hang this coat in front for you, and you can put your briefcase beneath the seat."

McAllister did as he was told.

The boy eyed him nervously. "This is Mickey," said the stewardess, placing a hand on his shoulder and gently sliding him past McAllister. "It's his first time on an airplane, so maybe you can help him a little with his seatbelt and things."

McAllister forced himself to smile, already computing the working time this boy was going to cost him. Mickey looked to be around six or seven, but McAllister had always been a bad judge of children's ages. He wondered if the boy was old enough to read; perhaps the stewardess could interest him in a magazine.

But she was already retreating down the aisle with his raincoat, leaving the two of them to make friends.

"Hi, Mickey," said McAllister, casting another glance at his watch. "So you're on your way to Los Angeles, eh?"

The boy nodded. "To see Daddy," he said. "He went out there last week. Grandpop put me on the plane." His voice was high, trembly, obviously nervous.

"Your first flight, eh?"

The boy nodded and remained silent, as if expecting further interrogation.

McAllister obliged. "How old are you?" he asked.

"Six," said the boy. And then, with evident pride: "But I'm already done with first grade."

"Well, that's nice." McAllister smiled. "I guess that means you've already—"

But at that moment the stewardess launched into her lecture on safety: "In the event of pressure loss, oxygen masks will drop automatically from the containers to the right of the cabin lights..." And while the boy listened with rapt attention and wide, fearful eyes, McAllister settled back, removed his notebook, and opened it to his price lists. He'd have dozens of model numbers and specifications to memorize in the hours ahead.

"Passengers should familiarize themselves with the emergency exits," the stewardess continued, laying aside the oxygen mask and holding up a plastic-coated card. "There are seven on each side of the airplane, two in the rear, and two in the front. In the seat pack in front of you, you will find a card showing the location of each of these exits..." Her voice sounded pre-recorded. McAllister glanced at the boy next to him before returning to his lists; Mickey was studying the card with the intensity of a doomed man, looking up to check the location of every exit.

"Mister?" the boy said suddenly. "Which is ours?" He waved the card at McAllister.

"Ours? Oh, you mean the exit," said McAllister. "I think there's one a couple of seats in front of us." Then, deciding the boy needed more reassurance: "But don't you worry about a thing. You'll never need it." He laid aside his notebook and began fastening his seatbelt; the great jet had begun to move, the whine inside the cabin growing louder, more insistent. "Believe me, son, you're safer here than on the ground. I know, I've ridden in these things thousands of times and I've never had any trouble. So just sit back and enjoy the view." He pulled the small fiberglass curtain all the way back from the window, then leaned over to help Mickey with his seatbelt.

The plane rolled sluggishly onto the runway and paused there, waiting its turn. Suddenly, with an almost deafening roar, it began to move, engines racing, picking up speed. McAlister let himself enjoy the sensation of being pressed back in his seat; he would normally be immersed in work by this time, but today, with the boy beside him, he allowed himself the childish sense of adventure. Looking over at his companion, he was pleased to see the boy's eyes were wide with excitement.

"Just like Flash Gordon, eh?" said McAllister.

The boy nodded, smiling uncertainly. "Wow!" he gasped. Then, with a touch of panic: "When's it gonna stop?"

"Any second now," McAllister said. "Whoops! Here we go!" The plane had given a little leap from the ground and now, tilted skyward, it was speeding toward the clouds. "See? We're off the ground now. Look."

The boy pressed his face to the window and gazed at the airport vanishing below. Already thin wisps of cloud were obscuring the view.

"Looks pretty nice from up here, doesn't it?" said McAllister. Maybe riding with the boy would be more fun than he'd expected. "I remember the first time I ever went up, we passed over—"

"Gee, it's not like I thought," the boy interrupted. "It's too hard to see."

"What's the matter?" asked McAllister. "Clouds got in the way? You can't help but have a few clouds. That just shows how high we are."

"I thought I'd be able to see better," said the boy. "I thought it would be like a magic carpet, and I'd be able to look down and see all the towns, and the people like ants... But I can't see anything out of this little window."

McAllister smiled indulgently. "Well, kid, I'm afraid that window's the best we can do, unless you can find yourself a magic carpet someplace. And when it comes to that, I'm afraid you're out of luck."

"Uh-huh," said Mickey. "You mean there's no such thing, right?" Perhaps he'd already been through this with his father.

"I'm afraid not," said McAllister. At the boy's look of disappointment, he reconsidered. "Oh, it's possible that maybe, once upon a time, there were things like that." He paused. "Do you know where India is?"

The boy nodded. "That's what Columbus was looking for."

"Well, aren't you smart!" said McAllister. "That's exactly right. And in India there used to be stories about magic carpets, and rope tricks... Have you ever heard of the Indian rope trick? A man makes a rope stand straight up in the air like a flagpole, without attaching it to anything, and then his assistant climbs right up to the top. People claimed they saw such things, but there's not a shred of proof. Western scientists spent years trying to find a rope that really stood up, and a carpet that really flew...but they never found one." He shrugged. "They think it's just some kind of mass hypnosis. You know, like magic? The magician casts a spell on everyone in the crowd, and they think they're seeing things that aren't really there."

The boy looked slightly crestfallen. "You mean it's all a trick?" he asked.

"I'm afraid so. Or else... Well, the Indians themselves argue differently. They say carpets *can* fly, and ropes *can* stick straight up in the air, just so long as everyone *believes* they can. You might say they're held up by the faith of the crowd—and then along comes a Westerner who doesn't believe such things, and poof!, the spell is broken, and they don't work anymore."

The boy looked confused; he probably thought "Westerner" meant a cowboy. McAllister attempted to explain. "It's like an unbeliever breaking a séance," he said. "Some people claim they can join hands and talk to spirits, but only when everyone in the room believes they can do it. When there's a doubter in the room, a skeptic, the whole thing falls apart. It's a pretty convenient way of getting yourself off the hook when the trick doesn't work."

He wondered if all this was over Mickey's head, for the boy seemed to have lost interest; he'd turned away and was staring out the window at the broad expanse of wing.

"And this plane," he asked suddenly, "it works by magic, too?"

Apparently the boy hadn't understood a thing he'd been saying. McAllister searched his memory for relics of high school physics. It had been a long time.

"No," he said, "it's not magic, it's...it's scientific. You see those big engines out there?" He pointed toward the wing. "Well, air comes in the front and gets forced out the back a whole lot faster, and that pushes the plane forward." He recalled a demonstration he'd seen on TV. "It's like when you let go of a balloon, it flies around because there's air being pushed out the back. Every action has, um, an equal and—"

"You mean that's how this plane stays up?" the boy interrupted. "Like a balloon?"

"Oh, no, no, you're thinking of helium-filled balloons, like at the circus. No, the reason this plane stays up is because of the shape of the wing. You see, the wing is flat on the bottom and curved on the top, so it takes longer for the air to pass over the top. And that creates...well, something called a vacuum."

"You mean like a vacuum cleaner?"

"Yeah, that's right, something like that. It sucks the plane up into the air."

"Where is it, then?" asked Mickey.

"Where's what?"

"The vacuum cleaner!"

McAllister wondered if he was being baited. Controlling his patience, he began again. "There's nothing you can actually *see*. It's the way the plane is built, that's all. The shape of the goddamn wings."

He immediately regretted his language, but the boy appeared not to have heard. He was still clutching the plastic card, peering intently at the schematic drawing of the jet, his lips moving as he read to himself. After a moment he looked up. "But it says here this plane weighs sixteen hundred...no, sixteen thousand tons. That's an awful lot for those wings to hold up."

"Believe me, kid," said McAllister, "everything's been measured very very carefully. That's what they have scientists for, to take care of things like that."

"But those wings," Mickey persisted. "They're metal, too?"

McAllister nodded. "They're metal, too."

"And they can still hold up this plane?" He looked highly dubious. "It sure sounds like magic to me."

McAllister smiled and picked up his notebook "Take my word for it, kid," he said.

Mickey nodded—but McAllister suspected it was more out of politeness than conviction. The boy returned to studying the card.

McAllister opened his notebook and ran his eye over the figures. They looked long and monotonous. He would never memorize them all; it would take hours. He shook his head. He had to admit, the kid had a point. Here they were, sixteen thousand tons of steel flying miles above the ground, with nothing but air to keep them up... It really *did* seem impossible, now that he thought about it.

Looking out the window, at the tons of steel that formed the airplane's wing, he frowned and shut his notebook. What if the kid was right? What if it *was* magic that held this thing up? What if this plane were flying on faith— the accumulated faith of everyone on board? Just like a magic carpet.

And what if one person on board—a person like him—suddenly *stopped* believing? Suddenly *lost* his faith? Wouldn't that break the circle?

It occurred to him, suddenly, that it was true. It really *was* like a magic carpet. When you believed in them, they flew.

And when you stopped believing...

He screamed as, with a sudden, stomach-wrenching cessation of movement, the plane faltered, stopped dead, and plummeted like a stone.

# S.F.

**S.F.** *n., abbrev. Geog.*: San Felipe, city, Chil.; San Fernando, city, Chil., U.S., Philip., Argent.; Santa Fe, city, riv., U.S.; prov., Argent.; San Francisco, earthquake site, U.S. *Other*: Sinn Fein (Ir., *lit.* 'we ourselves'), Ir. pol. movement, early 20th cent.; sacrifice fly *(baseball)*; sinking fund *(econ.)*; survival factor *(ecol.)*; science fiction; selective forgetfulness.

— *Oxford English Dictionary*,
Fourth Supplement

Thursday 17 Sept '39

Willie, precious:

How's my little snookums? How's my snookums today? As happy as I am? I hope so, because I'm sure there's never *been* such a wonderful day! I woke up this morning feeling like a young girl again, and when I looked at your picture above my bed and the sun shining outside my window, there were tears of happiness in my eyes.

And do you know why, precious? Because today I've decided to sit down and write you a letter. Imagine, Willie, a letter of your very own! Baby's First Letter!

There's so much I have to tell you, and I'm so excited I can hardly begin. Why, I don't *remember* the last time I felt so good! Just thinking about you now, and putting your picture here on the table where I can see it better, I feel as if... as if you're right here in the room with me! Of course, it's only an old photograph, not one of those holograph things they have nowadays— but it's a pretty picture just the same. Your Mommy and your Daddy, bless their hearts, are standing behind you looking oh so proud, the light gleaming off their chromium Helmets, and there you are in front of them, in your little plastic sunsuit, fast asleep with your thumb in your mouth, just as cute as can be! It's as if you're sitting right here beside me, your Great-Granny can almost reach out and touch you... And if she were with you right now, do you know what she'd do? She'd just give you the biggest kiss you ever saw—and a big hug, too! That's how much she loves you.

And even though they've put her in a Home (it's for my own good, I know) and she can't come round to see you like she used to, writing you this letter makes her feel so *close* to you... Why, so close I think I'll just reach out and tickle your chinny-chin-chin! There!

I remember the last time I saw you—I'm *sure* it wasn't very long ago—you were just the eentsy-weentsiest little baby, all swaddled up in your baby-sheath and looking ever so huggable! You were smiling in your sleep, with nothing but your precious little head sticking out of the top of the plastic like some relic in a museum. Your dear Mommy (God bless her) switched off the vibrator under your crib and went to get your vitamilk bottle, and just as I was leaning over to give you a Great Big Kiss, you woke up and, oh!, did you let out a howl! I guess you'd never *seen* such an old woman before! (Yes, Willie, your Great-Granny is old— so old she sometimes forgets her age.) Well, your Mommy had to come running back from the kitchen to turn the vibrator on again, so you'd stop crying and go back to sleep. She was a little cross with me, I'm afraid, and I felt sorry that I'd scared you, really I did. Now I'm in this Home, and I won't be able to come visit you anymore. But maybe after you've read this letter, you'll come visit *me!* Won't that be fun!

But oh, Willie, your Great-Granny forgets. You *can't* read this letter—I mean, not now, the 17th of Sept, 2039. You haven't learned to read yet! I'm sure you're nowhere *near* three years old... When I was a little girl, no one knew how to read before they were at least five or six—or even seven. Children nowadays are so smart, they're able to read much *sooner* than we did! Why, I'll bet my little Willie is reading and writing and multiplying and dividing by the time he's two-and-a-half, just like all my other great-grandchildren! There must be nearly a dozen of them by now. Funny that you're the only one I remember; I guess that's because yours is the only picture they've let me keep.

But it's a *lovely* picture, Willie, snookums, and I don't *care* if you're too itty-bitty to read this now. I have such important news for you that I'm going to write it anyway, and Mommy and Daddy (bless their hearts) can save it for you till you're old enough.

But they're not allowed to read it themselves. This is *your* letter, Willie, and it's just for you. No Grown-Ups Allowed! That's because what I have to tell you concerns those shiny metal Helmets your Mommy and Daddy wear—and why they make Great-Granny afraid.

Maybe they frighten you, too, those Helmets. I think if they'd had such things when *I* was little, *I'd* have been frightened... But that was ever so many years ago, and I'm growing a little forgetful.

Or maybe you don't even think about the Helmets at all; maybe you just "take them for granted," precious—that means not noticing things—because Mommy and Daddy wear them all the time, and you've never seen them with their Helmets off…

Or maybe you think they're pretty. Yes, that's it, you think, *What pretty Helmets!* (And they *are* pretty, too, snookums, especially when they're freshly polished. But they're not as pretty as a certain baby I know!) You'd like to wear one of those pretty Helmets yourself, am I right? You can hardly wait for the Big Day to arrive when, five years old, you're taken on a Little Trip to the Clinic and come back wearing a Helmet of your own, just like Mommy and Daddy (God bless them) and all the other big people.

Why, I'll bet you're counting the days till your Fifth Birthday!

(That's true, isn't it, snookums? Don't tell me you're five already. No, please don't tell me that! If I recollect, you should be… still a little baby. Five is a long way off, isn't it? Sure it is. You'll be reading this long before you're five. I know that because I know what a smart baby you are!)

But Willie, precious, even though you're so looking forward to that Little Trip, even though you want a Helmet of your own more than anything in the world, please listen to what your Great-Granny has to say, because you know your Great-Granny loves you, even if she did make you cry that time, and you know her only thought is what's best for you. Willie, precious, don't let them put one of those Helmets on you. They aren't good for you. You can trust Great-Granny, Great-Granny knows. Don't go with Mommy and Daddy when they take you down to the Clinic. There are men there who will hurt you, Willie. Great-Granny knows.

Instead, a few days before your Fifth Birthday, sneak out of the house and don't tell Mommy and Daddy where you're going. Put some food in your pockets, in case you get hungry. Maybe you could run away and come live with Great-Granny at the Home, wouldn't that be fun? Wouldn't you like to live here with me? They take very good care of you here, it's always quiet and there's plenty of heat in the winter. And I'd give you all the candy and cake you wanted, even for breakfast. I promise, Willie. Cross my heart.

But the important thing, precious, is not to tell Mommy and Daddy about this part of the letter. Don't tell them what I'm saying here. And most of all, don't tell them you're going to run away before the Big Day. That way, no one will know but you and me. And then we'll have a Secret! Secrets are fun—but only if you don't tell anybody about them. Then… Why, then it wouldn't be a Secret any more!

A Secret is much more fun than a Helmet, Willie. Helmets are no good for you. *I know* you want one, I *know* they look pretty, but you mustn't let Mommy and Daddy take you to the Clinic. They love you, Willie, but I'll bet you a giant chocolate cake with candy, flowers, and five birthday candles that they don't love you as much as Great-Granny does. They mean well, but they don't know what's best for you.

Great-Granny does. I'm 110 years old, or was the last time I looked, and they say I'm getting a little senile, but I know a thing or two. I know why more people are going to the movies than ever before—and why no more movies are being made. I know why people in this country walk around smiling—and why all the other countries laugh at us. Oh yes, I know a thing or two.

I also know what Feb 24th is. That's right, Willie, it's Keyes Day, the day of the big treasure hunt—aren't you the smart one! But I'll bet you don't know what it *really* is. I'll bet you think the same as every other child, that Keyes Day is when Mommy and Daddy hide little gifts around the house, locked inside closets and boxes and drawers, then give you a set of keys and turn you loose.

But Keyes Day means more than just getting presents. It's a very special holiday, for it celebrates the birthday of Alonzo Keyes. (Isn't that a funny name? I think William is so much prettier!)

And because Great-Granny knows that you like stories—of course you do, snookums, all children like stories—she's going to tell you one about Alonzo Keyes.

Story-time, snookums.

Once upon a time there was a young man named Alonzo who lived on an island named Trinidad, where he spent all day playing with his pets. His pets were called guinea pigs, but they weren't *real* pigs, and they didn't go "oink oink!" They were fat, furry little things, like hamsters, only bigger, and Alonzo liked nothing better than watching them as they scampered around their cage, feeding them all sorts of delicious food and teaching them the most wonderful tricks. He taught them to find their way through long twisty tunnels, and to ring a bell when they got thirsty, and to guess which trapdoor led to their supper.

Alonzo was what was called a Brain Researcher.

You know what a brain is, don't you, precious? It's the lump of meat that fills the inside of your head, and it's what hurts when you try too hard to remember something that happened long ago. It's colored grey and wrinkled all over like a soyburger, but the really strange thing is that, just as people's faces wrinkle as they grow older, so do their brains. My face and brain are very, very wrinkled.

Every morning Alonzo used to look inside the brains of his pets. I'm sorry to say that, to do this, he usually had to cut them open, but I'm sure he did it in a nice way. Sometimes he also had to give his pets injections in their brains. Injection means sticking someone with a needle, and then squirting some sort of drug into the hole you've made. (When I was a girl I was very scared of needles—but they don't use them anymore, not even for sewing. In fact, I'll bet you've never even seen a needle, so don't go having nightmares. Nightmares—yes, that's something else brains are good for.)

Alonzo was brown as a walnut and very, very smart. He worked in a building called a laboratory—a little red-brick building filled with glasses and cages and needles on the inside and palm trees on the outside—where he spent his time teaching his guinea pigs so many wonderful tricks that they'd forget the ones they'd learned the week before. Then he would inject different sorts of drugs into their brains to see which ones helped them remember the trick they'd forgotten.

Alonzo was working on a Memory Drug.

So far, he hadn't found a single one that worked.

Some people thought that Alonzo was doing all this for a Good Cause: if he could find a way for guinea pigs to remember their old tricks, he could find a way for people to do the same. But the truth was, he was doing all this for money—that is, he was getting an allowance, just like someday *you'll* get an allowance.

Your allowance, though, will come from Daddy or, better yet, from me. (I'll start giving you one just as soon as you come live with me here in the Home.) Alonzo's allowance, though, came from a group of men called the Trinidad Police Department. You know what Police are, don't you, snookums? They're men dressed in blue sunsuits who hit people who are bad. You've seen them on TV, and if you'd lived thirty years ago you'd have seen them on the street.

The Chief of the Trinidad Police Department—the Daddy of the Department, the man who told everyone else what to do—was a fat black man named Jubal. Jubal's tummy was so big that he always had to sleep on his back; if he'd tried to sleep on his tummy, or so the story goes, he would have tipped back and forth like an old-time rocking horse, a kind of wooden toy. Jubal loved to eat more than anything else in the world, and I'm sure he always cleaned his plate. Next to food, he loved his wife; for unlike him, Mrs. Jubal was thin and very pretty. Everyone on the island thought so, in fact. So did Alonzo.

The Memory Drug was Jubal's idea; he decided that if the men in the laboratory could make him such a drug, it would help in his Police work by making it easier to catch Criminals. (A Criminal is a grown-up who does something naughty. The only place you can see them now is on TV, along with Police.) When the Police caught a Criminal, they would hit him. But before they could catch him, they had to know what he looked like. Sometimes, when a Criminal did something naughty, other people might see him do it; but after a few days they'd often forget what they'd seen—and if they saw the Criminal again, they might not know him. Jubal wondered if a drug might help people remember, and he set Alonzo to work finding out.

This very thing had once happened to Jubal himself: he had seen a Criminal with his very own eyes and, only a few days later, had forgotten what the man looked like. His memory must not have been very good—though of course, the whole thing had happened in the dark... It seems Jubal had walked, or rather, rolled into his bedroom late one night, long after his wife was asleep, and in the moonlight pouring through the curtains he'd seen the dark shape of a man standing over his wife's bed. The man looked as if he'd just given Mrs. Jubal a Big Hug and a Kiss. When Jubal yelled, the man scampered across the room and climbed out the window—but not before Jubal saw, for barely a second, his face outlined in the moonlight.

Mrs. Jubal told everyone she'd been fast asleep and hadn't seen the Criminal. Jubal wondered if maybe she was Telling a Fib. But anyway, he knew he wouldn't need his wife's help—not if Alonzo came up with a Memory Drug.

But Alonzo seemed stuck. He worked hard, injecting the brains of guinea pig after guinea pig—yet maybe he didn't work hard enough.

True, if he found the drug, it would make him rich and famous, and Alonzo very much wanted to be rich and famous; he wanted people to point and stare, to know his name, to smile at him. And above all he wanted Mrs. Jubal to smile at him.

But it was *Mr.* Jubal he was worried about. He didn't want Mr. Jubal to point and stare; he didn't even want Mr. Jubal to look at him too closely. Because you see, precious, Alonzo had been the man in the Jubals' bedroom, and Mr. Jubal was the only one who didn't know it.

Alonzo went on testing drugs, but he never found the one he'd been paid to find—or if he did, he poured it down the sink. His guinea pigs remained as forgetful as an old woman.

He did find a drug, though, that had a very interesting effect: it made his guinea pigs forget even more.

Remember what I said about the brain, snookums? How it looks as wrinkled as a lump of grey soyburger? (Sure you do, *your* memory's OK!) Well, even though everyone's soyburger is special and belongs to them alone, they're all just about the same shape and have wrinkles in just about the same places. And there's one certain place, a little lump on a bigger lump, where everyone has a certain set of wrinkles for remembering things. Do you know what we call it? Why, IT, of course! Isn't that funny? IT is short for a certain complicated name you'll learn when you go to school. (In fact, it will probably be the first thing they teach you, though I didn't learn it—or IT—till much later.) The name is Inferior Temporal Gyrus—that's funny too, isn't it?—and Alonzo found that when he injected a certain drug into that certain set of wrinkles and then stuck two wires into the hole and did a certain complicated thing to them (sort of like touching them to a wall socket; do you know what electricity is?), he could make his little pets forget the trick they'd just learned.

He called it "snuffing a memory," and it worked almost every time.

As for the drug, he called it simply Number 57, which we sometimes write like this: #57. (That little tic-tac-toe board means Number.) He'd been searching for a Memory Drug, but even though #57 was exactly the opposite—a Forgetfulness Drug—Alonzo decided that it had its uses.

He didn't tell anyone about what he'd found; he worked alone for the rest of the year. Then, on New Year's Eve, just as 1976 was turning into 1977, he brought a batch of #57 to the Chief of Police.

The Jubals were in the middle of having a big party, and the house was filled with policemen and their wives. There were broken bottles everywhere—bottles that had once held a certain kind of old-time drink called rum—and everyone was doing the thing he liked best: the policemen were drinking rum and laughing and fighting, their wives were drinking rum and laughing and talking, Mrs. Jubal was dancing, and Jubal himself was in his private room upstairs doing his own Favorite Thing, which was eating his New Year's dinner. There was too much food for even a man as big as Jubal to eat, but he didn't mean to eat it all himself. Every year at this time he would stuff himself full of goose and chicken and pork and lamb and other precious meats that today only kings can eat; and after he had stuffed himself just as full as a soy sausage, he would give what was left over to his guests.

After saying hello to Mrs. Jubal and giving her a little wink (can *you* close just one eye at a time?), Alonzo went upstairs, where Mr. Jubal was busy eating, and showed him the #57. I'm afraid, though, that he Told a Fib: he told Jubal that #57 would help him remember the man in the bedroom.

The Chief of Police asked Alonzo to pour some of the drug into the tall glass of rum he was drinking, and Alonzo did as he was told. He also taped some wires to the man's head and ran them to a little machine he had made. Jubal drank his glass of rum, just like a good little boy drinking his vitamilk, and then nodded to Alonzo, who pressed a little button on his machine. All of a sudden Jubal's eyes closed, his mouth hung open, and he hiccupped. Alonzo let go of the little button, and the man's eyes opened again.

"What am I doing here?" he asked. "And what are these wires on my head?"

"You're just sitting down to your New Year's dinner," said Alonzo. "Don't you remember? You'd been waiting so long for it that you fainted from hunger. These wires brought you back."

"Well, leave them on," said the Chief of Police. "I don't want to faint again, I want to *eat*." He reached for a leg of lamb with one hand

and his glass of rum with the other. The glass was empty, but Alonzo quickly filled it with rum and #57.

As Alonzo watched, Jubal ate till he could eat no more. "Strange," he said, blinking, "I seem to get filled up faster than I used to." Alonzo pressed the little button, and again the Chief's eyes closed, his mouth hung open, and he hiccupped. When he woke again, Alonzo told him the same story and refilled his glass. Once more the Chief began to eat his New Year's dinner.

An hour later, as the New Year was almost upon them, the people downstairs heard a loud crash, followed by the tinkling of breaking glass. They rushed into the kitchen to find Alonzo bent over the shape on the floor. He seemed to be reading the dial of a little machine from which two wires dangled.

"Just as I thought," said Alonzo, and shook his head. He put the machine in his pocket. "We're too late, friends. The man's dead."

He was right. Indeed, Jubal had split open like an overstuffed soy sausage. He had eaten himself to death.

And that, snookums, is the story of Alonzo Keyes. Please don't let it frighten you. I do hope, though, you can learn something from it: A Good Boy Always Cleans His Plate, but he doesn't make a pig of himself.

Death? You don't know what Death means? Not now, precious...

I wish his story ended here, but I'm sorry to say that Alonzo Keyes went on to marry Mrs. Jubal. He put aside his guinea pigs and brain machines and lived happily—but not happily ever after. Within a few years, Alonzo and Mrs. Jubal took to fighting, and with great bitterness and gloom they decided to break up. The entire marriage had been a Mistake.

It was Mrs. Jubal's idea to bring out the old machine and the #57. She thought that all her sadness could be erased if, somehow, Alonzo could make her forget she'd ever seen him. Alonzo agreed; it seemed like a fine idea, and after "snuffing" their memories of the marriage, they could go their own ways without regret. So the very next day he cooked up some #57 on the kitchen stove, took out the little machine, and gave it a few adjustments (which means turning the knobs an eentsy-weentsy bit). Then he and his wife sat down on the living room sofa, drank a glass of the drug, and fitted the wires to their heads. After giving his wife one last angry look, Alonzo pressed the button.

The machine worked. Both closed their eyes, sagged to the floor, and hiccupped. The wires fell away, and when they awoke they didn't know one another.

But Alonzo had made a bad mistake: he'd forgotten that people tend to repeat their *own* bad mistakes. As soon as he came to his senses and saw the beautiful stranger on the floor beside him, he immediately fell in love with her all over again.

Can you guess what happened, snookums? That's right: they got married, and then broke up, and then erased their memories of the marriage, and then got married again, and then... Well, it took Alonzo almost twenty years to realize what had happened.

When he did, he took the #57 and the wonderful machines and put them On the Market; that means he put together a lot if them and left them in stores for people to buy. Once again it seemed he had done it for a Good Cause: he went on TV and told everyone that, used correctly, his little machines could cure troubled thoughts. He saw the day, he said, when every Clinic and Home would have one, and they would be used to make people happy—people who were worried and fearful and full of regrets for things that had happened in the past. (Sometimes, you see, a memory gets "locked away" deep inside us like a Keyes Day Treasure Hunt, and it gives us Problems years later. A boy whose Mommy made fun of him while he was learning to talk might, years later, have a stutter, a kind of shivering, at certain words. A woman whose Daddy had hit her when she was little might, years later, find it hard to fall in love. Alonzo thought his machines could help people like this by "snuffing out" the unhappy memories.)

But once again he'd made a bad mistake. People went out and bought them, but not to cure their troubled thoughts. They bought them, rather, as a toy. Correctly adjusted, with the drug taken at just the right time and in just the right amount, the machines could be made to snuff the tiniest and most recent memories. It gave many people the chance they had been looking for all their lives: to repeat, as if for the first time, whatever they liked best. A young girl whose happiest moments had been the first time she sat through *Gone With the Wind* (a popular movie which I'm sure you'll see someday) could sit through it again—for the first time. A man who liked reading could select his favorite book and, after correctly adjusting the machine, could read it again as if it were brand new.

There had never been anything like this before. Once upon a time, people used to "drink to forget." That meant that they drank glasses of rum, just like Jubal, and for an hour or two could escape from the past. But suddenly, overnight, everyone was drinking #57—and rum itself was forgotten. There had even been a rum-drinkers' club (it was known as the AA) where, night after night, sad people met and talked about their troubled thoughts. Now it changed its name to the Nepenthe Society. People came for just one night and went home cured.

As you might expect—since the drug's first use had been to commit a murder, a terrible thing, Willie—Criminals immediately saw the drug as a useful tool. A Criminal would walk into a shop, force the shopkeeper to give him all the money in his money-box (which was called a cash register), and then make the man forget he'd just been robbed. The poor shopkeeper would go about his day, never thinking to summon the Police, and only that night—after he'd looked inside his cash register—would he know that a Criminal had visited him.

(Finally somebody very very smart went to the Police with a good idea: whenever they caught a Criminal, instead of hitting him, they would simply snuff the man's whole past away. He would forget all the people and places that had taught him to become a Criminal and, inside his head, would become a little child again—a child who could be trained in Good Habits the way Alonzo had trained his guinea pigs.)

Those were memorable days, those first days of the Forgetfulness Drug.

I, too, was caught up in the craze, and so was my husband, your dear Great-Grandaddy (God bless him). We were much younger then, and saw no danger. We returned to Paris, a beautiful city in another country, and there we visited a certain garden named Versailles—a garden we had always loved because we'd spent the day after our wedding there. As we walked the broad paths, passing statues buried in greenery and bushes in the shapes of animals, gazing at ourselves in the reflecting pools and dodging the spray from the fountains, we knew somehow that we'd done it all before—that much the machine had not erased—yet it was just as wonderful as if it were the first time. Once again we thrilled to the vistas; once again we felt the vague Presence wherever we walked...

Pardon me, Willie. Great-Granny does go on. It's you I should be thinking of. I see I've written of the Presence. That's not the same as Presents, Willie, like the kind you get for Keyes Day, the kind I'll give you when you come visit me. I mean that your Great-Grandaddy and I had the feeling we were being watched by Something...

Well, Something was watching us *all*, I guess, because less than a month after Alonzo's machines appeared in the stores, the Government passed a law calling #57 a Dangerous Drug and stopping sales of the wonderful machines. (If you want to know what the Government is, snookums, I'll tell you when you get here. Don't ask Daddy about it, he doesn't know. He'll only tell you a fib.) Policemen went from house to house searching for machines that had already been sold; most of them were taken and melted down like oleo on a slice of soy toast, and the drug was dumped into the ocean. But your Great-Grandaddy (bless his heart) unscrewed the machine into little pieces and hid them inside our TV set, where they looked like they belonged, and he poured the #57 over an aspidistra plant we had in the bedroom, where it seeped through the soil and collected in a little puddle at the bottom of the dish long after the Policemen had gone.

We weren't the only ones who found a way to "save our snuffer" (as the machines came to be called). Many others did, too, and some men even made their own machines and drugs in their basements. I guess it wasn't so very hard to do.

So when the Government saw that its laws weren't working, and that Alonzo's snuffers were themselves hard to snuff, it quickly passed some new laws saying that people *were* allowed to own snuffers—but only if they bought them from the Government.

The ones the Government made were much better than Alonzo's; all you had to do was press them against your head, and there was no drug to worry about. The snuffer did it all.

Soon the new snuffers became as popular as TV and as common as cars. Everybody owned one—everybody, that is, but your Great-Grandaddy (God bless him) and me. Some might say he was too cheap to buy the new model—I'm sure that's what your Mommy and Daddy would tell you—but the truth is, he just plain didn't trust the Government.

In a way, I think he may have been right. There was something very funny about those snuffers… They'd been On the Market for a year or two, and suddenly they all began breaking down. People had to take them to be repaired—you know, the way a man comes to fix the air-conditioner—only the repairs weren't made at offices. No, you had to take your broken snuffer somewhere else.

To a Clinic.

And when you came back, you'd be *wearing* the snuffer.

The new models, it seems, were made to fit over the head, covering all the hair, like the chromium Helmets your Mommy and Daddy wear. This way, it was easier for people to have their snuffer with them all the time. And that's just the way people wanted it; they liked to keep their Helmets on all day and all night, when they were handy for snuffing out nightmares.

In short, SF had become a way of life.

(Some people think SF stands for snuffers. It doesn't. It stands for Selective Forgetfulness, which is what snuffers are for.)

And it's still a way of life today. Thanks to SF, certain books have become amazingly popular; others have been left to crumble into dust. People find the book they like best and spend all their time reading it, over and over, snuffing out each previous reading. The Classics are doing well, and so is something we call Adult Fiction, which means it was written for lonely people. Mysteries are doing best of all; every home and Home, it seems, has a copy of *The Murder of Roger Ackroyd*. I know it's a big favorite with your Mommy and Daddy—I remember seeing a copy of the special plastic-coated "Permanent Edition" at your house—and maybe someday it will be a favorite of yours. I hope, though, that you choose to read it only once.

As your Great-Grandaddy used to say, SF has made it possible for a man to find a well-thumbed book on his bookshelf, a book almost falling apart from years and years of reading, with his own thoughts written in the margins—a book he knows he's read dozens of times, and studied dozens of times, and discussed, and *loved*—and still not remember ever having read it.

A funny feeling, right, snookums?

Most people, of course, don't have bookshelves anymore. After all, they own only one book. That's all they'll ever need.

In movies the same thing has happened, only worse, since reading's too hard for many people. Young men and women quit their jobs and spend all day in downtown movie theaters, growing pale, living on popcorn and orange drink, watching the same film again and again, reel after reel, until they sicken or starve.

And there's no longer any question of spending time and money on a film that turns out to be bad; there are no more unhappy surprises. All the uncertainty has been taken out of it, and whenever people go to the movies, they know they're going to see their Favorite Film. There's no further need for new films, and no interest in them. No one's made a film in years; the Old Greats are good enough.

TV has been even crazier, maybe because each part of the country has its own choice. In Birmingham, England, episode #114 of *Coronation Street* was at one time shown every day for more than a year, and no one complained. But the record goes to the citizens of Calhoun County, Arkansas, who voted twenty-six years ago to have a favorite segment of *I Love Lucy*—"Lucy Buys a Dachshund"—shown every morning, seven days a week, rerun after rerun.

You guessed it, snookums. It's still on the air.

Live-action sports were hard-hit, too; men have taken to watching "instant replays" of their favorite football games on TV. There was even a terrible tragedy many years ago (that means something that ends badly) during the National Crew Races of 2024. During a crew race, Willie, eight men sit in a long thin rowboat and row as fast as they can, while a ninth man cheers them on. And in the races of 2024 the men *did* row as fast as they could—nine times, after which six men on one crew and four on the other died of heart attacks. It seems the audience was so excited by the races that they snuffed them, and persuaded the crews to do the same. The men in the boats couldn't understand why, the sixth and seventh and eighth time around, the race seemed so *tiring*…

Of course, bad mistakes like that had to be stopped, and they were. People have learned to be more careful. And then, a lot of things, such as music, seem almost unchanged. People listen to good music—and bad music—pretty much as they did before SF. The reason, I guess, is that music depends on repetition to be enjoyed; that means hearing it over and over, snookums. I'll bet you didn't like your nursery rhymes the very first time you heard them.

Of course, there are certain pieces that are just made for snuffing. The most popular is something by a man named Haydn; it's called *The Surprise Symphony*.

As you can see, everything has slowed down; in fact, we're standing still. People are too busy reliving the favorite days of their pasts to worry about the future. When someone asks, "What's new?" there's only one answer: "Nothing."

And it's been this way for...for twenty, thirty years now. Oh, snookums, it's been awful! The past was never like this! We're in a kind of Living Death. (It's not necessary that you know what Death means, snookums.)

The rest of the world smiles at us and shakes their heads, yet the Government doesn't seem to care. I guess they're happy they've been re-elected time and again for the past two decades. (All this may be too complicated for you, Willie, but I simply mean everyone seems to like the Government now.)

I've never voted for them myself; and now, of course, they won't let me, because I'm 110. Your Great-Grandaddy (God bless him) never voted for them either. I wonder what he'd say if he were alive today.

No, we didn't vote. But then, neither of us ever wore the Helmets. Everyone else bought them, but we were...afraid, I guess. Those Helmets don't work right. They snuff things even when nobody's asked them to, as if someone else is holding the switch. And so people these days forget things you'd think they'd want to remember. Like the time the Government promised all that money for the cities, and the cure for cancer, and the solar energy plants in every county. (That meant that your air-conditioner would work whenever the sun shines on your house.)

The Government seemed to forget those promises—but the people did, too. All the people with Helmets, that is. They were busy watching *TV Greats* and *The Classics Hour*. I'd tell your Mommy and Daddy about the Mayor's promise to leave office six years ago, to "give someone else a chance"—and they'd only smile and vote for him again...

That's one reason I'm afraid of the Helmets. Oh, please don't think I'm just an old scaredy-cat, Willie; it's *you* I'm afraid for. I don't want you to make that Little Trip to the Clinic, and I'm so glad it won't happen till you're five. Someone here at the Home said that soon children will be fitted with Helmets when they're born, and I said I didn't see how that could be true, because during the first five years the head grows too fast... But she said it'll be a new kind of Helmet that grows right along with it.

That means that someday *everyone* will wear a Helmet. But not me, I don't want one and I don't need one. I still have our old machine, the first one we bought, and what's left of Alonzo's #57, and sometimes, when the need is great, I take it out. But I only use it for very special things, precious. Harmless things. Like the time someone (I forget who) died—someone I must have loved—and I wanted to erase the pain from my memory.

Sometimes the need is very great.

But I've never worn one of the Helmets. They frighten me. And I wish they frightened you as well. Listen and I'll tell you another Secret: I know why your Mommy and Daddy never take their Helmets off.

They can't. The Helmets are part of their heads.

It's true, I know it's true. A few days before they put me in this Home, I saw a man jump from the roof of his building. He fell toward the sidewalk, ten floors down. He fell on his head. And when it hit the sidewalk, the Helmet cracked open, and there was no head under it, so that everything that was inside ran out, and the wires were exposed.

So Willie, precious, please come visit Great-Granny before your Trip to the Clinic. Please come to the Home and live here with me. I won't let them find you, and I'll let you try out my #57, and that will be good enough.

I'm so glad I've written you this letter, teaching you, warning you, scaring you, perhaps, but that's all to the good, because it means you'll come to me. Writing has made me feel so close to you, but it's nothing like having you here with me would be, having you here safe with your old Great-Granny who loves you so dearly. I'd give you all the cookies and cake you could eat. I'd even let you try the #57; it will be good enough…

Sorry, snookums. Great-Granny repeats herself.

I'll end here, praying for your reply, and I'll be waiting, even if it takes years.

Your loving Great-Granny

*     *     *

Friday 18 Sept '39

Willie, precious,

How's my little snookums? As happy as I am? I hope so. I woke up this morning feeling like a young girl again, and when I looked at your picture above my bed and the sweet rain beating against my window, there were tears of happiness in my eyes, because today I've decided to sit down and write you a letter. Imagine, Willie. Baby's First Letter!

There's so much I have to tell you, and I'm so excited I can hardly begin. Why, I don't *remember* the last time I felt so good…

# GROWING THINGS

"Hey, honey, listen to this one. It's downright scary."

The magazine, drawn from near the middle of the pile, was yellowed, musty-smelling. Herb licked his lips with a fat tongue and squinted at the page with the corner turned down. " 'Dear Mr. Fixit: Early this spring a peculiar roundish bulge appeared under the linoleum in my bathroom, and now with the warm weather it's beginning to get larger, as if something is sprouting under there. My husband, who is not well, almost tripped over it yesterday. What is it, some sort of fungus? How can I get rid of it without having to rip up the linoleum? As we cannot afford expensive new flooring, we are relying on you.' Signed, 'Anxious.' "

"I shouldn't wonder she was anxious," said Iris from her cloud of lemon oil and beeswax. She'd been giving the old end table a vigorous polishing and was slightly out of breath. "Who wants to share their bathroom with a bunch of toadstools?"

"Don't worry, Fixit's got it under control. 'Dear Anxious: Sounds as if you have a pocket of moisture trapped between the floorboards and the linoleum. Often a damp basement is the culprit. Simply drill a hole up from the basement to release the moisture buildup, then seal the area with flash patch or creosote.' " Herb rubbed his chin. "Sounds simple enough to me."

"Not in *this* house."

"What do you mean?"

"We don't have a basement, remember? You'd have to get down on your belly and slither beneath the house, with all that muck down there."

"Hah, you're right! Certainly wouldn't want to do that!" Herb's stomach shook as he laughed. "Thank God the damned bathroom's new."

In fact, the bathroom, clean and professionally tiled, was one of the things that had sold them on the house. Herb liked long showers, and Iris—who, unlike Herb's first wife, had never had to make time for children—was given to leisurely soaks in the tub.

The rest of the place was in, at best, an indifferent state of repair. The rain gutters sagged, the windows needed caulking, and if the house were to serve as anything more than a summer retreat from the city, the ancient oil-burning furnace in an alcove behind the kitchen would have to be replaced. Eventually, too, they'd have to add more rooms; at present the house was just a bungalow, a single floor of living space crowned by a not-too-well-insulated attic littered with rolls of cotton wadding, damaged furniture, and other bric-a-brac abandoned by the former owners. Who these owners were was uncertain; clearly the place hadn't been lived in for years, and—though the real estate lady had denied it—it had probably been on the market for most of that time.

The two of them, of course, had hoped for something better; they were, in their way, a pair of midlife romantics. But Herb's alimony payments and an unexpected drubbing from the IRS this April had forced them to be practical. Besides, they had four acres' worth of woods, and stars they could never have seen from the city, and bullfrogs chanting feverishly in the marsh behind the house. They had an old woodshed, a swaybacked garage that had once been a barn, and a sunken area near the forest's edge, overgrown with mushrooms and moss, that the real estate lady assured them had been a garden. They had each other. Did the house itself need work? As Herb had said airily when a skeptical friend asked if he knew anything about home repair, "Well, I know how to write a check."

Secretly he nourished the ambition of doing the work himself. Though he had barely picked up a hammer since he'd knocked together bookends for his parents in a high school shop class, he felt certain that a few carefully selected repair manuals and a short course of *This Old House* would see him through. If fate had steered him and Iris toward that creature of jest, the "handyman special," well, so be it. He would simply learn to be a handyman.

And fate, for once, had seemed to agree; for among the artifacts left by the previous owners was a bookshelf stacked high with old magazines.

Actually, not all that old—from the late 1970s, in fact—but the humidity had aged them, so that they had taken on the fragile, jaundiced look of magazines from decades earlier. Iris had wanted to throw them away—"Those moldy old things," she'd said, curling her lip, "they smell of mildew. We'll fill up the shelves with books from local yard sales"—but Herb refused to hear of it. "They're perfect for a country house," he had said. "I mean, just look at this. *Home Handyman. Practical Gardener. Growing Things Organically. Modern Health.* Perfect rainy day reading."

Luckily for Herb, there were lots of rainy days in this part of the world, because after three months of home-owning it had become clear that reading do-it-yourself columns such as "Mr. Fixit"—a regular feature in *Home Handyman* magazine—was a good deal more fun than actually fixing anything. He'd enjoyed shopping for tools and had turned a corner of the garage into a rudimentary workshop; but now that the tools gleamed from their hooks on the wall and the necessary work space had been cleared, his enthusiasm had waned.

In fact, a certain lassitude had settled upon them both. Maybe it was the dampness. This was, by all accounts, one of the wettest summers on record; each week the local pennysaver sagged in their hands as they pulled it from the mailbox, and a book of stamps that Iris bought had long since stuck together. Dollars had grown limp in Herb's wallet. Today, with the summer sky once more threatening storms, he lay aside the *Handyman* and spent the afternoon with his nose buried in a back issue of *Country Kitchen*, while Iris, unable to transform an end table from the attic into something that passed for an antique, put away her beeswax and retreated to the bedroom for a nap.

It was growing dark by the time she awoke. Clouds covered the sky, but the rain had not come. Despite the afternoon's inactivity, they were both too tired to cook; instead they had dinner by candlelight at a roadside inn, along a desolate stretch of highway several miles beyond the town. They toasted each other's health and wished that they were just a few years younger.

The house felt chilly when they returned; the air seemed thick with moisture. They'd already had to buy themselves wool mattress pads to keep their sheets from growing clammy. Tonight, to take the dampness off, Herb built a fire, carefully examining the logs he carried inside for spiders and insects that could drop off and infest the house. He remembered a line he'd seen in *Practical Gardener*, something about being constantly on watch for "the blight on the peach and the worm in the rosebud."

This evening, though, it was *Home Handyman* that drew him back. He'd started weeks before with the older issues at the bottom of the pile and had steadily been working his way upward. While on the couch Iris yawned over a contemporary romance, he engrossed himself in articles on wood-stove safety, building a patio, and—something he was glad he'd never have to worry about—pumping out a flooded basement.

The issue he'd just pulled out, from the top half of the pile, was less yellowed than the ones before. "Here's a letter," he announced, "from a man who's had trouble removing a tree stump next to his house. Mr. Fixit says he'd better get rid of it fast, or it'll attract termites." Herb shook his head. "Christ, you can't let down your guard for a second out here. And here's one from a man who built a chimney but didn't seal it properly." He chuckled. "The damn fool! Filled his attic with smoke." He eyed their fireplace speculatively, but it looked solid and substantial, the flames merry. He turned back to the magazine. The next page had the corner folded down. "Some guy asks about oil stains on a concrete floor. Mr. Fixit recommends a mixture of cream of tartar and something called 'oxalic acid.' How the hell are you supposed to find... Hey, listen to this, here's another one from that same woman who wrote in before. 'Dear Mr. Fixit: The advice you gave me previously, on getting rid of bulges under the linoleum in my bathroom by drilling up from the basement, was of little use, as we have no basement, and due to an incapacity my husband and I are unable to make our way beneath the house. The bulges—' "

Iris looked up from her book. "Before it was just *one* bulge."

"Well, hon," he said, thinking of her in the tub, "you know how it is with bulges." He made sure he saw her smile before turning back to the column. " 'The bulges have grown larger, and there's a definite odor coming from them. What should we do?' Signed, 'Still Anxious.' "

"That poor woman!" said Iris. She stretched and settled back into the cushions. "You don't suppose it could be radon, do you?"

"No, he says they may have something called 'wood bloat.' " Herb shuddered, savoring the phrase. " 'Forget about preserving the linoleum,' he says. 'Drill two holes deep into the center of the bulges and carefully pour in a solution of equal parts baking soda, mineral spirits, and vanilla extract. If that doesn't do the trick, I'd advise you to seek professional help.' "

"She should have done that in the first place," said Iris. "I'd love to know how she made out."

"Me, too," said Herb. "Let's see if the story's continued."

He flipped through the next few months of *Home Handyman*. There were leaky stovepipes, backed-up drains, and decaying roofs, but no mention of the bulges. From the couch came a soft bump as Iris lay back and let the book drop to the rug. Her eyes closed; her mouth went slack. Watching her stomach rise and fall in the firelight, he felt suddenly and peculiarly alone.

From outside came the whisper of rain—normally a peaceful sound, but tonight a troubling one; he could picture the land around the house, and beneath it, becoming a place of marsh and stagnant water, where God knows what might grow. The important thing, he knew, was to keep the bottom of the house raised above the ground, or else dampness would rot the timbers. Surely the crawl space under his feet was ample protection from the wetness; still, he wished that the house had a basement.

Softly, so as not to wake his wife, he tiptoed into the bathroom—still smelling pleasantly of paint and varnish—and stared pensively at the floor. For a moment, alarmed, he thought he noticed a hairline crack between two of the new tiles, where the floor was slightly uneven between the toilet and the shower stall; but the light was bad in here, and the crack had probably been there all along.

By the time he returned to the front room, the fire was beginning to go out. He'd have liked to add more wood, but he didn't want to risk waking Iris. Seating himself back on the rug with a pile of magazines beside him, he continued his search through the remaining issues of *Home Handyman*, right up until the point, more than three years in the past, when the issues stopped. He found no further updates from "Anxious";

he wasn't sure whether he was disappointed or relieved. The latter, he supposed; things must have come out okay.

The issues of *Handyman* were replaced by a pile, only slightly less yellowed and slightly less substantial, of *Modern Health*, with, predictably, its own advice column, this one conducted by a "Dr. Carewell." Shingles on roofs were succeeded by shingles on faces and legs; cracked plaster and rotting baseboards gave way to hay fever and thinning hair.

"I have an enormous bunion on my right foot," one letter began, with a trace of pride. "I have a hernia that was left untreated," said another. Readers complained of plantar warts, aching backs, and coughs that wouldn't quit. It was like owning a home, Herb thought; you had to be constantly vigilant. Sooner or later, something always gave way and the rot seeped in. "Dear Dr. Carewell," one letter began, where the page corner had been turned down, "My husband and I are both increasingly incapacitated by a rash that has left large rose-red blotches all over our bodies. Could it be some sort of fungus? There is no pain or itching, but odd little bumps have begun to appear in the center." It was signed "Bedridden."

All this talk of breakdown and disease was depressing, and the mention of bed had made him tired. The fire had almost gone out. Glancing at the doctor's reply—it was cheerily reassuring, something about plenty of exercise and good organic vegetables—he got slowly to his feet. From another room came the creak of wood as the old house settled in for the night.

Iris snored softly on the couch. She looked so peaceful that he hated to wake her, but he knew she'd fall asleep again soon; the two of them always slept well, out here in the country. "Come on, hon," he whispered. "Bedtime." The sound of the rain no longer troubled him as he bent toward her, brushed back her hair, and tenderly planted a kiss on her cheek, rosy in the dying light.

# IMAGINING THINGS

"When Dr. Blanke turned off the current, the woman said the strange presence had gone away."
— *New York Times,* October 3, 2006

I once saw a scary movie on TV. Maybe you've seen it, too. It was about a babysitter who, one night, gets a series of threatening telephone calls from someone unknown. She's in this big spooky house with a couple of little kids asleep upstairs. At first she thinks the calls are just a prank, but as they continue she becomes more and more frightened. Somewhere out there, she realizes, lurks a dangerous psycho. She phones the police and has them put a trace on the line. After she gets still another call from the psycho, the police phone her back. Quick, they tell her, get out! We've just discovered where the calls are coming from—right inside the house with you.

My little brother and I were watching that movie in our basement, sprawled on the broken-down old couch, and we were so stunned we almost fell onto the floor. We had no idea, at the time, that the movie was based on a popular campfire tale that had been told to generations of Boy Scouts and summer campers. It caught us completely by surprise. The notion that the thing you feared most might be hiding inside your own house, practically *beside you*—well, neither one of us ever forgot it.

Weezy—that's my brother—was always more affected by things like that than I was. Mom once said he was more "sensitive." I still remember that; I remember looking up the word in the dictionary and trying to figure out whether it meant she liked him more. His real name is Eugene, but when I was little I couldn't pronounce that—it came out "Weezy"—and the name stuck. I guess that sort of thing happens in a lot of families.

Sensitive or not, we both watched the same type of movies—the type where, if half the cast isn't either dead or bloody by the end, you haven't gotten your money's worth. Probably the main reason Weezy watched those movies was because I did. He liked them well enough when I was sitting there on the couch next to him, but afterward, at bedtime, he'd regret it, like someone addicted to the very thing he was allergic to. In fact, Weezy had to sleep with a pink seashell night-light. I didn't need one—night-lights were for babies—and I slept with my door closed, because the light spilling from Weezy's bedroom would have kept me awake. Mom and Dad's room was around the bend in the hall, so the light must not have bothered them.

I was thirteen when they split up, which meant that Weezy was eleven. Dad moved to the city and hardly ever came to see us, and when he did he looked sheepish and uncomfortable. There's no getting around it, it was a rotten thing he did, and all the explanations in the world don't make it better. Mom had to pull Weezy and me out of school at the end of the term. We ended up in a different school district on the other side of town, in an apartment upstairs from a family called the Mundlers. (Weezy and I immediately dubbed them the Mumblers.) He and I had to share a room now, or as Mom put it, making it sound jolly, "bunk together." At least we were spared the indignity of bunk beds; there's only so much togetherness a guy can stand. Also, since he regarded me now as his protector, Weezy agreed to give up his night-light; I wouldn't have put up with it.

Mom had to go back to work. She hadn't held a job since before I was born, and she was relieved to find one at a bank less than half an hour's drive from where we lived. I've heard people joke about "banker's hours," meaning a short workday of nine to three, the time banks used to close; but that wasn't true of our mother. She'd be out before eight in the morning and wouldn't be home till after six—or later, if she'd been shopping for groceries. She was tired all the time, and out of patience.

There's a word for a change like the one we'd just gone through: "traumatic." A father leaves, a family gets uprooted, and the kids are supposed to go wrong. The funny thing is, Weezy began going wrong before any of this happened. Even when all four of us were living in the old house and life seemed relatively secure, he had begun to have what my mother called "episodes."

For example, there was the episode at the zoo, when he wouldn't go near a cage of monkeys and instead dashed behind my father and hid. He was young then, but not so young that this behavior didn't draw puzzled stares from the people around us. He said the monkeys were whispering things to him—"bad things" was all he would tell us—and then, more mysterious still: "They keep saying they've been expecting me."

And there was the time he broke the tall mirror in the downstairs clothes closet—smashed it with his fist. Mom had to drive him to the doctor, and I think he got nine stitches in his hand. He claimed he'd seen someone in the mirror that wasn't him.

I knew my brother was odd. "He's certainly an *odd* duck, isn't he?" my father once said, and when I was with Weezy, I often found myself repeating that expression to myself: "an odd duck." But some things didn't become apparent till I actually began living in the same room with him. Like how little he seemed to sleep. We usually went to bed around the same time, but I would almost always drop off before he did, and if I'd wake in the middle of the night, he'd often be lying there with his eyes open. Once, or maybe more than once, I woke to hear him talking softly in his sleep. I couldn't make out the words.

"Weezy!" I said. "You're having a nightmare. Wake up!"

"I *am* awake," he said.

Mostly, he was fine. In school he got better grades than I did. His teachers described him as "impulsive," "erratic," "prone to fantasizing," but they also found him "a delight" and "a real asset to the class," which is more than they ever said about me.

That's why it was so shocking when he went after one of them with a microphone stand.

It was in the new school district, our third year there. I didn't hear about it till I got home, because I was in high school by then, and Weezy was still in middle school.

Weezy had shown up for Tuesday afternoon chorus practice as usual, only to find that Mrs. Morton had been replaced that day by a substitute— some man from outside the district. No sooner had Weezy laid eyes on him than, in front of everyone, he ran to the heavy steel microphone stand, picked it up base and all, and swung it at the man's head.

He'd missed; it was way too heavy for him to control. I came home just in time to see Mom driving up with Weezy in the car, both of them looking stunned, neither looking at the other. He'd been expelled, would probably be sent to a special school, and would have to be monitored by youth counselors.

We never found out what had set him off, and he never chose to explain it. There'd been nothing special about the new chorus master, certainly nothing threatening. From what I heard, he was just an ordinary man, not very tall, with glasses, dark hair, and a beard.

I confess that, when I heard Mom talk about a "special school," my heart leapt—just for a moment—at the thought that Weezy would be going away and I'd have our room to myself.

That's not how it worked out. He was transferred to a different school but got to live at home. In fact, for all his trouble with the authorities—his weekly appointments with a therapist at the county clinic, his prescription medications, and his official new status as a youthful offender—Weezy's day-to-day existence didn't seem to change much. He just seemed to have less homework. Thanks to the pills, he slept better at night, which meant I slept better as well.

When, a year later, I found a minimum-wage weekend job checking inventory at J&G Industries, an easy couple of bus rides from where we lived, Weezy soon managed to get one, too, in the company mailroom; Mom had forced me to recommend him. It was, if anything, a cushier job than mine. I had to spend my Saturdays pushing a wagon through the aisles of a warehouse full of lawn-care products, insect spray, and fertilizer. Weezy worked in the adjoining building, sorting mail-in cards from potential customers. He didn't even have to get his hands dirty.

He held that job at J&G until the weekend before he was due to start high school—the local branch where I was about to be a senior. Maybe he was stressed out by the prospect of entering the normal world again, of returning to an ordinary school, not the one for "special needs" kids that he'd been attending. All I know is that Phil, one of the guys I worked with, hurried up to me in the warehouse that afternoon and told me there'd been some trouble with my brother and that I was to take him home.

"He went after Mr. Healy with some bug spray," Phil told me. "They're not gonna press charges. No one was hurt."

Mr. Healy was Weezy's boss. He wasn't a bad guy, either—just a mild, inoffensive old man who, because of a breathing problem, barely raised his voice above a whisper. Later that day I heard my mother on the phone with him, apologizing over and over. It was still light, but Weezy had already gone to bed.

"Do you think it has anything to do with Dad?" I asked her when she'd hung up. I'd been reading stuff on a family psychology website. "I mean, dealing with a male authority figure?"

"I wish it did." She looked grim. "More likely Eugene's problem is organic—the chemistry of the brain. That's what Dr. Shulman thinks."

I wondered uneasily, just for a moment, if the same chemicals that flowed through my brother's brain might be seeping into my own.

Sometime after midnight, I woke to find Weezy crouched at our bedroom window. It was late August, with a sliver of moon, and in its light I could see that he was staring intently at something outside. As a rule, he now slept soundly, but maybe he hadn't taken his meds, or maybe he'd just gone to bed too early. And of course, it had been a pretty upsetting day.

"Weezy," I said, "what are you doing?"

"C'mere." His voice was hushed, frightened. I got out of bed and crossed the room. "Can you see it?" he said, not turning his head.

I peered into the night. There isn't much of a view—mainly the neighbors' house and, between it and ours, a twisted old maple.

"I don't see anything."

"Something's out there, clinging to the tree," he said. "You don't see it? You don't *hear* it?"

"No. What is it?"

"I'm not sure," he said, squinting as if to see better. "It's big—like some kind of big dark furry caterpillar, covered all over with..." He searched for the word. "You know. Like our brushes."

I knew what he meant—the two matching hairbrushes Dad had given us one Christmas. They were labeled GENUINE BOAR'S BRISTLE, and I remember asking Dad what that meant. "Pig hair," he'd replied, grinning.

"Weezy," I said gently, "there are definitely caterpillars in that tree. *Little* ones. Maybe gypsy moths from last spring."

He took no notice. "It's whispering things."

"What's it saying?"

He paused, caught his breath.

"It's—it's promising to come for me." He turned. "You can't hear it?"

To humor him, I listened. I could hear the crickets, a soft breeze, nothing more. But moments later, I couldn't be sure; it's never hard to hear word sounds in the breeze. The tree was just a dark, shifting mass with an occasional flicker of moonlight on the leaves. Who knows what might have been hiding in it? Was that a dark face I saw? Who knows?

The last time I'd been taken to the eye doctor, he had measured my vision for glasses. As I stared at the chart on the opposite wall, he would slip a lens into the mechanical device I was looking through and he would say, "Now, is it better this way—" He would slip in another lens. "Or this way—" He would remove the second lens. "Or hard to tell?" He would do it again. "Is it better this way? Or this way? Or hard to tell?"

Tonight was a case of hard to tell.

"Weezy, there's nothing out there. It's all in your mind."

"Honest?"

"Believe me, you're imagining things."

He gulped, seemed to relax a little. "So it's just in my head?"

"Trust me."

"Well... all right, then." He stood up. "Don't tell Mom, okay?"

"Of course not."

The next morning, as she was driving me to the mall to buy school clothes, with Weezy at home blinking sleepily in front of the TV, I told Mom.

The hospital where they sent him was on the other side of the county, but it could just as easily have been in another country, because for at least the first three weeks, he was supposed to have no visitors and no communication with family members. It sounds harsh, but I guess it was for his own good.

With Weezy gone, I set up my computer at his desk and used mine for homework and books. I piled my extra clothes on his bed. I missed Weezy in some ways, I really did, but it was good to have my own room again.

Only two weeks had passed when I heard, from Mom, that he was going to come home. She got off the phone with a smile. "They say he's been making great progress."

"Great," I said.

The next day, when I came back from school, I saw a letter addressed to me in Weezy's handwriting. Across the back of the envelope, he'd written CONFIDENTIAL. He wasn't supposed to communicate with us, and I wondered how he'd managed to get it in the mail. Mom wouldn't be home for an hour or two. I took the letter into my room and read it at my desk. It was written in pencil on a piece of lined paper yanked from a notebook, leaving the three holes torn.

*Hey, bro,* he wrote,

> *I've been thinking about what you told me. There's not much else to DO here. I mean, except think. And make nice for the doctors. Which I'm getting very good at. I know just what to tell them. And what NOT to tell them. Because they're jerks. Blind. They know nothing, and less than nothing.*
>
> *I'm imagining things—that's what you said. It's all INSIDE MY HEAD, right? And maybe that's supposed to be comforting. But remember that movie we watched together? The one about the babysitter? It was a warning, that movie, to keep the things OUT. To keep them OUT THERE—in the night. You don't want to let them in the house, you don't want to turn around and find them inside with you, right there beside you, because once they're inside, they're MUCH WORSE. Because they're REAL. Because I IMAGINE them. To imagine means to INVENT—and what you invent becomes real.*
>
> *I'll be home soon, and I'll show you what I mean.*

He had drawn a sort of picture at the bottom of the letter—a kind of stick figure seeming to reach out, maybe in friendship, maybe not—only the figure had little jagged lines scribbled all over, giving it a certain bulkiness.

There's an expression I've heard in old crime movies: "dropping a dime" on someone. It means, basically, tattling on someone—ratting on him. It comes from the days when a call at a pay phone cost ten cents. You want to turn someone in, you drop in your dime and call the authorities.

Well, you might say I dropped Weezy's letter on him. I folded it up and put it back in the envelope, took the bottle of Elmer's from the kitchen drawer, and carefully resealed the flap. I left the letter lying with the rest of the mail and went out for a bike ride.

Mom was holding the envelope when I got home, but she hadn't opened it. She watched me as I pretended to read the letter for the first time.

"What does he say?"

"I really shouldn't tell you."

"*Tell* me."

"I really shouldn't."

She was as upset, when she read it, as I'd known she'd be. Before the week was out, it was decided that Weezy wasn't coming home after all, and once again communication ceased.

"They're planning to run some tests on him," she announced one October evening over dinner. "To see if they can find out what's wrong."

"I thought they agreed it was schizophrenia," I said, proud of my ease with the term. I'd been spending more time on the web.

"No one's sure," she said. "Apparently a Swiss doctor with a name like Bland or Blank has been doing some experiments…"

"They're flying Weezy to Switzerland?" Awful as it sounds, I instantly felt a twinge of jealousy.

"Hardly!" she said. "They're just hoping to use a similar method here. Something very up-to-date."

That night I Googled the name. Olaf Blanke—how appropriate, I thought. Blank slate. Fill in the blanks. Mind went blank. It appears that over the past few years, he and his team have been doing some groundbreaking experiments at a lab in Lausanne involving electrical stimulation of the brain.

I had no trouble finding a paper of Blanke's on the net, in a medical journal called *Brain*. You can probably find it yourself. I tried to read it, but it was filled with lines like "Presurgical epilepsy evaluation suggested right occipito-parietal seizure onset partially overlapping and anterior to a dysembryoblastic neuroepithelial tumor."

Why do they have to use all those five-dollar words? I couldn't even make my way past the summary at the beginning, with its weird parentheses: "We suggest that OBE and AS are related to a failure to integrate proprioceptive, tactile and visual information with respect to one's own body (disintegration in personal space) and by a vestibular dysfunction leading to an additional disintegration between personal (vestibular) space and extrapersonal (visual) space."

I soon gave up; even homework seemed more fun. Weezy had always been better at science than I was. Maybe he could have figured it out—if he hadn't, at this very moment, been on the receiving end of it.

I got a glimpse of what those tests he was undergoing might be like when, less than two weeks later, I received some unexpected news. It was a chilly grey Saturday morning, and I had just arrived at my job at the J&G warehouse. Grinning as he ambled up to me, Phil, my coworker, handed me a pale blue printed card. "Hey, pal," he said, "this showed up in the mailroom yesterday. It's addressed to you."

I saw immediately what it was—one of those free postpaid cards that the company stuck in magazines alongside their ads. If you wanted further product information, you filled out the card and dropped it in the mailbox.

On the address side, above the words "J&G Industries," someone had penciled in my name. I recognized the handwriting.

"I think it's from that crazy brother of yours," said Phil. He stood regarding me curiously as I turned the card over. The printed words—"Please rush me FREE information about..."—were not what caught my eye. Rather, it was the message scrawled in the spaces meant for name and address:

> *They've got me wired up here—in more ways than one. It doesn't hurt, though. It's like a game. They tell me I'm producing good results.*

There was no signature, but I didn't need one.

The card itself probably dated back to Weezy's days in the mailroom, or else he'd ripped it from a magazine at the hospital. It was a clever way of reaching me without a stamp—and without Mom knowing. I decided not to tell her, at least not yet.

At night, after dinner, I made myself a cup of instant cocoa and sat down at the computer, ready to give Dr. Blanke another try. I skipped ahead to where he described the actual experiments. From what I could make out, he'd been treating epileptics and people with histories of everything from migraine headaches to hallucinations. His team had implanted dozens of electrodes in these patients' brains and, on others, had experimented with something called "low-intensity magnetic stimulation." While the patients were awake and fully conscious, the current was turned on for a couple of seconds, during which they were asked to report what they felt.

That much didn't seem especially new. But Blanke's team had discovered that when they stimulated an area called the angular gyrus, in a part of the brain an inch behind and above each ear called the temporoparietal junction, they got some rather startling reactions.

Most of the patients said they felt themselves floating: sometimes right there in the hospital room—the classic "out-of-body experience"—but in one woman's case, floating outdoors, over hills and meadows. That sounded nice. Another saw and felt her legs moving when they weren't.

Still another, identified only as Patient 3, had "the distinct feeling" that something—a shadowy figure—was standing behind her, "although upon turning round, there was nobody there." The researchers discovered that the effect was "counterlateral": when the left side of her brain was stimulated, the patient reported that the unseen figure was on her right; when they did it to the right side, she sensed the figure to her left.

It's this mysterious presence that seems to have caused the biggest sensation. Though the experiments had been going on for several years, they weren't well known till the British journal *Nature* published an article on them in September of 2006: "Brain Electrodes Conjure Up Ghostly Visions." I couldn't find that article online, but I found plenty of others, some with headlines out of a horror movie: "Creepy Experiment Exposes Paranoia and Sense of Alien Control." "Inducing the Shadow-Self by Stimulating the Brain." "Brain Stimulation Creates Shadow Person." The *Chicago Tribune* spoke of "Brain Zaps" and "Eerie Feelings," and the *London Daily Telegraph* reported " 'Shadow' Sheds Light on Schizophrenia." I felt rather proud when I saw that; I'd been right about Weezy after all.

I was glad I'd taken the time to read up on this stuff, because at work the following Saturday, Phil walked over and, with a sympathetic little nod, gave me a second card from my brother. I suppose it should have occurred to me that if Weezy could get his hands on one blank card, he could obtain more. Maybe he'd stolen a pile of them before he'd been fired and had smuggled them into the hospital. Still, his message came as a surprise:

*I was right. It exists.*

That's all it said. Once again there was no signature, and this time, I noticed, Weezy hadn't even bothered to write my name on the address side. "Good thing that guy in the mailroom recognized it," said Phil. "Otherwise it would've got tossed in the trash."

I almost wished it had been. I thought about the message all day—the simple certainty in those words.

Of course, how could Weezy be expected to understand? Surely, from what I'd read, he was prey to a delusion, a phantom conjured up in his brain by a two-second jolt of electricity.

I found more about that phantom—or at least about one that might as well be its brother—in the library the next day; in fact, I spent my whole Sunday afternoon there. *The New York Times* had run an article on the subject: "Out-of-Body Experience?" the headline read. "Your Brain Is to Blame." It confirmed my suspicion that what Weezy was going through was nothing new. Blanke's patient had expressed "an uncanny feeling that someone was behind her, intent on interfering with her actions." When she tried to lie down, she felt the figure lie down beneath her. "When Dr. Blanke turned off the current," the *Times* reported, "the woman said the strange presence had gone away. Each time he reapplied the current, she once again turned her head to try to see the shadow figure... Some schizophrenics, Dr. Blanke said, experience paranoid delusions and the sense that someone is following them."

Another news report provided more details about what this "presence" was capable of. "When the patient sat and embraced her knees, she noticed that the 'man' was now also sitting and clasping her in his arms, which she described as 'unpleasant.' " When she'd been handed a card and asked to read it, she could feel the figure try to snatch it from her. "He wants to take the card," she had explained. "He doesn't want me to read it."

Blanke had concluded that this shadow figure was simply the patient's illusion of her own body. There were only two things this theory failed to explain: why a woman had described the figure as being of the opposite sex—and why, if it was merely a projection of herself, it seemed to treat her with such hostility.

Weezy's next message, the following weekend, suggested, against all reason, that the figure might be more than just a product of his mind:

> *I couldn't see it—it was standing behind me. But I think the doctors saw it.*

There was no card waiting for me the weekend after that, and I was relieved. Maybe the experiments were at an end.

But the next weekend brought a new message:

> *Felt it today. It was behind me, and I felt it on the back of my neck. I heard a doctor say, "What the hell is that?"*

A week later:

> *Felt it again. It's the thing from the tree.*

And the next:

> *It tried to put its arms around me. I could feel it even after the current was turned off. Not pleasant. I'm getting out of here.*

No word came from Weezy for the next two weeks. I wondered if maybe he had actually gotten out—if anyone was clever enough to find a way, he was—and night after night I wrestled with the thought of warning Mom about it, or of contacting the hospital. But I didn't. Maybe I was reluctant to betray him a third time. Or maybe I just figured that this time I'd get caught.

December had arrived. Midterms occupied me, and when I got home from school, I'd pull down the shades in my bedroom to shut out the early darkness and would try to study. Whenever I'd ask Mom about how Weezy was doing, she'd say, "They tell me he's doing fine," but she'd look worried.

"Do you think he's getting out soon?" I asked her once, careful to keep all emotion from my voice.

She shook her head. "Not for a while."

Yet each day, when I entered the house, I almost expected that I'd walk upstairs and find him standing there to greet me. I imagined him asking me to hide him, or to give him some money so that he could escape, and I wondered what I'd do.

Eventually I put him from my mind. The holidays were coming, and I looked forward to a week of vacation. Weezy was safe where he was, with the best of modern medical science to vanquish his demons.

And then, that Saturday, came another pale blue card with another message from him, the shortest one of all, yet the one that most haunts me. The card's heavily printed commercial text seemed to fade into insignificance, framing the area of blank white space, in the middle of which, scrawled in pencil, were four simple words:

*It has a friend.*

Since then, the cards have stopped. Their absence—the resumed silence, you might call it—has been welcome. Mom has been making preparations to visit Weezy for the holidays, and I can see that the thought makes her happy.

She wasn't yet home when I came upstairs after school today, my last day of classes now behind me, vacation ahead. I pulled down the shades and was sitting at Weezy's desk in our room, alone in the apartment, though I could hear, below me, the Mumblers going about their evening business and the sound of carols from their TV; and as I sat listening, I could swear I felt something brush the back of my neck. I turned, but no one was there. The room was empty.

But for a moment, I had felt a touch, tentative but oddly familiar. And bristly.

# THEY DON'T WRITE 'EM
# LIKE THIS ANYMORE
## A TV Treatment in Two Versions

**Version One:**

A bleak day in early spring; evening. The rather cheerless city block is dominated by an expensive modern high-rise. Inside its plush elevator stands Martin Stone, tired, graying, his face half hidden behind the financial column of a newspaper. He is returning home from a hard day at the office; he wears a trench coat and, in his free hand, clutches a sleek leather briefcase.

The door slides open. Stone lets himself into an apartment at the end of the hall. It's posh, well-furnished, a bit impersonal. So is the peck on the cheek that Stone gives his wife, who greets him in the living room. She's middle-aged, attractive, somewhat distant. Perhaps a photo or two may hint of a grown-up daughter somewhere—grandchildren, even—but there's no sign of children in this sterile apartment. Somewhere there's an old-fashioned picture of Stone's Aunt Marian, dead these twenty years.

Stone looks through the pile of mail waiting for him on the coffee table: *Time, Fortune, Vanity Fair,* a few bills, some glossy corporate reports… and then his brow furrows. "What's this?"

"I don't know, dear—it just came in the mail. Some kind of promotion, maybe."

It's a large, colorful pulp magazine, *Science Marvel Tales* emblazoned on the front—and it's in spanking new condition. On its cover, a tentacled creature reaches for a partially-clad blonde; behind them, a futuristic city glows beneath the stars.

"April 1939," he says wonderingly, reading it on the cover. "Obviously a reprint." He flips through the pages. "Hmm, good job, too! A perfect facsimile." Holding the issue to his nose, he closes his eyes, takes a deep breath, and smiles like a man smelling a food he hasn't tasted for years. "Mmm… Smells just like they used to, that wonderful pulp smell!" He stares at the cover, shakes his head. "God, I haven't seen one of these since… I must have been twelve! Sure, that's right—I remember using my birthday money to send away for a subscription."

The magazine's arrival stirs a flood of memories, which he recounts to his wife. Perhaps we see some of them in flashback: memories of a small-town boyhood during the Depression, when Stone lived with his stern and pious Aunt Marian. He remembers waiting for the postman each month, snatching the newly arrived issues of *Science Marvel Tales* out of the mailbox before his aunt saw them, sneaking into the house with them concealed beneath his jacket, and reading them under the covers at night with a flashlight. (He kept a secret hoard of back issues behind the Sunday-school texts on his bookshelf.) The magazine's illustrations—especially the covers—were so enticingly lurid, worthy of a Margaret Brundage. His aunt would never understand…

He remembers the day he got to the mailbox too late—and the look on his aunt's face as she eyed a particularly salacious-looking cover. She was greatly put out: not furious, perhaps, but troubled. The cover, the interior artwork, the very titles of the stories—"Spawn of the Vampire Queen," "White Slavers from the Stars"—convinced her that the magazines were the sort of trash no twelve-year-old should read. She wouldn't believe his protestations that the stories themselves were wonderful.

"I remember she wrote to the publishers and had the subscription terminated," says Stone.

"That wasn't very nice of her," says his wife. "After all, it was your birthday money."

Stone nods, trying to remember. "I know," he says. "It's hard to picture Aunt Marian doing a thing like that. It wasn't like her. She was strict, but she was fair."

(Perhaps he also recalls her finding the issues hidden behind the book-shelf. "She made me give my precious collection to the Salvation Army," he'd say, "but she bought me a set of Dickens to make up for it.")

"At any rate," he says, flipping through the pages, "she was dead wrong about this—it all seems pretty innocent now." Smiling, he scans one of the stories and begins to read a passage aloud to his wife. Distracted by some household matter, she barely listens as he savors the fantastic imagery and deliciously florid prose.

At last she interrupts: "Who do you suppose sent it to you?"

Stone looks up, puzzled, and peers at the address label on the cover. "I can't imagine."

"Maybe they still have your name on the mailing list."

Stone smiles. "Ha! Not likely! The magazine folded back in the forties, just like the rest of 'em, thanks to the wartime paper shortage—it was probably on its last legs by then anyway. Besides, I doubt they could have traced me here. I'm a long way from Rutherford's Corners now."

A touch of sadness; he's remembering how family fortunes had changed with the Depression. They'd had to move; the boy, growing up too fast, hungry for money, had forgotten things like vampire queens and starships.

He gazes down at the magazine. "In fact, this must have been one of their last issues."

The pages before him reveal a magnificent 1930s illustration nearly crowding out the text, a lush pen-and-ink spread of a space explorer coming upon a beautiful woman on a world with two suns. He reads a few lines to himself and sighs with satisfaction. "Wow! They don't write 'em like this anymore!"

Eagerly he settles down to read.

In the coming months, the issues continue to arrive, each cover stranger and more enthralling than the last. May '39, June '39, July '39, on into the fall—representatives of another age, yet every issue crisp and new as if printed that very morning.

A cold evening in late fall. Stone and his wife, laden with luggage, tote bags, etc., from some weekend excursion, stop in the mailroom off the lobby to pick up the weekend's mail.

Amid the bills and circulars he finds a new issue of *Science Marvel Tales*— October '39. He hurries into the elevator with all the pleasure of a schoolboy. "I haven't seen you smile like that in years!" his wife sniffs.

A small white piece of paper flutters to the elevator floor; it had been stuck inside the magazine. It proves to be a note, written in the smudged and jumpy lettering of an old manual typewriter, on stationery bearing an ornate old-style logo: *Uncanny Productions—Publishers of Science Marvel Tales.*

"Dear Sir," it says, "We hope you have enjoyed our publication, and are sorry for the interruption in your original one-year subscription, which will terminate with this issue." It's signed, "M. C. O'Dowd, Circulation Manager."

"Impossible," Stone mutters. "After half a century..."

"What do you mean?" asks his wife.

"They're claiming it's the subscription I had when I was twelve! The one Aunt Marian canceled." He laughs. "Somebody's pulling my leg."

The next day, at the office—an imposing modern workplace, at once plush yet high-tech—someone notices the magazine on Stone's desk and ribs him: "What's this? Are you reliving your boyhood?"

Embarrassed, Stone puts the magazine away, like a schoolboy caught reading a comic in class. But later, noticing it in his desk drawer, he calls his secretary in. "There's an outfit in Chicago I want you to check on for me." He reads her the name from the front of the issue. "Uncanny Productions..."

"What's that?" asks the secretary. "A video house?"

"No, it's a publishing company. It's in something called The Blake Building, at—" He reads her an address in Chicago.

"Are we thinking of buying it?"

"No, no. Just find out if it still exists."

She reports back to him: there's no listing for it. He's disappointed. "Oh well, I didn't think there would be," he says. "I doubt if the address even exists anymore."

"I wouldn't know," she says, "but you could check on it yourself. You're scheduled to fly out there on Thursday."

Thursday finds him in Chicago. Traveling from his hotel to a corporate meeting, he asks the cab driver to make a detour to the address he'd read in the magazine. "You sure you want to go over there, mister?" the driver asks dubiously. "It's a bit out of the way. That whole area's due to be demolished. It's like a ghost town these days."

"Yes, let's go. I want to see for myself."

The street is empty, but the tiny six-story Blake Building is still standing, its bricks black with age. "I hear they're tearin' it down in a week or two," says the driver. He waits as Stone peers inside the darkened entranceway. The building appears to be abandoned, but a directory on the wall still bears the names of various small-time establishments of a bygone age: a dry-goods firm, a hat-maker, radio repair, voice lessons. The fifth floor lists Uncanny Productions. It's a walkup. Grimacing, Stone heads for the stairs.

Four flights later he emerges from the shadows, panting heavily, and comes upon the offices of *Science Marvel Tales*. He tries the door; miraculously, it opens, and he enters. He finds himself in what the *Weird Tales* offices must have looked like in the days of Farnsworth Wright: small, shabby, quaint—a total contrast to Stone's super-smooth corporate headquarters. Dusty framed paintings from *Science Marvel* covers adorn the walls. A thin, ragged-looking writer sits near the entrance, nervously cradling his manuscript. A secretary in high-necked 1930s garb is pecking at an ancient black manual typewriter that's clearly an antique.

She looks up. "May I help you, sir?" Stone gives his name and asks to talk to Mr. O'Dowd. He notices, through a doorway, an editor in bow-tie and spectacles poring through a tottering pile of manuscripts.

O'Dowd appears, young, sandy-haired, and harried-looking. "Trouble with your subscription, Mr. Stone?" There is something curiously knowing in his eyes.

"No, no trouble at all," says Stone, then smiles—"aside from a short delay."

O'Dowd regards him gravely. "Well," he says, "if I recall correctly, we had some correspondence on this matter from a Miss Marian Stone."

"You're absolutely right," says Stone, astonished. "You folks certainly have long memories! Marian Stone was my aunt. She's the one who canceled my subscription."

"I beg your pardon, sir," says O'Dowd. "Not canceled—interrupted. You'd paid for that subscription in good faith—with your own money, if I'm not mistaken—but your aunt felt you were a tad too young for it. So she asked us to hold the remainder of your subscription 'pending further notification,' as she put it... And that accounts for the delay."

"But who notified you to start it again?"

"She did."

"Aunt Marian? When?"

"Why, it was, let's see... around six or seven months ago."

"Impossible!" cries Stone.

"I saw her face to face, Mr. Stone. She was right here in this office."

"She's been dead for nearly twenty years!"

"That may very well be, sir," says O'Dowd, "but she was here this spring, standing right where you are now... and she told me she thought it was time to reinstate your subscription. She said you were finally old enough to appreciate it." He stares at Stone intently. "I know it's run out now... but any time you want to, you can renew. Whenever you decide."

"I don't want to renew," snaps Stone, his head suddenly aching. "I want an explanation! I want—"

"Remember, Mr. Stone," the other interrupts, "it's *never* too late for a renewal. It's just a matter of wanting it badly enough." He glances at his watch. "And now, if you'll excuse me..."

He turns to a nervous young man who has just hurried through the door carrying a large artist's portfolio. "Chief!" O'Dowd calls, and the editor emerges from his office. Ignoring Stone, the two examine the young man's illustration, a shimmering pen-and-ink spread similar to the one Stone had savored in the magazine, depicting spaceships, monsters, a wide-eyed young woman, a futuristic cityscape, a sky festooned with stars.

Dazed, his head swirling with the strange conversation and the images from the picture, Stone sinks weakly into one of the shabby leather chairs.

"Sir?" the artist asks. "Sir? Can I give you a hand down the stairs?"

Stone looks up, confused. "What? Oh... Oh, yes. Thanks."

Half staggering, he allows himself to be led toward the stairway. "It's so encouraging to find my work appreciated by someone like yourself," the young man is saying earnestly, "someone who's old enough to know how badly we need beauty in the world. That's what makes working for Uncanny Productions so special—the possibility of reaching people, people of all ages, from all walks of life. There are a lot of magazines on the stands, but there's nothing quite like *Science Marvel Tales*."

Stone finds himself back in the cab. The driver turns to him.

"Where to, mister?"

"Oh, uh… back to my hotel."

"Good. Glad to get outa here. These old ruins give me the creeps!"

Dissolve to December: a snowy street scene near Stone's downtown office. Passing a dusty little second-hand bookshop, he stops and peers inside. A tattered copy of *Science Marvel Tales* is lying in the window.

"That's a valuable one," says the shopkeeper. "The last issue—they didn't make it through the war. It'll cost you a bit."

"That's okay," says Stone. "The cost doesn't matter. All I'm looking for is a form, a piece of paper, something… some way to renew."

He turns the stiffened pages, yellow with age—and there, opened before him, is the haunting illustration he saw in the Uncanny office.

**Version Two** is set in a suburb of Chicago, where an elderly man is living in bored retirement with his daughter and young grandson. The high point of his day is the arrival of the mail.

"Grandpa, what's this!" says the boy one afternoon. In the mail is a brand-new issue of a 1930s pulp, *Science Marvel Tales*, addressed to the old man. He has the same reaction as above: the issue "even smells right." Though he soon concludes that it's some sort of reprint edition, at first he half believes that it's his old 1930s subscription, somehow lost in the mail for half a century. He'd actually subscribed to the magazine at age sixteen, using money saved up from his newspaper route. How he'd loved it then! But the subscription had been interrupted by the family's moving during the Depression. "I remember how broken-hearted I was when I had to sell off my collection," he recalls. "Probably got all of 75 cents for it!"

He, too, soon receives a note from the Circulation Manager: "Dear Sir, We're sorry for the interruption in your subscription due to your change of address, but we've finally located you."

"They must have gotten your name from their old subscription rolls," says his daughter. "You know how mailing lists are. Once you're on, they never take you off!"

Over the next few days, the old man loses himself happily in the action-packed stories and fantastic illustrations. His grandson is equally intrigued. "You really love those tales, don't you, Grandpa?" he says.

"I sure do," says the old man. "They don't write 'em like this anymore." He recalls how he'd always wanted to be an author, even wrote up a bunch of stories—but he'd never had the confidence to submit any of them. "I probably still have a few in the trunk upstairs."

"Why don't you send them one, Dad?" asks his daughter.

"Oh, no, they're not looking for *new* submissions." he says. "These are obviously the original stories, you understand? From the thirties."

"Well," says his daughter, "so are yours. And they're certainly not doing anyone any good sitting up there in the trunk. Why not show them one? You never know until you try."

But the old man does not; he's sure that the downtown address at the front of the magazine is long since gone. The boy, however, is unaware of this; to him the address must be real. Dusting off an ancient manuscript from his grandfather's trunk, he takes it into the city.

The *Science Marvel Tales* office is as described above. The boy has an amiable encounter with the editor, who assures him that the magazine is always looking for the work of new, undiscovered writers. After a discussion of rates—

"A quarter cent a word."

"Wow, writers sure aren't paid much, are they?"

"You're absolutely right, son. It's a very tough way to make a living."

—he leaves his grandfather's story atop a huge pile of manuscripts.

The following month, the magazine fails to arrive, and the boy is dismayed to learn that the office building he'd visited has just been demolished for a new high-rise. He wonders where the publishing company has gone.

Later, passing a dusty secondhand bookshop, he notices a flyblown copy of a 1939 *Science Marvel Tales* in the window and attempts to buy it.

"That one's pretty valuable," says the bookseller. "It's the last issue."

"Oh, no! You mean they went under?"

"Afraid so, son. That's the way it is with magazines. This one'll cost you seven bucks."

"That's a lot of money," says the boy. "How do I know it's really so old?" He's sure the issue isn't really from 1939, like it says on the cover; it looks like just another one of Grandpa's reprints, one that simply got yellowed from the sunlight. Then he turns the pages—and his eyes widen with excitement...

Cut to the family at home. "So even though I knew it wasn't really old," says the boy, "I paid him anyway—because look..." Featured in the magazine, suitably illustrated, is his grandfather's story.

We leave the old man happy... but wondering, just the same, how long he's now going to have to wait for the check.

# THE BOOK OF HIERONYMUS BOSCH

Although no atlas maps the world of Bosch,
The wanderer knows it: Hidden in the heart
There lurk the crowded images that dance
Across the paintings; and within the pit
Of even sane men's souls there lies the mad
Arena, Bosch's carnival of pain.

Impaled on harp-strings, sinners sing in pain,
As taloned apes (those pets beloved of Bosch)
Take wing and swoop about a sky gone mad—
A throbbing furnace. Trumpets shriek! The heart
Drums faster as the show starts. In the pit
A cortege of the damned joins in the dance.

Around a bagpipe fools and demons dance,
Carousing beasts that celebrate men's pain.
A duck-billed monk emerges from the pit
Of hell to join this dancing throng; and Bosch
Knows every step those dancers take by heart,
Where some go with God's love, and some go mad.

Nearby this red arena lies a mad
Putrescent garden. Thorns on vines that dance
In grotesque tangles pierce a human heart,
Like fruit that's swollen red as if in pain.
But is this tattered plum the heart of Bosch?
Or is it but a plaything of the pit?

The wanderer through this world within the pit
May first dismiss its architect as mad.
In time he comes to understand that Bosch

Has drawn the tune to which all mortals dance;
For each man dreads the demon-prod of pain,
And each must dance to bagpipes in his heart.

So Bosch has ripped these horrors from his heart
To make a Traveler's Guidebook to the Pit:
The thorns a symbol of the spirit's pain,
The monk a faith denied and driven mad.
And that tremendous bagpipe in the dance?
An emblem of the body's lust, said Bosch.

The traveler sees that Bosch has searched his heart
To illustrate our dance around the pit.
And who that's witnessed pain dare call him mad?

**NOTE:** Invented at the end of the thirteenth century by the Provençal trouba-dours, the sestina is among the most complex of verse forms, consisting of six six-line stanzas traditionally written in iambic pentameter. Its rhyme scheme fol-lows a strict mathematical order—

$$A\ B\ C\ D\ E\ F$$
$$F\ A\ E\ B\ D\ C$$
$$C\ F\ D\ A\ B\ E$$
$$E\ C\ B\ F\ A\ D$$
$$D\ E\ A\ C\ F\ B$$
$$B\ D\ F\ E\ C\ A$$

—to which is appended a final stanza of three lines.

"Rhyme scheme" is perhaps misleading, for in fact the same six end-words are repeated throughout the poem; and in the final three-line stanza, all six end-words must be used, three at the ends and three in the middle. The task is addi-tionally complicated by the fact that the final end-word of each stanza becomes the first end-word of the next, producing a repetitiveness that is difficult to dis-guise. (The result, unfortunately, is sometimes more puzzle than poem.)

# Lament of an Aging English Instructor

What irks:
Soon my students will
speak of me
(if they speak of me
at all)
in the third person
past tense. And I
shall not be around
to correct them.

# THE FATHER OF THE WITCH

— in which —
a proud papa,
having read "Porphyria's Lover" six times
and
having seen "Rosemary's Baby" seven times,
is pleased to report
the success of his experiment.


"Where did we go *wrong*?" the woman cries.
How like my wife to trust the poor clichés
Of Dr. Freud. Do you read Dr. Spock
Or Dr. Cagliostro? Dr. Seuss
Or Dr. Nostradamus? The good wife
Was always half-agreeing with those slobs
Who told us "what an imp" our daughter was—
As if an Imp is cute! I realized
Our restive girl was *right* to run away
(Or fly away?) from our suburban block,
Where school and church conspired to seduce
My changeling child to duller paths of life.
"Lord knows where she *is* these days," she sobs,
While I smile—for I'm not so sure He does!

The "mischief" that they caught her at, of course,
Was nothing to the misdemeanors done
As soon as that fat cop had brought her home.
(That very night the station-house burned down!)
He should have let her study without fear
Of interruption by the law. And she did worse
Than *that* to those who crossed her, like the one
Who made such vicious fun of my last poem.
(He disappeared the night that she left town.)
A bed is always waiting for her here.

"She was such a *good* girl," neighbors sigh.
Forgive them, Nick, they know not that they lie.
But *let* those who know better call her bad—
Even a witch has someone she calls Dad.

# ARTHUR MACHEN'S
# 'THE HOUSE OF SOULS'

One of my longest-held ambitions—not a particularly lofty one, but the sort that all too easily gets put off, decade after decade, until one suddenly discovers it's too late—is to spend a year or so motoring around the British Isles, from Penzance to John o' Groats, stopping wherever I please. The back seat of my car would of course be filled with books: with the dozens of travel guides, highway atlases, and gazetteers of haunted houses, prehistoric sites, battlefields, and castles that I've been collecting all my life.

But in addition to the carload of reference works, I'd want to take three volumes of memoirs and a book of supernatural tales. The memoirs are those of Arthur Machen and, together, they constitute a rambling autobiography: *Far Off Things, Things Near and Far,* and *The London Adventure.* The story book is Machen's *The House of Souls.*

Machen (rhymes with "blacken") was a Welsh clergyman's son who, as a young man, left the countryside behind and moved to London in the hope of becoming a writer, nearly starving in the attempt; later he toured with a company of Shakespearean actors, but for most of his eighty-four years he made his living as a journalist. He was born in Caerleon-on-Usk on March 3, 1863, and died in Amersham, near London, on December 15, 1947. I was privileged to share the earth with him for precisely five months.

Machen is, to my mind, fantasy's preeminent stylist. What makes his work so special is the rhythmic quality of his prose: one hears in it the short, seductive cadences of a fairy tale or the Bible. With the eye of a visionary and a language that is, for all its simplicity, at times truly incantatory, he reveals the wonder—and frequently the terror—that lies hidden behind everyday scenes. No other writer's work so perfectly blends the two elements of Walter Van Tilburg Clark's phrase "the ecstasy and the dread." (Indeed, Machen's longest foray into literary criticism, *Hieroglyphics,* sees the key attribute of great literature as "the master word—Ecstasy.") Jack Sullivan has noted that in Machen's best tales "beauty and horror ring out at exactly the same moment," and praises Machen for "his ability to make landscapes come alive with singing prose." Philip Van Doren Stern saw Machen's imagery as "rich with the glowing color that is to be found in medieval church glass." No one is better at evoking the enchantment of the Welsh hills, or the sinister allure of dark woods; no one makes London a more terrifying or magical place, a latter-day Baghdad filled with exotic dangers and infinite possibilities. Wherever he looked, he saw a world filled with mystery. Every word he wrote, from youth to old age, reflects his lifelong preoccupation with "the secret of things; the real truth that is everywhere hidden under outward appearances."

But perhaps this "secret of things" is too shocking for the human mind to accept. That, at least, is the premise of *The House of Souls'* best-known story, "The Great God Pan," in which a ruthless scientist seeks to rend the "veil" of everyday reality. ("I tell you that all these things—yes, from that star that has just shone out in the sky to the solid ground beneath our feet—I say that all these are but dreams and shadows: the shadows that hide the real world from our eyes.") In a laboratory set amid "the lonely hills," he performs a delicate operation on the brain of a young girl, reawakening atavistic powers and enabling her to glimpse that real world—a process he calls "seeing the god Pan." The result is not enlightenment but horror: the child goes mad from what she's encountered and dies "a hopeless idiot," but not before giving birth to a daughter, a malign being who, decades later, in the form of a seductive woman, causes an epidemic of sin and suicide in Victorian London.

Today, for all its power, the tale's decadent frissons may seem rather dated, but at the time, "Pan" outraged the more prudish English critics. Machen, who took a perverse pleasure in his bad reviews (he even collected them all in a book, *Precious Balms*), relished "the remark of a literary agent whom I met one day in Fleet Street. He looked at me impressively, morally, disapprovingly, and said: 'Do you know, I was having tea with some ladies at Hampstead the other day, and their opinion seemed to be that..."The Great God Pan" should never have been written.' "

Two other stories in the book, "Novel of the Black Seal" (part of a longer work, *The Three Impostors*) and "The Red Hand," can still provoke a shudder, even today. They theorize—as do later Machen tales—that the so-called "Little People" of British legend, the fairy folk, were in fact the land's original inhabitants, a dark, squat, malevolent pre-Celtic race now driven underground by encroaching civilization, yet living on in caves beneath the "barren and savage hills" and still practicing their unsavory rites, occasionally sacrificing a young woman or some other luckless wanderer they can catch alone outdoors at night. Writers such as John Buchan have also made use of this theme, but none so chillingly.

The book's most remarkable story is "The White People." (It was the direct inspiration, incidentally, for my own novel *The Ceremonies,* which quotes from it at length.) Most of it purports to be the notebook of a young girl who, introduced by her nurse to strange old rhymes and rituals, has a series of nearly indescribable mystical visions involving supernatural presences in the woods. We learn, at the end, that she has killed herself. The girl's stream-of-consciousness style, at once hallucinatory and naive, lends a spellbinding immediacy to the narrative, and for all its confusion and repetitiveness, it remains the purest and most powerful expression of what Jack Sullivan has called the "transcendental" or "visionary" supernatural tradition. Most other tales of this sort, such as Algernon Blackwood's "The Wendigo," E. F. Benson's "The Man Who Went Too Far," and Machen's own "Black Seal" and "Pan," merely *describe* encounters with dark primeval forces inimical to man; "The White People" seems an actual product of such an encounter, an authentic pagan artifact, as different from the rest as the art of Richard Dadd is different from the art of Richard Doyle. Lovecraft, who regarded Machen as "a Titan—perhaps the greatest living author" of weird fiction, ranked "The White People" beside Blackwood's "The Willows" as one of the best horror tales ever written. Machen, who often denigrated his own efforts, and who once wrote "I dreamed in fire, but I worked in clay," himself termed the tale merely "a fragment" of the one he'd intended to write, "a single stone instead of a whole house," but acknowledged that "it contains some of the most curious work that I have ever done, or ever will do. It goes, if I may say so, into very strange psychological regions." E. F. Bleiler's assessment strikes me as more accurate: "This document is probably the finest single supernatural story of the century, perhaps in the literature."

# ABOUT THESE STORIES...

When *Reassuring Tales* was published fifteen years ago, in a limited edition, I added a rather grumpy introduction. The grumpiness was mostly a pose. I was, frankly, somewhat conflicted about reprinting these stories, and like an old performer pretending to be annoyed by calls of "Encore!" before lumbering back onto the stage, I chose to blame the book on the urging of "a handful of meddlesome friends—well-meaning, I suppose, or maybe just polite"—as well as on the book's hardworking and totally innocent publisher, Bill Schafer of the Subterranean Press. I also suggested that what had finally convinced me to allow its publication was plain old financial inducement. Here's what I wrote:

> And then there's my stone wall; well, not exactly stone. You see, a couple of decades ago, shortly after *The Ceremonies* came out, I bought a house surrounded by woods in a little town upstate. (As I like to tell visitors, it's just across the dirt road from the cabin where Whitley Strieber claims to have been buggered by aliens.) On weekends, I've been building a low retaining wall, around forty feet long, where the side lawn slopes to the driveway. I'm constructing it out of concrete blocks that—at least in the catalogue photo—resemble roughly chiseled rocks. Very picturesque, in the right light. At any rate, these wonderful blocks cost five dollars each. There's also a delivery charge.
>
> Then, too, not long ago, as a sporadic autograph collector—or as an adherent, if you like, of what's called sympathetic magic—I bought a note signed by one of my favorite writers, George Orwell. I have the requisite items by Lovecraft, Machen, and other literary idols, as well as a smattering of Antarctic explorers (including captains Scott and Oates), but I'd never before seen an Orwell offered for sale, and this one doesn't even appear in the twenty-volume edition of his complete works (which contains nearly every stray jotting). Now, possession is a funny thing: After gazing with satisfaction at the note, I put it away in a cabinet, and I may never look at it again; and if a burglar had made off with it that very night, I'd be none the wiser. So what was it exactly that I bought? Still, it seemed a bargain at twelve hundred dollars.
>
> Or let's talk about an unfortunate habit of mine: nail biting. It's quite satisfying, and undoubtedly healthier than cigarettes, but after some fifty years of it, my front teeth were getting visibly worn down.

And Dr. Schaap, a genuine artist among Manhattan dentists, persuaded me of the need for—you know, I'm not even certain what they are. Caps? Veneers? Maybe a bit of each. Anyway, he did a lovely job, and I'm ready now for Hollywood. There were plenty of teeth for him to labor over; and this book you're holding will pay for…oh, maybe a couple of them.

All of which is a hoot, because, of course, books of this sort pay for absolutely nothing. Like fine words, they—as the old expression has it— "butter no parsnips."

Well, here you have a new edition of *Reassuring Tales,* and damned if I'm not still somewhat conflicted about it; only this time around, just as unfairly, I'm blaming Ed Stasheff of Pickman's Press, who—along with a lot of keenly intelligent advice and encouragement—pointed out that the earlier limited edition is extremely hard to find today and quite costly, and that, whatever my mixed feelings about them, these stories were being pirated online.

Speaking of old expressions, in the introduction to the previous edition I acknowledged my uneasiness about the project by bringing up, at the start, an expression I first heard years ago from my friend (and fellow Anglophile) Kathy Murray. It's one I've become quite fond of, and that perhaps applies to this collection: "a curate's egg." As I noted then, it's an expression not generally known in America, nor even in England these days except among the hopelessly bookish. Its origin is a *Punch* cartoon of the 1890s in which a timid young clergyman, dining at a bishop's home and asked if his egg is bad, nervously assures his host that "parts of it are excellent."

The point of the joke, of course, is that the egg is rotten and that the clergyman's words are faint praise indeed. But as the phrase has come to actually be used—when, for example, a critic refers to some book, play, or exhibition as "a bit of a curate's egg"—what's meant is simply "good in parts, not so good in others."

Well, I think you may be holding just such an egg in your hands: not, I hope, the bad one the curate was stuck with, but—in that latter, more forgiving sense—one with at least a couple of digestible mouthfuls.

And for what it's worth, in the hope of offering you slightly more substantial fare, Ed and I have included in this "Expanded Edition" a few additional items—an article, an interview, some poems, the young-adult story "Imagining Things," as well as three nifty illustrations by Gahan Wilson and one by Tim Kirk—and, as always, I've tinkered a bit with the texts, mainly trying to correct the usual infelicities of language.

One thing I enjoyed explaining, in that earlier introduction, was the title: why *Reassuring Tales?* Blame it, I said, on one of the living writers I admire most, Ramsey Campbell, who, back in 1980, in his collection *Dark Companions,* declared: "I believe that horror fiction cannot be too frightening or too disturbing. Too much of it seeks to reassure."

I hope it's clear, by the way, that Ramsey isn't warning that horror fiction should avoid being too frightening; he's saying, on the contrary, the scarier, the better. (You may recall a long-ago *Saturday Night Live* sketch that exploits this same quirk of language, in which a retiring nuclear engineer gives the staff taking over the power station some maddeningly ambiguous advice: something like "You can't give the reactor too much water.")

Now, seriously as I take whatever Ramsey says—and I'm proud of having written what may have been the first critical appreciation of his work—I don't share this curiously punitive sentiment. Personally, I've never had the ability, the temperament, or the intention of scaring the shit out of anybody, and I don't especially enjoy being scared myself. Where's the fun in that?

And here I added a footnote,[*] one in which, while the personal circumstances have changed, the opinions have not:

> I don't go to many horror movies, spending much of my time with a woman whose taste runs to Fred Astaire and for whom the pinnacle of violence is the Three Stooges. But friends sometimes lure me to the cineplex or lend me horror videos or DVDs; and I think it's interesting that the last four I happened to see—*They, Jeepers Creepers, Ju-on,* and *The Ring* (granted, a pretty mixed bag)— all pit innocent, indeed virtuous, mortals against malign supernatural beings who menace them, torment them, hunt them down, and ultimately vanquish them. They all left me feeling rather cheated, as if I'd been forced to watch a cat toying with, then killing, a mouse. Here it was humans struggling against vastly stronger predators. In the end the victims were defeated, and you realized that they'd never had a chance. What's the point? That supernatural evil triumphs? If so—to steal a line from the novelist Wilfrid Sheed—I don't see the point of the point.

I continue to think that it's a pretty rough world out there and that we need all the reassurance we can get. And so, for years, I played with the idea of naming a collection—by way of a joking nod to Ramsey— "Reassuring Tales." As it happens, I never actually sat down and wrote those tales, but I thought it would be fun at least to use the title.

In keeping with that idea, the initial edition's cover, by the veteran

---

[*] Yes, that introduction had honest-to-God footnotes!

illustrator Jason Eckhardt, was meant as a gag: In the style of a lurid pulp magazine, it depicted a quiet domestic scene in a suburban house—the man in his easy chair, smoking a pipe as he reads the evening paper, the wife washing dishes in the kitchen—with absolutely nothing out of the ordinary. Unfortunately, a surprising number of people didn't get it.

As you can see, the new one, by Ashley Cser, is distinctly less reassuring. It illustrates "The Events at Poroth Farm," my first published story—"a statement," I noted in a 1990 Necronomicon Press chapbook, "that would sound a lot grander if I'd written more than a handful of stories since then."

In that chapbook, I offered a quick sketch of the tale's inception. It was begun in the summer of 1971, amid surroundings—physical surroundings, at any rate—not very different from those encountered by my narrator. Since that now-distant time, rural New Jersey has gone through some pretty appalling changes, and farms have given way to suburban malls, developments, and factory outlets, especially in the section of Hunterdon County where the tale is set. But here and there, in certain quiet places, one still feels far from the city.

The major inspiration for "Poroth" came from Arthur Machen's "The White People," but it also owes its existence to the stories by Lovecraft and others that, ever since high school, I'd been reading in Arkham House collections; it was basically an attempt to duplicate for myself some of the pleasure I'd found in those seductive black-bound books. In fact, not knowing what else one did with a horror tale, I wrote it with the vague hope of mailing it off, when completed, to that publishing house's founder, August Derleth. It wasn't until later that summer, on a trip to Providence, that I learned from my friend and former thesis advisor, Barton St. Armand, that Derleth had died that July.

As it happens, Barton also had on hand copies of *Nyctalops,* a splashy Lovecraftian fanzine published in Albuquerque by Harry O. Morris, and—never having seen a fanzine before—I ended up mailing the story to him. I recall that I didn't feel comfortable sending it as a formal submission; instead I wrote some sort of hesitant, rejection-avoiding cover letter saying, in effect, "This isn't meant for your magazine, of course—I just thought maybe you'd be amused by it." Fortunately, Morris was not only amused but went on to publish it—with the striking illustration by Tim Kirk reprinted here—in the second issue of a short-lived sister magazine called, in the grand Lovecraftian manner, *From Beyond the Dark Gateway.* He also sent a copy to Richard Davis, then editing *The Year's Best Horror Stories* for Sphere Books in the U.K., who bought "Poroth" for one of the volumes in that series; later it was included in an American edition, as well as in *Gahan Wilson's First World Fantasy Awards.* (Davis, when Kathy and I finally met him in London, turned out to be exactly the sort of amiable eccentric you'd want your English editor to be. When we first arrived at his office, he stuck his head out of one of the inner rooms to greet us, and we were momentarily surprised to see that his head was pale and hairless as an egg. "I'll be right out," he called, withdrawing it, and moments later appeared wearing what looked like a dime-store fright wig and hastily crayoned-on eyebrows—and proceeded to take us for an enjoyable lunch at his club.)

"Poroth," as I've mentioned—like the novel based on it, *The Ceremonies*— is set in a now vanished world. I regret to say that other stories in this book are similarly dated (or, to put it more gently, are "of their time"). When "S.F." was written, 2039 seemed so unimaginably distant that you could make the most absurd claims for it. The events of "Well-Connected" are impossible today because the characters would all be walking around with cell phones. And does anyone on earth still use a Polaroid camera?

I bring up that particular piece of technology because another tale here, "Camera Shy," depends on it. A word about the tale's intended function: It was written for a glossy corporate magazine that Polaroid was publishing (was it to be the first issue? I forget), and the assignment was to write a horror story that would be illustrated with Polaroid photographs. Either the magazine never came out, or the notion of running a piece of fiction every issue was scotched once the editors saw "Camera Shy"; all I remember is that I was paid. You can see today where the pictures would have gone; and while, God knows, the story's all too obvious, dressed up with cleverly staged photos it might have been pretty cute.

Other stories here had an equally quirky genesis. The late Bruce Jay Friedman, introducing a collection of his fiction, noted with pride that "none of the stories were written either to or for anyone" and that he wrote only for himself. I can't make that claim. Just as virtually every job I've ever had has come to me because of some friend's timely intervention or invitation, almost all the stories in this book were written at someone's— usually a friend's—request. The truth is, without a little arm-twisting or guilt-tripping or ego stroking, it's never been easy to get a story out of me. I remember, for example, that a novella of mine, "Children of the Kingdom" (not in this book), was written because my friend and agent, Kirby McCauley, was putting together an anthology called *Dark Forces* that would contain, along with work by a multitude of excellent writers, an original story by Isaac Bashevis Singer, at that time an idol of mine (with the Nobel still ahead of him). The prospect of being in the same book as Singer was all the inducement I needed.

In the present collection, "Ladder" was written expressly for the premier volume of Tom Monteleone's *Borderlands* series because Tom had been so astonishingly nice as to write an essay about *The Ceremonies* in a compilation called *Horror: 100 Best Books.* I mean, how could I say no? (Please note that, in an attempt to justify the present collection's subtitle, I couldn't resist adding a brief appreciation of Arthur Machen that I wrote for that same *Best Books* compilation. Of all the writers of fantasy, Machen is closest to my heart.)

One of the strange things about "Ladder," incidentally, is that years ago it was supposedly translated into French for a foreign anthology; and someone has written me literally today (I swear!) asking to translate it into German. If you read the story—and I warn you, it may bring to mind Samuel Johnson's line "None ever wished it longer than it is"— you may wonder, as I do, how that feat of translation could possibly be pulled off.

"Well-Connected" was written for the first issue of a magazine called *Country Inns,* which my longtime buddy John Bensink was editing. (During my years at *Twilight Zone* magazine, John had been the editor of *Gallery,* a sort of poor man's *Playboy. TZ* had been one of its more respectable, but distinctly less profitable, offshoots.) Somehow John convinced *Inns'* publisher that just what their first issue needed was a ghost story set at a country inn. I had been reading L. P. Hartley at the time, and in places I catch myself trying to imitate him. The story originally appeared under the title "Hagendorn's House," which sounded properly country-innish. When it was reprinted in one of the latter-day revivals of *Weird Tales,* I gave it its present, more ramsicampbellian title.

"One Size Eats All" was written for yet another first issue, this one of a magazine called *Outside Kids,* a junior spin-off of the popular adventure magazine *Outside.* The editors, one of whom was my friend Robin Bromley, wanted a scary supernatural tale for children, and the story was duly presented as—though this may sound oxymoronic—a "campfire chiller." Later, I convinced Gahan Wilson that if he illustrated the story, we could market it as a children's book. (Although Gahan was celebrated, of course, for his *Playboy* and *New Yorker* cartoons, he'd been *Twilight Zone's* movie reviewer.) Alas, it never happened; I think I somehow dropped the ball. So the two sample drawings Gahan did are published here for the first time.

And speaking of Gahan, "Curtains for Nat Crumley" was written for a book Nancy Collins was putting together called *Gahan Wilson's The Ultimate Haunted House.* (Don't you just hate that *The?*) Each of the writers was invited to choose a particular room in a haunted house as the setting for a story, and then Gahan was supposed to illustrate that room with one of his signature antic-macabre cartoons. Again, how could I say no? Unfortunately, I think all the best rooms had been taken by the time Nancy got around to me, or maybe I was shy about asking for a place as obvious as the attic or the basement. Somehow, at any rate, though I ended up stretching the rules, I found myself officially assigned to the foyer (a word I've never even been sure how to pronounce, much less define).

"Growing Things" found its way, blessedly, into Al Sarrantonio's anthology *999* after a series of false starts and dead ends. Initially, *Parade* magazine—you know, the ubiquitous Sunday supplement?—asked a trio of writers for short horror tales on an ecological theme. Well, why not? I don't remember who my two compatriots were going to be, only that the tales were killed and we were paid off. Later, Ellen Datlow offered to take this one for *Omni,* but she asked me to cut two to four hundred words. Now, I don't claim it's a virtue, but I'm one of those people for whom cutting words is like cutting my own flesh; so this request irked me. I was in New Orleans at the time, and I left Ellen a stern message declaring, "No, the story can't be cut. Send it back." To my amazement, when I got home, there it was, in the mail. To this day, I don't know which one of us was the bigger jerk.

In blithe defiance of numerical precedence, the anthology *666* was in fact published eight years after *999.* The book was put together by Scholastic, aimed, I assume, at young adults; its full title was *666: The Number of the Beast.* "Imagining Things" was written for that anthology, and I don't think it's appeared anywhere since then. The scientific research that inspired the story is real, as are all the quotes.

As for "S.F."—probably inspired by the tall sci-fi tales in Arthur C. Clarke's *Tales of the White Hart,* a book no one reads anymore—it's hard to account for the fact that its first appearance was in 1975's edition of *The Year's Best Horror Stories.* It's not horror, and, to put it mildly, it's certainly not best. It's not even juvenilia, since I was hardly a juvenile in 1975; I'd already graduated from a perfectly good college and had an MFA from another. I was a grown-up. (Cute title, though.)

About those poems: I used to read a lot of poetry, when I was younger, and somehow managed to accumulate, over the years, four bookshelves of it. I thought of myself not as a poetry fan—which seemed too pretentious—but as a "poetry consumer." I seldom read it anymore; before even attempting to, I follow Mark Twain's method of reading the opening line, then the last, and not plunging in unless they seem to make sense. (And they rarely do.) I did once write an amusing poem about a poet sitting on the pot while composing a poem, "wondering if 'dappled' was too precious a word." I can no longer lay my hands on the rest, but I think it's a nice line.

The three poems you'll find in this book are just meant as an extra, take 'em or leave 'em; two already appeared in *Providence After Dark.* Strictly for the record, here's what I wrote about the first of them on one of its appearances:

The sestina above was written back in 1965 (and I've been revising it ever since) after my first encounter with the work of the fifteenth-century Dutch painter Hieronymus Bosch, creator of such bizarre masterpieces as *The Temptation of St. Anthony*, *The Seven Deadly Sins*, *The Last Judgment*, *The Descent into Hell*, and the celebrated triptych *The Garden of Earthly Delights*. About the man himself relatively little is known, except that he belonged to a mystical order called the Confraternity of Our Lady and was given, as an artist, to arcane religious symbolism. His paintings—lurid visions of salvation, sin, and retribution—are populated by a menagerie of monstrous hybrids that appear to be, as one critic has said, "part animal, part vegetable, part man-made object, part human." They are creatures out of dreams, denizens of an interior landscape once known as hell, and they explain why Bosch was a major influence on the twentieth-century Surrealists. There seems, in fact, something distinctly modern about the world he depicts; it is a world of carnage and carnality, a world at once fantastic and familiar.

"They Don't Write 'Em Like This Anymore," printed in the first issue of Robert Price's *Pulp Magazine* back in 1989, is a pair of treatments for what could be—in a better world than this—a half-hour TV fantasy in a mode I've come to think of as Serlingesque Sentimental. These treatments are half-baked, I admit, and pretty corny, but they're from the heart. They derive from conversations I had with Jon White, whom I met in 1984 (when, as a *Publishers Weekly* regular, he'd been the first person to review *The Ceremonies*) and who died in 2004. Aside from writing, Jon made his living as a second-hand book dealer specializing in science fiction, mystery, and pulps. He was an invalid for most of his life—often in considerable pain, in the end nearly blind—and seldom left his tiny, horrendously cluttered Manhattan apartment; you could call him up at practically any time and he'd be there. Over the twenty years I knew him, he and I spent literally thousands of hours on the phone, dreaming up various projects that never got past the talking stage; one was an anthology of supernatural tales about books and bookstores, which stalled because we could never manage to come up with a clever enough title. ("Hell-bound"? Nah, sounds like a railroad book.) Recently I noticed that someone has put out an anthology called *Shelf Life: Fantastic Stories Celebrating Bookstores*. We'd have rejected that one out of hand.

During these years of conversation, though we frequently argued over politics, our common currency was nostalgia; we shared a preoccupation with the past, and agreed, for example, that life in the 1930s seemed curiously appealing from our modern perspective. Obviously the Depression had been a period of terrible privation and anxiety that traumatized generations of Americans, yet it was also a time, as Jon pointed out, when popular culture had flourished; and the thought of somehow visiting that era, or of capturing some piece of it, had a powerful fascination for us. Jon's immersion in the world of pulp magazines was, of course, an expression of this; and so was the fantasy, one we discussed often, that animates those two short TV treatments.

As you might imagine, Jon and I often speculated about what it must have been like to enter the hallowed Chicago offices of *Weird Tales* back in its heyday. Eventually it occurred to me that somebody I knew, Robert Bloch, was one of the few people still alive who'd actually visited those offices. He was a fellow client of Kirby's; I'd met him at the First World Fantasy Convention in Providence in 1975, had shared authorship of a booklet on the convention with him and Fritz Leiber, and had published him in *Twilight Zone*. He was also a remarkably nice man. In 1991, yielding to a sense that time was short, I wrote Bloch asking if he could recall what those offices had looked like. (At the time, although I didn't know it, he was probably working on his autobiography, which came out in 1993—a year before his death—and contains a description that generally accords with what follows.) He sent me back a two-page handwritten letter, including a diagram showing where *Weird Tales* editor Farnsworth Wright and business manager William R. Sprenger had their offices. I'm going to give Bloch the last word; if nothing else, I'd like to think his brief account adds something to the value of this book. Here's what he wrote:

> ... Unfortunately (or fortunately) my recollection of the WT layout is very hazy. Not just because we're talking about almost 60 years ago, but because I've no memory for physical objects—and after twenty-five years in this house (27, actually!) I couldn't accurately describe our living-room. I still have to think about where wall-switches are located throughout the house.
>
> Anyhow, 840 N. Michigan was, I believe, about 8 stories high, dwarfed by surrounding structures because it was an older example of early-"skyscraper" architecture, rather more squat than its leaner companions. I recall nothing about a lobby—just a walk-in to the elevators, which I think were twins. The WT office was, I believe, opposite the elevator on the 5th floor. The office layout was like this:

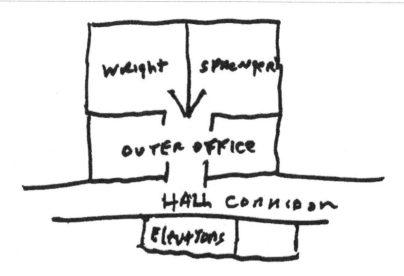

The secretary—part-time, I believe—was ensconced at a desk outside Wright's office. On the far right of the reception room was a couch: one or two chairs flanked the outer door. I never saw any other waiting visitors. The only writer I ever met there was Otto Binder, on the occasion of an early visit, circa 1935. Wright's office had a desk and filing cabinets—it was small and unimpressive. Sprenger had a desk: left, I believe, an adding-machine on a table. Right wall has shelves containing run of WT issues bound in multiple units in green leather. In one of the offices—I don't recall which—was a cupboard housing copies of back issues. No pictures or artwork on the walls—no exotic or eerie appointments—all quite ordinary and a bit on the private-eye seedy side as far as furnishings were concerned. Sam Spade would have loved it: I know I did!

# Interview with T.E.D. Klein

by Dejan Ognjanović

First published in *Vastarien*, Vol. 2, Issue 3, Fall 2019

Theodore Donald Klein was born on July 15, 1947, on St. Swithin's Day—by a strange coincidence, he shares his birthday with the protagonist of his novelette "The Events at Poroth Farm" (1972), his first major work. He studied literature at Brown University in Lovecraft's Providence, where he got infected with cosmic horror. In 1975, Klein accompanied his friend and agent, Kirby McCauley, to Providence, where he watched as McCauley and local officials planned the first annual World Fantasy Convention, complete with a World Fantasy Award bearing Lovecraft's visage.

From 1981 to 1985 he was the first editor of the new *Twilight Zone* magazine, and made it the premier newsstand magazine that published mostly horror fiction. The mid-1980s were his heyday: in 1984 he published his first and, so far, only novel, *The Ceremonies*, laureled with many blurbs, including one from Stephen King. It was on the *New York Times* bestseller list, got the award from the British Fantasy Society, and was selected among *Horror: 100 Best Books* (2005). Klein's stellar collection of novellas and novelettes, *Dark Gods*, was published in 1985. The novella "Nadelman's God," original to the collection, brought him the World Fantasy Award. That same year, in Douglas E. Winter's *Faces of Fear*, Klein was one of seventeen major contemporary horror writers interviewed.

He also wrote some entries for *The Penguin Encyclopedia of Horror and the Supernatural* (1986), announced a new novel, *Nighttown* (still unfinished), and tried to make sense of Dario Argento's treatment by writing the screenplay for the messy *Trauma* (1993). After that he basically fell under the radar, and the promises of his two excellent books sadly did not lead to more of those. In 2006 his second collection, *Reassuring Tales*, was published; the author's introduction contains what is probably the harshest self-deprecation in the history of horror, but it is true that the stories, mostly early stuff, were not up to the highest standards of those in *Dark Gods* (with a strong exception in "The Events at Poroth Farm," although it would have fit better in *Dark Gods*).

The incoherent and lugubrious "study" *T.E.D. Klein and the Rupture of Civilization: A Study in Critical Horror* (2017) by Thomas Phillips is, so far, the only attempt at a book-length study of Klein's contribution to contemporary horror. A far worthier and heavier volume appeared in November 2019: *Providence After Dark and Other Writings*, from Hippocampus Press, bringing together 600 pages' worth of Klein's nonfiction (essays, introductions, reviews, interviews). This excellent book, brimming with insights into all things horror (and more), provides a perfect occasion to talk to Klein and attempt to sum up his views on this genre.

**DO:** Please tell me about the shape and contents of *Providence After Dark*. Are these your *collected* or *selected* nonfiction writings, and if selected—who made the selection, you or Mr. Joshi?

**TK:** It was S. T. Joshi who gathered and arranged the material—and he cast such a wide net that "collected" is probably more accurate than "selected." Plus I added a few items that he didn't know about, e.g., some letters, a few of them somewhat crankish, to various magazines.

**DO:** In your roles as a critic and especially as an editor of *Twilight Zone*, you must have had a "yardstick" for measuring quality—for distinguishing between "masterpiece," "excellent," "very good," "good," etc. How did you make this distinction? What is it that distinguishes a masterpiece from, say, a very good story?

**TK:** I wish I could offer you the sort of yardstick A. E. Housman claimed to use as to whether or not something was successful poetry—that it gave him goosebumps, interfering with his morning shave—but the closest I can come is that, after reading the final words of a terrific story, I would literally hear myself say out loud, "Wow!"

**DO:** Have there ever been clashes between personal taste and publishing demands? Specifically, were there cases when you thought: "This is a wonderful story but is not right for the magazine"? Or, "This is average, but will be liked by the readers, or will it bring good sales because of a Name Author"?

**TK:** Yeah, I think that's inevitable; an editor's always making compromises. I know I've complained in the past about how the owners of *Twilight Zone*—who also owned, more significantly, *Gallery*, a sort of poor man's *Playboy*—would urge me incessantly to fill the magazine with Stephen King, or at least to figure out a way to stick his magical name on the cover of every issue. They had no interest in what was inside; I doubt they did more than glance at the contents. But I really shouldn't gripe, because that generally gave me the freedom to do as I pleased.

Ironically, when you ask about material "not right for the magazine," it's a story of King's—"Survivor Type"—that immediately comes to mind. It was one of the few tales I wanted to run but was discouraged from buying (by Carol Serling, Rod's widow, among others), because the subject matter— a shipwrecked doctor who survives by cannibalizing his own body parts— was, perhaps rightly, considered too grisly for something bearing Serling's imprimatur.

**DO:** How come you never edited an anthology with what is, according to you, the very best in the genre—either classical or modern? I guess it has never been offered to you? But if it had been, would you have liked to try it?

**TK:** Well, first of all, there are so damned many anthologies already. I grew up on them; if you include science fiction and suspense, I must own hundreds—cheap paperbacks, big fat hardcovers. And the level of most of them is frankly pretty low. As *TZ*'s editor, I'd get hastily typed permission requests to pass along to writers from some of the greedier, more debased anthologists, guys who churned out these books on an assembly-line basis; they'd actually misspell the authors' names and get the stories' titles wrong, and would offer, say, all of $35 for the reprint rights.

And then, too, of course, by editing a magazine, I was essentially playing anthologist already, issue after issue.

For several years, with my good friend Jon White, I toyed with the notion of putting together an anthology of supernatural tales about books and bookshops. As you might imagine, there are a lot of them, and they're great fun; and since readers themselves are by definition book lovers, the subject seemed a natural. However, we never got far with the project—in fact, we never even got to square one—because we were unable to think up a clever punning title, which seems to be a prerequisite for such books. I'm still open to suggestions.

P.S. The late Tom Disch reviewed books for *Twilight Zone*, and he and I used to joke about someday publishing an anthology titled *Great Tales of the Supernatural That We've Never Had Time to Read*. The introduction was going to say something like, "We still haven't gotten around to any of the stories in this book. Could you kindly drop us a line and tell us if they're any good?"

**DO:** Robert Aickman once said that there have not been more than about forty first-rate ghost stories ever written. Since you have read quite studiously the major works of this genre from its Gothic beginnings onwards, can you offer your own rough subjective estimate? How many first-rate horror stories are there?

**TK:** In many ways, Aickman's estimate sounds reasonable. Really good stories are rare. It's certainly been the case, all my life, that I've read many a horror anthology—or, say, a mystery digest of some kind—without finding a single story in it that truly impressed me. And I remember once searching the work of Algernon Blackwood for something of his that I could reprint in *Twilight Zone:* something considerably shorter and less famous than "The Willows." Here was one of the acknowledged masters—yet what a hard time I had finding anything that worked! (Incidentally, I just checked; the story I ended up using was "The Occupant of the Room," a fairly charming old tale, but far from first-rate.)

Conversely, however, I just mentioned above that good stories made me go "Wow!" and I've claimed through the years, maybe a bit extravagantly, that each issue of *Twilight Zone* could easily have been two or three times longer without any diminution of quality—which more or less suggests, if you take this claim seriously, that I must have uttered "Wow!" hundreds of times. Maybe, indeed, there really are hundreds of top-notch stories out there.

You know, there used to be joke in the film world about how it was really simple to cast the male lead: You just started with Laurence Olivier and worked down from there. In a sense, that's a reminder that we tend to mark on a curve, and that as you descend in quality, the field of possibilities inevitably grows larger.

So I guess I'm dodging the question by acknowledging, in a roundabout way, that if you ask me for the Dozen Greatest Stories, I'll come up with a dozen, and if you ask for the Fifty Greatest Stories, I'll come up with fifty. Or even a hundred and fifty.

I did once take the opportunity to suggest thirteen of them, in a series *Twilight Zone* magazine was running. I'm afraid I was pretty conventional; inevitably I had to list "The Willows," as well as a Machen ("Novel of the Black Seal"), a Lovecraft ("The Dunwich Horror"), and a James ("Casting the Runes"). I also mentioned Ramsey Campbell's "The Trick," John Collier's "Bird of Prey," Anthony Boucher's "They Bite," Richard Matheson's "First Anniversary," three s-f tales (John W. Campbell's "Who Goes There?," Michael Shea's "The Autopsy," Raymond F. Jones's "Stay Off the Moon!"), a creepy psychological horror (George Bamber's "Ottmar Balleau X 2"), and Jack London's classic adventure tale "To Build a Fire."

Of course, these things are so subjective. Aickman himself, the one time I met him, seemed to greatly revere a little Joseph Payne Brennan tale called "Levitation," in which a hypnotist dies on a carnival stage in the middle of levitating a man, and so the man ends up sailing off into the clouds.

I don't know whether Aickman regarded that as among the forty "first-rate" stories, but he liked it enough to include it in one of his anthologies.

**DO:** Since you've written one very long horror novel and many short stories and novelettes/novellas, what are your thoughts on the connection between form and genre in horror? Specifically, do you agree with a pretty prevalent opinion that shorter forms are better suited to the horror genre, while, by contrast, it is pretty difficult to write a great, effective horror novel, because of length?

**TK:** It certainly makes sense in theory, and I've maintained, over the years, that horror is ideally a short form, one that's hard to sustain over the course of a novel, much less a long novel. Which, of course, suggests—and I'm sure this is true—that *The Ceremonies* is far too long.

**DO:** Even more specifically, what were the difficulties you encountered while writing your one (for now) published novel? What was the process like of expanding your novelette into a novel?

**TK:** Sorry, Dejan, this would involve such a long, tedious, detailed answer that I'm just reluctant to go into it. Suffice it to say that the problems I had putting *The Ceremonies* together are, I assume, pretty much the same ones any first-time novelist has.

By the way, though, I have to tell you, perhaps to your annoyance— since you've only recently finished translating *Dark Gods* into Serbian—that I've just finished ever so slightly revising two of its four tales for eventual republication in Britain, and will soon begin revising the other two. (I learned of the British sale only last week.) My revisions amount merely to some word changes, a few lines of dialogue, and a couple of details. I'm congenitally unable to reread something of mine without wanting to make changes, even if it's only to add or delete a comma. And this endless dissatisfaction is what makes my writing process so lengthy—which was also, needless to say, the case with *The Ceremonies*.

**DO:** Is it at least partially counterproductive to set horror stories in a very specific time, with a date (say, June 1977), or to link them to a specific historic event (say, the New York blackout), as you did in "Children of the Kingdom"? Remember how in older tales they used dashes ("It was in the year 18—")? Can one read a story like "Children of the Kingdom" as a piece of "historical fiction" today, safe at a distance of more than four decades from its events, as opposed to some other story which takes place in a very vague "present"?

**TK:** Personally, I find it effective to mention real places in a horror tale—and sometimes, as in "Children," even real events, like the blackout of 1977. For me, that was one of the things that made Lovecraft's stories so effective: They were set amid actual Providence streets, even actual houses. As a young reader, I recall believing that the books Lovecraft quoted from might also be real. Classic stories set vaguely "in the year 18—" and featuring "Mme de G—" have always distanced themselves behind a pane of glass, so to speak, as in a museum; modern writers—is King the best example?—realized that it made for a better connection to say "He bought a Milky Way" than "He bought a candy bar."

P.S. Reality, or a semblance of it, is so important to me, in fact, that I may have lost my ability to enjoy fiction. I remember how, at a friend's recommendation, I tried reading Michael Chabon's award-winning *Kavalier & Clay*. When I found myself slogging through page after page chronicling the history of some nonexistent New York comic-book publisher, I lost interest. It occurred to me, Why am I wasting my time on this imaginary corporation (and its imaginary line of superhero comics), when its main claim to our attention is that it more or less parallels the real ones?

**DO:** I was intrigued to find you calling the ultimate academic darling, "The Turn of the Screw," "the most overrated ghost tale ever written." Would you care to elaborate on that?

**TK:** Well, I simply maintain, after many attempts at trying to read him, that James writes in airy abstractions, when what moves me in fiction—and what presumably moves most readers—are sense details of specific concrete things. You know, there's that William Carlos Williams line about "No ideas but in things"? That certainly doesn't seem like a doctrine James would have subscribed to, or to the old creative-writing-class maxim, "Show, don't tell."

By the way, you've encouraged me to provide lengthy answers, which may be rather dangerous. I was actually tempted to quote a long passage from the opening chapter of "The Turn of the Screw," describing how the governess wins over the little girl. I'll spare you, but trust me, it's amazingly vague and tedious, and gives you no sense of precisely how the two of them looked and sounded and behaved.

**DO:** Connected with it, but not necessarily, what are your thoughts on the dichotomy (or balance?) between suggestiveness and explicitness in horror fiction? Why is suggesting seemingly better than outright showing? And can one exaggerate with suggestiveness—making a tale that's too vague, too open, as, perhaps, the case may be with "The Turn of the Screw"?

**TK:** Exactly. You know, a basic question in fiction is what to tell, what to leave out; it's a perpetual conundrum. This is off topic, but I'm thinking of something that struck me when I read a couple of Raymond Chandler mysteries: how every time his detective enters someone's house or an office building, we get tons of surprisingly unnecessary architectural description; or how, in *The Book of Ebenezer Le Page* (which, if you're curious, happens to be The Great Guernsey Novel), we find similarly excessive descriptions of characters' clothing, from boots to bonnet ribbons. I guess Chandler and G. B. Edwards were simply interested—maybe too interested—in architecture and fashion.

Now, James, too, has plenty of such detail—I just looked at his descriptions of a couple of country houses, and admittedly they're way more specific than I'd remembered—but he's awfully reticent as to other things (like where and how the narrator of *The Aspern Papers* has his meals), and his descriptions of human emotions are so abstract as to be, at times, almost impenetrable.

**DO:** In your essay *Horrors! An Introduction to Writing Horror Fiction* you write with disapproval about "Clive Barker's wildly popular *Books of Blood*," which for you typify "the current trend toward explicit violence and gross physical detail." Do you still feel that way? Some might argue that they are about much more than mere violence and gross-out, or that the gross physicality is part of some purpose, idea, worldview.

**TK:** At the risk of affirming my fogeyhood, yes, I still believe that.

**DO:** You also worked on *The Penguin Encyclopedia of Horror and the Supernatural*. What was it like? Did you select the entries/authors you covered, or were you assigned without question? Who did you write about?

**TK:** Glad you mentioned that; I'd forgotten about it. It's a handsome and valuable reference book, marred a bit by some unfortunate design. I'm pretty sure I selected the various writers I wrote about, and as usual I enjoyed the chance to air plenty of opinions—though I do feel a little guilt over the slightly snarky entry I wrote on Basil Copper; I'd met him in England and didn't like him very much.

For the record, since you were kind enough to ask, in addition to Copper, I wrote about Arkham House, Charles Birkin ("For many readers, this genteelly tricked-up sadism is exactly what horror is all about"), William Peter Blatty, Anthony Boucher, Fredric Brown, Robert W. Chambers ("Early works such as *The King in Yellow* still create a powerful atmosphere of futility and doom"), John Collier ("Because Collier's writing looks so easy, he is often imitated—almost always in vain"), W. F. Harvey ("The terror a creature inspires is often in inverse proportion to its size"), Robert Hichens, William Hope Hodgson, Jerome K. Jerome, Henry Kuttner, Jack London, my late friend and agent Kirby McCauley, Arthur Machen ("justly praised as one of supernatural fantasy's great stylists"), John Metcalfe ("Metcalfe's stories, typically, rely upon fragments of letters, snatches of half-remembered conversation, liquor-dulled reminiscences, murky dreams, fleetingly described photographs, and veiled references to messages never actually quoted"), Saki ("There's absolutely no room for sentiment in a Saki tale; humankind is ruled not by love but by hatred"), Steven Spielberg, "Belief and the Writer," *The Twilight Zone*, Edward Lucas White, the Rev. Henry S. Whitehead ("He seems to have treated 'vodu' with a kind of wary respect, as a rival religion that, for its practitioners, given the condition of their lives, makes very good sense"), and Colin Wilson.

**DO:** Would you like to bring your booklet *Raising Goosebumps for Fun and Profit* back in print? Have there been any motions in that direction by either you or some publisher?

**TK:** Well, this new collection reprints a *Writer's Digest* article that was later expanded into *Goosebumps*, including a list of what I claim are the Most Familiar Horror Plots. Unfortunately, the book can't reprint Peter Kuper's striking illustrations; they're the best reason I can think of for reissuing *Goosebumps*. It's an appealing idea.

**DO:** Tell me about your "Anxiety of Influence," if any, towards H. P. Lovecraft. You wrote a thesis on him; your first tale was a sort of homage to him and Machen; one of your most praised tales ("Black Man with a Horn") was written specifically for an anthology of Lovecraftian tales. The latter even deals, explicitly, with a writer who lives in the shadow of a greater one. How did you feel about this shadow back then?

**TK:** Nothing new here; as a writer, you try to imitate something from the authors whose work you admire, yet you also struggle to find your own voice. When I first came upon Ramsey Campbell's work, in a Lovecraftian anthology published by Arkham House, what struck me was how his tale— "Cold Print"—stood out because, in both style and content, it was the least Lovecraftian piece in the entire collection.

**DO:** Why do you think Lovecraft has cast such a big shadow to begin with? Why are so many authors, both his contemporaries and later ones, including the freshest ones, from the 21st century, so obviously inspired by him?

**TK:** I've always felt that what made Lovecraft so special, at least for me when I encountered him as a youngster, was the way he combined cosmic horror—not mere ancestral ghosts but extradimensional deities threatening all humanity—with specific quaint and colorful New England settings. I'd never seen anything like that before. And those books he'd quote from seemed to provide an additional authenticity; I was at a stage when there was nothing that excited me more than the thought of rare, dusty old books brimming with forbidden lore.

**DO:** In recent years Lovecraft-bashing has become popular, due to Lovecraft's "racism" and "xenophobia," his treatment of women and minorities, etc. How do you feel about this aspect of his personality and his writings? How much does it take away, if at all, from his greatness?

**TK:** It's funny, racism has practically become the aspect of Lovecraft that fascinates people most. Looking through this year's NecronomiCon program book, I noticed that every one of the guests of honor was asked about it.

Actually, there are two separate questions: whether racist elements within HPL's fiction detract from it, and whether our opinions about the fiction are, or should be, affected by what we know of his personal prejudices. We could talk about these subjects for hours, but I'll confine myself here to a few stray thoughts.

For several reasons, I don't take Lovecraft's racism all that seriously. And it's hard to know, at times, just how seriously he took it himself. When, in early letters, this spindly, nerdy, pale, decidedly unmanly mama's boy writes, with seeming gusto, about his sword-swinging Nordic ancestors who drank foemen's blood from human skulls, this pose can seem so pathetic that you cringe, or else you may regard it with an indulgent pitying smile; but you may also sense that Lovecraft himself was smiling along with you, that his tongue was in his cheek, and that he enjoyed poking fun at himself.

This also seems to be the case when, in a notorious 1924 letter, he appears to work himself into a frenzy describing the populace of Manhattan's Lower East Side: "They were monstrous and nebulous adumbrations of the pithecanthropoid and amoebal; vaguely molded from some stinking viscous slime of earth's corruption, and slithering and oozing in and on the filthy streets or in and out of windows and doorways in a fashion suggestive of nothing but infesting worms or deep-sea unnamabilities. They—or the degenerate gelatinous fermentation of which they were composed—seem'd to ooze, seep, and trickle thro' the gaping cracks in the horrible houses… and I thought of some avenue of Cyclopean and unwholesome vats, crammed to the vomiting point with gangrenous vileness, and about to burst and inundate the world in one leprous cataclysm of semi-fluid rottenness."

Sorry, but that's basically a hoot, a performance akin to "the dozens," demonstrating—as I suggest in my introduction to Arkham House's *Dagon* collection—a schoolboyish delight in stretching language to exaggerated lengths.

Finally, I suspect that for some of us, racism in the abstract simply doesn't count for much; what matters more is how we're regarded personally. I have plenty of prejudices myself, but I'm always prepared to make an exception; in truth, I'm delighted when some prejudice of mine is proved wrong. So, okay (I tell myself), HPL didn't care for Jews in general—but how would he have felt about me? After all, he married a Jewish woman and had a few Jewish friends. I'm vain enough to think that he and I would have gotten along fine.

P.S. Would I force "Herbert West: Reanimator" on a black reader? Definitely not. One doesn't want to hurt people's feelings—and that goes for what one writes as well. In my own story "Children of the Kingdom," with its description of rioters during the '77 blackout, I was torn between, on the one hand, a reluctance to offend, and on the other a desire to tell the truth about that night as I'd experienced it, and let the chips fall where they may. In the end, I followed what my old friend Kirby used to say: The book is boss.

**DO:** Since you witnessed the founding of the World Fantasy Award, and were years later one of its recipients, what do you think about the recent decision to take away Lovecraft's visage (as re-imagined by Gahan Wilson) from it and replace it with an inoffensive stylized tree?

**TK:** I think what they did is shameful. So that's what they have now—a tree?

**DO:** One of your powerful leitmotifs is inadvertently bringing "Evil" into the world: like the protagonist of "Poroth," who does some strange signs (pointless and meaningless even to him) and thus invokes Something from the woods, or "Nadelman's God," where a piece of juvenilia comes to unexpected life in its author's adulthood. Why did this specific trope appeal to you? Did you sometimes feel that you, as a writer, might bring some unexpected horror into the world through your writing?

**TK:** As I mentioned above, I admire Lovecraft's ability to combine seemingly inconsequential mundane events with shocking preternatural results—and that sort of connection was very much on my mind when I wrote those stories.

Speaking of bringing horror into the world, I may be confusing two incidents, but I seem to recall that there was a murder in the woods years ago, possibly on Long Island, involving two or three teen cultists who may have taken *The Ceremonies* as, if not a guidebook, at least as nonfiction. And I also recall a friend informing me that a copy of my novel had been found among the books belonging to some cult broken up by police in the Puget Sound area. Obviously one doesn't want one's fiction to be misconstrued and cause harm; yet one also would prefer not to self-censor.

**DO:** One of constant complaints against horror is: "We have enough horrors in the world such as it is; do we really need *more* of it in books, films, comics, video-games…?" What do you think about that? Can real-life horrors and fictional ones even be meaningfully compared?

**TK:** I keep seeing variations on the idea—and it makes sense to me—that we try to lose ourselves in horror fiction as an escape from the real horror.

My father told me that as a combat soldier in World War II, in his foxhole, he would read a book of Sherlock Holmes stories—likely one of those armed forces paperbacks, made to fit in a GI's pocket. As the war in Europe began to wind down, he developed a superstitious belief that if he finished the book, he'd be killed. So as he drew closer to the final pages, he would read just a paragraph each day. Fortunately, the war ended before the text ran out. It's occurred to me that instead of Doyle, he might just as easily have been reading Lovecraft; there was a popular armed forces edition, *The Dunwich Horror and Other Weird Tales*. And I'm sure that Yog-Sothoth and company, for all their monstrousness, would have afforded him just as much relief from the war as Holmes did.

**DO:** Should horror really be disturbing, which seems to be its *sine qua non* in order to be truly effective—or should it be reassuring, as you sometimes claim? But wouldn't reassurance take away from its effect and make it powerless, inefficient?

**TK:** Good question; see above. I often, against my better judgment, check out the *Daily Mail* online. In print it was a typical British tabloid, but now it's the go-to site for disasters, scandals, and lurid crimes. And almost every time I look at it, there's some sort of murder or atrocity that makes me want to simply ring down the curtain on the universe. There's been unimaginable horror throughout human history, and for millions of years before human history. There was unimaginable horror sixty-five million years ago, when an asteroid wiped out three-quarters of the life on earth, including all the dinosaurs. Each day something happens in the world, or merely within this city, so disturbing that, if I didn't possess the ordinary human ability to put it from my mind, I'd want to blow my brains out (a sentiment that makes me sound like one of Lovecraft's narrators).

My own life has, I think, been lucky and privileged—quite sheltered, even coddled—yet I can't forget that we all come to a bad end.

So I'd prefer, in what I read and what I write, to keep the horror down, if possible, to a civilized, mildly unsettling tingle.

**DO:** In his study *The Modern Weird Tale*, S. T. Joshi says that "Klein's notions on the function of weird literature stand in antipodal contrast to his actual practice as a weird writer" (re: your predilections for happy endings, reassurance, horror as a light-hearted amusement, etc.). He also calls you "a sort of schizophrenic writer or, at the very least, a writer torn between what he wants in life and literature and what he is somehow compelled to do once he actually sits down to write a tale. *Klein likes happy endings in literature, but where are they in his own work?*" So, how do you explain this apparent division between your horror theory and horror practice?

**TK:** It's an excellent point. Sometimes the tale just requires a bleak conclusion and you can't get out of it, much as you'd wish to. In general, though, there's nothing more satisfying than that seeming oxymoron, a horror tale with a happy ending.

**DO:** Describing the appeal of horror, you wrote, "It's the pleasure of the carnival 'house of horrors'—more commonly known as the 'fun house.' And fun is what this genre's all about." What do you think about this genre's deeper and more serious potentials? Can it be subversive to dominant discourses? Can it be disturbing to the status quo? What about its spiritual aspects (questioning religious dogmas, offering alternative spirituality—even, sometimes, of a nihilistic kind, like in Lovecraft and Ligotti)?

**TK:** Stubborn as it may seem, I continue to regard horror tales as merely innocent entertainment. "Subversive to dominant discourses"? That sounds like a phrase overheard at some MLA panel. Remember, as Auden said, "Poetry makes nothing happen." The same goes for horror.

**DO:** Recently you've been the subject of a book-length treatise called *T.E.D. Klein and the Rupture of Civilization: A Study in Critical Horror*. Have you read it? How do you feel about it?

**TK:** Maybe someday I'll have a chance to sit down and chat with the author, who seems, via email, an extremely nice guy. Meanwhile, I confess to having had a hard time getting through his text. But then, odd as it may sound, I'm clearly not that book's intended audience; I never lasted even half a semester when going for a Ph.D. in English.

**DO:** How important is Jewishness to your personal identity? I notice that most, if not all of the main characters in your major tales are Jewish. Related to that (or not?), why did you choose to end "Nadelman's God" in a synagogue? Although you seem to be an atheistic writer (and your character is patently atheistic), that ending might suggest the synagogue as a possible shelter from Evil which, at least temporarily, seems able to protect the protagonist.

**TK:** My Jewishness, or lack of it, is another subject I could talk about, and happily bore you with, for hours. My sister and I were raised in almost no religion—both parents Jewish but nonpracticing, father somewhat ashamed of his Jewishness and at times even antisemitic. I did not go to Hebrew school and was not bar mitzvahed; we had a Christmas tree, Christmas stockings, Easter eggs. The only religious symbols to be seen were not Jewish but Catholic.

In fact, you might say I grew up in a house filled with Catholic trinkets. For generations, the Klein family business was manufacturing rosaries. The firm was founded in the 1870s by, I gather, a Jewish street peddler from Bohemia. Both my father and grandfather worked for years as traveling salesmen, selling rosaries to churches, convents, and parochial schools up and down the East Coast. Until it went belly-up around 1960, the company's headquarters was in downtown Manhattan, the factory in Providence. The latter is still there and still called the Klein Building.

Before I went off to Brown—where, incidentally, my father had been rejected, perhaps because he was Jewish—he bought me a three-piece tweed suit and warned me that when fellow students learned my last name and that I came from Woodmere, Long Island, I would immediately be despised. Needless to say, this filled me with dread, until I discovered that none of it was true. (P.S. I don't think I ever wore that suit.)

Religion has never been a part of my personal beliefs. Once, when I was little, I asked my mother if Santa Claus was real, at which point she divulged the terrible truth. I asked her some years later if God was real, but I don't recall her answer—probably something like "If you want him to be."

So, yes, I'm pretty much a lifelong atheist. However, I have no love for that familiar argumentative character, the so-called "village atheist." I've always agreed with the philosopher Sidney Hook, who, though an atheist himself, noted that he would certainly not want to disparage the faith of a grieving mother comforted by the thought of being reunited with a dead child in heaven.

You're right about that synagogue in "Nadelman." I think it's basically a pretty typical horror story, one that, beneath all the digressions and complications, follows the classic pattern, in which a supernatural incursion is initially explained away by a rational protagonist until, in the end, he has to acknowledge the presence of the supernatural (and in many tales is overcome by it). Instead of noting the seeming disparity between my personal preference for happy endings and my stories' unhappy ones, S. T. Joshi might have asked why, as an atheist, I'm attracted to tales in which rational heroes are forced to admit they're wrong!

Although I'm often ashamed of my fellow American Jews, particularly of their politics, I'm quite proud today of being Jewish—I mean culturally, ancestrally—and am fervently pro-Israel. If I've identified some of my main characters as Jewish, it's mainly because I think, Come on, this is me. Who am I trying to kid?

A lifelong New Yorker, **T.E.D. Klein** was the founding editor of *Twilight Zone* magazine from 1981 to 1985. His first (and so far only) novel, *The Ceremonies,* was a *New York Times* bestseller and won the 1984 British Fantasy Society award. In 1985 he published *Dark Gods,* a collection of four novellas, one of which, "Nadelman's God," won the 1986 World Fantasy Award; another, "Children of the Kingdom," was cited by Victor LaValle in the *New York Times* as "the greatest New York City horror story of all time." He later edited the true-crime magazine *CrimeBeat* and wrote the screenplay for Dario Argento's thriller *Trauma.* His nonfiction writing has been collected in *Providence After Dark.* In 2012, the World Horror Convention bestowed on him its Grand Master award. "In close to 25 years of writing," says literary critic S. T. Joshi, "Klein has only two books and a handful of scattered tales to his credit, and yet his achievement towers gigantically over that of his more prolific contemporaries."

# More Books from Pickman's Press

## THE AVEROIGNE ARCHIVES

All of Clark Ashton Smith's weird tales of Averoigne—the sinister, monster-haunted province of medieval France—are collected into one volume. Werewolves and satyrs stalk dark forests, witches and necromancers lurk in swamps, and giants terrorize the cathedral city of Vyônes in the heart of Averoigne.

## THE AVEROIGNE LEGACY

Over two dozen tribute tales and poems set in Clark Ashton Smith's world of Averoigne. Revisit Vyônes and Périgon, meet Luc le Chaudronnier and Azédarac once again, as tales of harpies and vampires, ogres and giants, changelings and cockatrices await you!

## CORPORATE CTHULHU

Just like the Great Old Ones, corporations are powerful but unseen entities we have no control over, yet subtly manipulate our lives and our world—and we don't even realize it. Endure twenty-five Mythos tales of bureaucratic nightmare, but remember: it's nothing personal—just business.

## SORCERY AGAINST CAESAR

Simon of Gitta, escaped slave turned magician, roves the Roman Empire battling dark magic and demons, all while pursued by Caesar's soldiers in sixteen stories by Richard L. Tierney and others that combine historical fiction, sword & sorcery, and Lovecraftian Horror.

Made in the USA
Coppell, TX
10 November 2022

86142877R00098